MEN WITH NO MASTER: THE COMPLETE
ADVENTURES OF ROBIN THE BOMBARDIER

Roy de S. Horn

Kingdom Come

BY MARTIN MCCALL

Henry Rides the Danger Trail: The Complete
Tales of Sheriff Henry, Volume 3

BY W.C. TUTTLE

Z is for Zombie

BY THEODORE ROSCOE

The Bait and the Trap: The Complete
Adventures of Tizzo, Volume 2

BY MAX BRAND

Minions of Mars

BY WILLIAM GRAY BEYER

Swords in Exile: The Rakehelly Adventures
of Cleve and d'Entreville, Volume 2

BY MURRAY R. MONTGOMERY

The Torch

BY JACK BECHDOLT

King of Chaos and Other Adventures:
The Johnston McCulley Omnibus

BY JOHNSTON MCCULLEY

The Blind Spot

BY AUSTIN HALL & HOMER EON FLINT

MEN WITH NO MASTER

THE COMPLETE ADVENTURES OF ROBIN THE BOMBARDIER

ROY DE S. HORN

ILLUSTRATED BY

V.E. PYLES

STEEGER BOOKS • 2019

TABLE OF CONTENTS

MEN WITH NO MASTER

*Hail to the heroes of New Forest—those
defiant, stout-hearted freemen, whose
longbows and bombards shall write high glory
for England in the Hundred Years War.*

CHAPTER I

GIBBET RULE

AT THE CROSSROADS it stood, gaunt and gruesome, like some evil harbinger of the times. High and stark rode the great gibbet, full twenty feet above the sward, its stout timbers limned against the sky. And ever the breeze puffed, the gruesome thing suspended therefrom twisted and spun. Its dangling toes danced until the gibbet chains clinked and clanked to catch the ear of every passerby.

So unexpectedly had he come upon it, rounding the outthrust shoulder of the forest, that Robin Santerre stopped stock-still in his tracks and all but dropped the scrip bag on his shoulder and the traveler's pack on his back.

"God save us!" he mumbled. "And yet the jongleurs sing of Merrie England!"

In truth it was not fright but the sudden shock of coming on it so unexpectedly that had shaken him. For crossroads were few in all England that did not carry each its gibbet and dangling fruit. It was a time when hanging was the common penalty for every crime from striking the king's men to stealing a flitch of bacon or poaching a deer or hare from the royal forests.

And thickest of all were the gibbets on this road adjoining the New Forest that appeared so dark and so dense from the very roadside. Fair and green were the trees and the bracken where the road cutting let in the sunlight. But a hundred feet, and the light was barred off by the somber depths, stretching through thicket and fen and tangled wildwood all the leagues from the

1

There on the forest green the free
man and the lord fought lustily

Salisbury Road to the Solent and Southampton Water. Leagues visited only occasionally by the King's hunting parties and those of the Lord Warden of the Forest and his guests. Woods inhabited solely by charcoal burners—and by the masterless men.

The twenty years up to this year of grace, 1346, had brought grievous days to England. Shattered castles and burned peasants' rooftrees marked the paths of the armies that had ravished and fought through the length of the land. First as the rightful King Edward III had waged righteous war against his own mother, the wicked Isabella of France, murderer of his father and usurper of the throne, and against her paramour Mortimer and their evil French favorites; and then the wars against the Scots. And now for the past few years the constant forays into France.

From those wars had returned ribald soldiers, as well as reckless yeomen and archers from the noted Free Companies. Men who, having known pay only in the form of pillage and loot, found it hard to change habit and exist by villein's work even when returned to their own people.

Disbanded, taking no baron's *livraison,* and calling no man master, they roamed the land, a wild and doughty crew. Dense wildwood, like the New Forest where they found companions of like feather in the reckless poachers, was their favorite haunt.

Hence timid travelers tarried not even on that stretch of king's highway between Salisbury and Romney and Rye that skirted and even penetrated the great forest, lest sundown catch them outside the safety of castle, abbey, or walled town.

AFTER HIS second glance Robin saw that the dangling man was very dead indeed. And since his own feet were weary from the miles to Salisbury town and he had not broken his fast since sunrise, very calmly he sat down in the leafy shade beside the road and lightened himself of his back-pack and his scrip bag. Then taking out of the scrip his dinner of bread and beef and a flask of wine, he began to eat, studying the gibbet gravely the while.

While gibbets were somewhat new to him, sudden death was not. Even an Oxford student knew his sword and hauberk as well as he knew his *aves* and his Aristotle. And from the new College of the Scots in Balliol Hall, Robin had often sallied forth into blood-drenched St. Giles's Street to repel with sword and pike the raids of the southern students against the northern.

"By his doublet and his hose yon gibbet dangler is a forest man and not a villein," he decided, "even if the stag head atop the gibbet did not mark him for a poacher. And by the pull on the chains and the length of his swing, he would be twelve stone weight, no more!"

Suddenly both his meal and his arithmetical calculations were broken in upon by a rustling from the forest at his right. And out of it slipped three men, as nimble of foot as they were swift of action.

The first of them was a great red-headed man, full six feet tall, with freckles like a pied piper. The second was lean and scarred, with pinched lips, and cheeks as gaunt as a gray wolf. The third, who bounded and laughed as he walked, was agile and slender and of no more years than Robin's own twenty.

All of them wore the doublets and green hose of forest men. Long bows were in their hands and knives at belt, while slung to their backs were their round archer's shields and baldric and quiver, with great clustered arrows with goose-quills showing.

Not observing of the youth who sat so quietly in the shade, the three crossed the road and were at the gibbet foot in a twinkling. Evidently the red-headed giant was leader of the three, for quickly he gave his orders.

"Thou art the youngest, Peter Joy, and the nimblest, if thy feet will cease bouncing long enough to climb. I will stand to the post and give a hand up, while John the Wolf keeps watch adown the road."

"A post that suits me well." Plucking a feathered shaft from his quiver, the gaunt archer notched it to his string and stepped into the road.

"I would like it better if it should be the Lord Warden himself who comes. Hanging from gibbet or buried by clergy, no doubt Lory of the Longbow would find the hell-fires cooler if Butcher de Brenn toasted in them alongside."

"Stand still, Hubert, thou great ox," said the agile Peter, as he leaped atop the huge archer's shoulders. "You squirm worse than a villein with a flea in his doublet." Then wrapping his arms and legs around the post he was up it like a mountebank. Once there he set himself astride the gibbet crosspiece and swung himself along until he was at its center immediately above the chain. From his belt he drew forth a short but heavy armorer's hammer and chisel and set the cold steel to the head of the nearest rivet, the while talking amiably to the dangling body.

"Did I not tell thee, Lory, that a deaf ear and a greedy belly bring a man to grief? If thou hadst watched the glades behind as greedily as the pot venison ahead, the warden's foresters had not caught thee. And we would not have the labor of cutting thy bones down from this gibbet."

"Cease thy gabbling and cut the chain!" grunted the red-headed archer, Hubert, beneath. "The Lord Warden would like it little if he came upon us robbing him of his gallows-bait."

But Peter Joy only laughed, "I can see the road from here for furlongs on either side. There is a dust rising toward Salisbury, but it is a sizable way yet. Before that time—"

ALL AT once he stepped short and his eyes opened wide. From his high perch he had glimpsed for the first time the silent form of Robin.

At his halted speech, the gaunt wolf-faced John had spun around, the bow stave bending under his pull. The archer's fingers quivered as they prepared for the loose, and then they suddenly tautened and held firm as his eyes perceived that it was only a single being, and him a youthful traveler, who sat there harmlessly.

"Ho! A clerk!" he cried. "By my bow, a rascally traveling clerk!"

The red-headed giant, despite his size, was no less quick. He was across the road at a bound, had laid great hands on Robin before that squirming youth could even rise. It was the archer's hands that jerked him upright.

"Spying for the Butcher, is it?" roared the archer. "Skulking in the bracken and spying on his sweet gibbet?"

"Nay." Robin squirmed to break loose, at the same time watching the drawn shaft of John the Wolf. "Nay, I was but eating my nones-meal. I am a traveler just come from Salisbury."

"Slit his gullet for him, anyway, and leave him hanging in place of Lory," growled John the Wolf. "It will be but a fair exchange for the Lord Warden. But first, run hand in his scrip satchel. Mayhap there are groats there—even a shilling."

Taking the scrip bag from Robin, the giant Hubert dumped its contents in the dust, only to swear at their meagerness.

"See?" said Robin. "Not even a shilling—"

"Then what of his pack?" reminded John the Wolf. "If he be a clerk, what need has he of a great pack fit almost for a trades-man? Break open the pack Hubert—and mind thee that we all share and share alike!"

Dropping the empty satchel, Hubert laid hands to the pack and was grumbling at its stout straps, when a call from the top of the gibbet gave him pause. Peter Joy was looking away, over the shoulder of wildwood, and up the road toward Salisbury.

"They come, they come quicker than I had thought! Drag him into the bracken if you would strip him before they come!"

"Who comes?" John the Wolf swung around now to face this new direction.

"A party—a trading party. A goodly merchant at the very least, by his train. Burdened sumter mules—carts a half score—"

"A rich merchant makes even better pickings than a rascally clerk," said John the Wolf. "If we lay well our plans—"

But the red-haired leader cut him short. "How many?" he called to the man atop the gibbet. "Escort men, I mean."

"A round score. And hard men, by their looks. I can even see their pike-staves, the windlasses of their crossbows!"

"Too many then, even for we three. Haste thee down, Peter!"

Peter Joy was already scuttling down like a scared squirrel. As he reached the road, Hubert gave a great push that sent his captive spinning. "Back to thy nones-meat! And keep a shut mouth what times it is not chewing! For we shall have an eye on thee from the bracken—and even a shout or a leap is not as swift as a full-feathered shaft!"

CHAPTER II

THE LORD WARDEN

THE NEXT MOMENT Robin was left blinking in the road, as the three archers dived headlong into the wildwood. But though they had vanished from sight, he could still see the bracken quaking, and the keen arrow-point covering him from the brush.

He had scant time to observe, however, for just then around the forest Corner a short score paces away came the jingling merchant train. Sumter mules, covered carts so laden that their wheels creaked, a score of escort men and drivers with crossbows to hand and pikes out-held. And alongside the foremost cart, a white-bearded, rounded-bellied man, riding on a jennet— evidently the merchant owner himself.

All this he saw at one full glance, and had not time for a second one.

For all at once the lead mule snorted, threw up its head, and spun halfway across the road in one frightened plunge. In an instant the whole road was a mêlée of confusion. Sumter mules were kicking and rearing, their packs bursting open and the rich goods scattering everywhere. Cart horses plunged amid their tangled harness. One of the carts overturned, lay with spinning wheels at the side of the road. The cursing carters were struggling with their animals, while the trader himself, springing down, was wringing his hands and filling the air with shrill prayers to the saints in garbled half-English, half-foreign phrase.

Forgetful for the moment of the archers' warning and the drawn arrow-shafts, Robin left his pack and scrip bag and sprang into the mêlée.

Catching a plunging horse by one ear, he jerked him down and straight in the harness again. To a refractory mule he gave such a great blow on the rump that it mended its ways forthright and joined its fellows in orderly place. Then setting his sturdy shoulders to the overturned cart, he heaved with such right good will that it came upright on its wheels once more.

The fat merchant stared, and then he burst into voluble thanks.

"My son, my son! Your coming must be the answer of the good Saint Christopher himself! These foolish mules and those knaves of carters had quite undone me. Thy name, my son, that I may remember thee when I say my credoes, this vespers!"

Smilingly the youth brushed away the dust of his recent exertions. "As to my name, it is Robin. And any prayers for me would be welcome, though I fear you give me too much credit."

"Nay, nay, the prayers shall be said!" The foreign looking merchant thanked the saints again and mopped his brow. "This terrible England! Two score candles will I burn in the cathedral at Bruges if I leave not my bones here as well as my goods! Two score candles for the safe return of Jacob Algelt—"

"Two score candles for the cathedral, and only empty thanks for this youth who saves a whole cartload?" It was a new voice, a merry, laughing voice, that suddenly broke in. "Shame it is to Bruges if its cloth is as poor as its misers!"

WHIRLING, ROBIN stared at the cart whose concealing canvas towered almost alongside him. There was a slit there, and through it poked a head. The eyes were merry, as the voice had been, and the lips were red and curving. Yet belying them was the matted hair of an old crone, her bonnet coif all but shielding her ears and cheeks.

"Eh? What? Thou shameless hag! Keep thy mouth shut ere it be shut for thee!" The fat merchant rolled his head from side to side, turned hurriedly to the smiling Robin. " 'Tis but a sharp-tongued crone I gave room to, in pity for her weary years."

Nevertheless he was fumbling in his great leather pouch as he spoke. Drawing out several coins he regarded the silver ones covetously for a long moment, then dropping them hastily back into the pouch, he made shift to hand the other ones to Robin.

"There—that will buy thee ale and meat at the next inn. And if in saying vespers thyself, thou shouldest remember the name of Jacob Algelt of Bruges—"

Smiling at the trader's miserliness, Robin dropped the coppers into his scrip bag. "If it were not already past nonestime, I would bide with you a while, lest the sumter mules be frightened again."

"Nay, nay," the merchant said hurriedly. "Before night we should be in Rye, and safe, both as to goods and bones. In truth it has been but a sorry venture—to London and back without profit.... This road—it leads to Rye?"

"Rye?" Robin shook his head. "Nay you took the wrong turn two leagues back. Did not your carters recognize this wildwood here to the right as the New Forest?"

"The New Forest!" Apparently the evil reputation of the New Forest had spread even across the Channel.

"If you will proceed straight ahead to Bewly, however," said Robin, "I doubt me not you will find direction there how to get to Rye."

With one more fearful glance at the gibbet and its fruit, the merchant of Bruges shouted to his carters who straightway began to harry the animals forward again. Before the whole party was straightened out in orderly file again, however, it was overwhelmed in still greater catastrophe.

For from the forest depths to the right suddenly broke out a great baying and crashing, followed by the winding of a horn. Then full into view burst a lordly stag with seven-point antlers wide spread, its eyes rolling and its flanks heaving from the hot chase. Close on its heels leaped and bayed a pack of great deer hounds; and pell-mell behind them came the mounted hunters themselves.

SO CLOSE pressed was the fleeing stag that the cart train before him seemed less danger than the harrying hunters behind. In between two carts he plunged, so close that his antlers all but brushed them as he sought the covert beyond. And hot after him raced the hounds, between cartwheels, under the legs of horses and sumter mules, so that immediately they were rearing and plunging again in fright, and the whole train worse tangled than the time before.

But that was not the end of it yet. Equally regardless, the hunters themselves rode down and through and over the train, putting their mounts to it as they would to mere gullies or fallen trees in their way. Mules plunged until they lost their packs, while two carts were completely overturned.

Some of the hunters had gained through and continued the chase, but most were checked short by the tangle of carts and mules. Instead of making apology, however, they showered the carters with oaths and curses. In particular the leader of them, a dark, nobly-dressed, hawk-faced man of over thirty, rained blows on the nearest hapless carters with his riding whip, all the time shouting in fury:

"Knaves! Varlets! Heard not the blast of the horn for clearing of the way? Ten lashes of the hangman's whip would teach thee better manners!"

The trader, Jacob Algelt, was wringing his hands again at sight of the new wreckage. Toward him the angry rider turned with whip uplifted.

At that Robin's lips tightened, and he was about to spring between, when someone else forestalled him. Out of the cart leaped the crone, her skirts flying, her eyes blazing beneath her matted hair.

"The devil's sorest murrain upon thee! Wouldst strike an old man, with hair already white with age?"

So spiteful was she that for the moment even the angry huntsman was taken aback. And before he could recover, one of the other riders, broke in with a ringing laugh.

"She has thee there, Hugo!"

He was a young man of thirty or thereabouts, and dressed in hunting garb like the others. But the fineness of his fur-trimmed mantle and cap was only matched by that of the hawk-nosed huntsman himself.

FOR ANOTHER moment the hawk-nosed hunter glared at trader and woman alike. Then with narrowed eyes he swung his mount aside and led his party down the road and around. In so doing he was caused to ride close past Robin. So fixed was that youth's gaze upon the trader and the crone that he did not glance up. And so the horseman came almost abreast him. And let out another great oath.

"By the great dragon's bones, it is beyond belief! Know you not enough, varlet, to doff thy coif before thy betters?"

And with a slash of his whip he not only cut the bonent-cap from Robin's head but left the mark of the leather on the tip of his ear as well.

For one second the youth stood, white-faced, trembling. Then his right hand plucked downward toward his belted tunic under his mantle.

"Seize him!" shouted the huntsman, turning to the three men in foresters' habit who rode close behind him. "To the gibbet there with him, and make a lesson for all such villeins!"

But the same pleasant-faced rider who had laughed before, now spoke again. "Hang him if you will, Hugo. But I ride on after yon stag. Who slays the deer wins the cask of wine—remember our wager!"

Grumbling, the hawk-nosed Hugo gave over then, and with a curse lashed his mount in the direction the hounds were still baying. But the pleasant rider, hesitating for a moment, looked down at Robin.

"Know ye aught of the whereabouts of a man named Wat the Armorer, whom rumor hath it is to be found not far from this forest and the masterless men?"

Robin slowly shook his head. "I am but new come from Salisbury. Ye must needs ask a more familiar man."

"Then ye had best get on with your carts." The horseman pointed toward where the carters, under their master's driving tongue, had gotten the animals straightened out once more. And then suddenly he leaned in his saddle, so that his lips were close to Robin's ears. "Warn thy sister that her mat of hair hath slipped—and that young eyes and a neat angle are illy fitted to a crone's rags. Especially when the Lord Warden, Hugo de Brenn, is no more blind than I!" The next moment he was galloping off after the rest of the racing huntsmen.

The merchant's carts were scarcely around the next bend, and Robin was just stooping to gather the scattered contents of his scrip bag, when from their place of concealment stepped the three archers again.

"By my bow, there is no luck in us!" John the Wolf was scowling toward where the merchant's party had vanished. "A rich merchant—and too many escort men to chance a foray! E'en Lory of the Longbow had no such murrain upon him as this!"

"The clerk's pack is still here," laughed Peter Joy. "And the clerk as well. Over timid he was of thy goose-feather warning, Hubert, or he would have snatched flight in one of those covered carts!"

"Then get at the pack," ordered Hubert, the red-headed one, "and after that up with thee to the gibbet again. If the Butcher rides too well covered by huntsmen and verdurers to risk losing a shaft upon, we can at least rob his gibbet from under his—Hola! What devil's luck is this now?"

Pounding hard adown the Salisbury road had come a new sound, the unmistakable thud of horses' hooves at a fast pace. Not one horse, but many, and with it the jingling of spurs and armor plate. Though they were still shut off from sight by the jutting forest fringe, the horsemen were undoubtedly close, and coming fast.

"Back to our bracken!" ordered the red-headed archer. "And, clerk, the warning before is still as meanful now."

CHAPTER III

THE MASTERLESS MEN

THE NEW COMERS who burst in cavalcade around the forest point were neither hunters nor merchant's men nor yet ordinary travelers. In the fore and in the rear rode men full-armed even to lance and helmet tightlaced to hauberk rings. They formed a compact group in the midst of which rode the only two who were not fully armed. One of them was a much scarred man in rich velvet and gold-plated shoes, but the other was a slender boy of scarce sixteen mounted on a dappled jennet. His clothing was plain black, though of the finest cloth, and his face and hands were unusual by reason of their fairness.

At sight of the gibbet with its dangling body they halted. And the boy's face clouded and his brows grew troubled. He spoke quick words to the older man. "Another gibbet? We have seen more such sights in the past three leagues than along all the rest of the road even unto London."

"The Lord Warden of the New Forest has troubles enough, I doubt not, what with the poachers and the masterless men." The scarred man pointed. "See? The varlet's crime is shouted from the gibbet over his head."

"None the less I like it not." For the first time the fair-faced boy noticed Robin standing on the opposite side of the road.

He waved him nearer. And now Robin, giving due regard to the heavy-armed men, did not delay about doffing his bonnet.

"Canst tell me how far it is to Romney?" The slender boy spoke in a voice tinged with a French accent. "And is there at Romney a seasonably place of abode?"

"I do not know Romney overwell," returned Robin. "But it is some several leagues distant yet. Bewly is nearer. And at Bewly is the Abbey, and inns in the town, and Bewly Castle, the holding of the Lord Warden of the Forest."

The cavalcade jingled on with Robin looking after them curiously. In fact, so curiously that John the Wolf's snarling voice was almost at his shoulder again when he heeded.

"A curse now on all hauberks and casques and those who wear them! Had it not been for those men-at-arms, I would have had the stripling's jennet and clothing ere now."

"But not worth fighting a dozen men-at-arms for, John, old Wolf." Red Hubert's voice was placid, but his eyes were fixed curiously on Robin, "The pack, the pack of this young sprig, Peter. Have a look in it."

So meek had their captive seemed through all this time, that neither Peter nor John the Wolf gave him a second's glance. Peter was reaching for the pack straps, when Robin's hand moved quickly to his waist, and up again. So fast it moved that the keenpointed knife was pressed tight against John's ribs before he could turn, could even gasp.

"You were so eager to split my gullet just now," Robin said crisply, "how would it seem to have thy own paunch opened? Shift but one step and thou wilt know the answer!" And he pressed the needle point a fraction inch to give weight to his words.

SO SWIFT and unexpected had been his action that even Red Hubert still held his bow with arrow unnotched. Peter Joy gawked from where he knelt over the pack. John the Wolf's eyes popped wide. And he let out a wild bleat.

"Spit him, Hubert! Spit him!"

But instead, the red-headed archer suddenly burst into laughter. Laughter in which Peter joined.

"How now, old Wolf? The joke is turned serpent and coiled back on thee! Ye had best been satisfied with the scrip bag, and let the pack be."

But the gaunt old archer continued to roll his eyes and shout, his body frozen against the knife point. "He is mad—the sniveling clerk is mad!"

"If he be sniveling clerk, then am I a tonsured priest!" retorted Red Hubert, again running his keen eyes over Robin. "What is it you really seek in these parts?"

"Now that you ask me civilly," said Robin, still keeping his knife pressed hard, "I seek a man. A man named Wat the Armorer. And if anyone of you know and will lead the way to him, I might even forego the letting of this gray wolf's blood."

"Wat the Armorer!" The giant archer repeated the name amazedly. "What want you with him?"

"That," said Robin tersely, "is my business—and also in some degree the business of John here, it would seem."

"And your name?"

"Robin. Robin Santerre."

Apparently Red Hubert was satisfied, for he slowly nodded. "So be it. Put up thy knife, clerk, and we will sheathe our shafts. John, hand him his scrip bag and pack, and be thankful that he asks no more. And now do you, Peter, climb the gibbet again that we may be finished with our work."

Quickly Peter Joy swung himself up and out on the crosspiece once more and resumed his chiseling. This time no interruption came, and with a sudden clank the chain gave way, dropping its burden on the ground beneath.

Swiftly lifting the dead man's shoulders while Peter and the grumbling John seized his feet, Red Hubert led the way into the forest. Within a few yards he located a little trail.

Down this for a half-mile they tramped, until they came to a storm-felled tree a little off from the trail. Into the hole between the uptorn roots Red Hubert rolled the body of Lory of the Longbow, kicked enough earth from the crumbling sides to cover it, then stepped back to the trail again. He led the way at a jog-trot now, delving deeper and ever deeper into the great forest.

EVEN BEFORE they came to the thinning of the forest, they could sense the nearness of the smithy, for the whole forest aisles resounded with its hammering. Then the red-haired archer thrust through the woodland fringe and the smithy stood immediately before them.

It was but a three-sided shed set at the edge of a little stream where a woods road crossed. Its front lay open to the weather, and there was the great anvil and the forge with its rising smoke and blowing bellows. On either side of the forge were racks with hammers and chisels of all sorts, and bars of metal stock, as well as the cunningly rounded and pointed anvil pieces for the curving and forming of helmets.

Behind the anvil, pounding at the glowing metal tonged in his left hand, stood the smith himself, bare of chest and bare of head. He was grimy, and grizzled of hair, but despite his age his shoulders were as wide as Hubert the archer's. His corded muscles bunched and rippled as he swung the heavy hammer. Between strokes he turned his head to bellow for more speed form the jerkin-clad helper who sweated at the leathern bellows.

"Hold, Wat!" shouted the archer.

Dropping his hammer and brushing the grizzled hair back from his sweating forehead, Wat the Armorer looked their way.

"Hast cut down Lory from the Butcher's gallows, or did leave him there for the Butcher to laugh at, in passing?"

"Cut down and buried," replied Hubert, grinning. "And almost under the eyes of the Butcher himself who came that way a-hunting."

"Good!" The armorer nodded approval. "Though had you hung the Butcher up in Lory's place it had been even better."

"Zounds!" exclaimed the archer. "Art never satisfied, old forest boar? Lory was fair caught, stealing the king's deer, and the Lord Warden gibbeted him for it. We have stolen the body from the Butcher's gibbet, so it seemeth to me a fair exchange all around."

"Nay!" said the armorer, "it is no fair exchange, for God put the deer in the forest for honest freemen as well as for kings and barons."

"A saying that would get thee drawn and quartered if it but came to the Butcher's ears," retorted the archer lazily. "For me, I am content to fill my own belly regardless of who owns the deer."

"Which is why the Butcher de Brenn still hangs men like Lory of the Longbow," growled the armorer. "Whereas if all freemen stood together—" Suddenly he broke off, his eyes catching sight for the first time of Robin. "Who is this young sprig you bring with you?"

HUBERT GAVE Robin a great thrust forward and laughed. "A traveler from the north, so he says. But John the Wolf asserts that he is a sniveling clerk—"

"A clerk!" The old armorer fastened keen eyes on Robin. "What does a clerk here? And from whence come you, clerk?"

"From—from Oxford," answered Robin, feeling himself suddenly all alone under the grizzled armorer's fierce gaze. "I came, seeking to learn more of the armorer's art from one whom men say is the master armorer of all England. Wat the Armorer—"

"From Oxford? Seeking me?" The armorer's eyes widened. "And what Oxford armorer did you serve under?"

"None—no one," said Robin hesitatingly. "But in Balliol— the College of the Scots—I found that while the books well stated the theories of iron, including the smelting of ores and the compounding thereof, they were deficient in the practice. Hence I came out to seek out Wat the Armorer to obtain that practice which I was lacking."

"And thy name?"

"Robin Santerre."

"Santerre!" At the French name, the armorer's brows lowered. He mouthed the word distastefully. "Norman-French—and a blight upon it! There is no place here among honest Saxons for Norman clerks nor yet Norman murderers!"

"Murderer, perhaps, but no sniveling clerk," put in Hubert, laughing. "He had his knife in John the Wolf's ribs here before a man might wink."

"Knife, eh?" The grizzled armorer flashed out a hand with speed that belied his age, and plucked the lean knife out of Robin's belt before he could move. He tossed it to Hubert. "Break me this blade, and then drive him from the woods. Let him seek his fellow Normans at the Butcher's Castle of Bewly."

Hubert the Red shrugged his shoulders, set the knife point upon a stone end, grasping the hilt in his strong hands and with his fool planted between point and hilt, gave a great tut. But the blade gave no whit. With a grunt of surprise the archer threw his whole weight onto the blade. But again the steel withstood the effort. A look of amazement spread over the archer's face.

THE SMITH was no less startled. Reaching for the knife, he studied it keenly. "How now? Whence did an Oxford clerk secure a knife of my own make to pare his meat?"

"It is no knife of thine." Robin shook his head. "It is of my own fashioning, from the little smelter and the forge off St. Giles Street. Though I doubt me that the books—"

"Books!" John the Wolf let up a howl of derision. "He hath thought to learn the armorer's trade by reading out of musty books!"

"Aye, the books of that Sir Mohun of Kent who followed our own King Richard to Jerusalem and Damascus—may God rest his soul," said Robin devoutly. "Scorn not the knowledge that lies in books, Archer John."

But Wat the Armorer was trying the keen edge of the knife with his thumb. Plucking a grizzled hair from his own temple, he passed the blade edge across it, and the hair sliced as cleanly as though it had been gossamer.

"Powdered charcoal!" he exclaimed, staring at Robin. "Powdered charcoal in the compounding of the second melting! Didst thou that?"

"Aye, and in the third melting as well. Then thrice heated and cooled for temper, in a bath of oil and not water—according to the precepts which Sir Mohun of Kent had from the Saracen sword-makers of Damascus."

"The very precepts which I had from my father—who had it from his own grandfather who was armorer to that same Mohun of Kent!" exclaimed the armorer. "In truth there may be somewhat in this matter of books, after all. What else didst thou learn at Oxford College, Robin the Clerk?"

There came a slight twinkle into Robin's eyes. "In truth there were other subjects that stole my fancy. The matter of fulcrums and weights, the science of levers—"

"Levers!" It was Peter Joy who interrupted, chuckling. "Such as levering thy shoulders under an overturned cart, perchance?"

"That is one sort of leverage, yes," said Robin soberly. "But a bow is also a lever, according to Roger the Franciscan, and the more powerful the lever, the stronger and longer the arrow flight."

"Now I know these books teach foolishness," said John the Wolf. "Because the flight of the shaft depends only upon the strength of the archer behind it."

"Yet it is still true that it is the leverage of the bow, and not the size of the archer that maketh for far flight," returned Robin. He turned to his back-pack which he had dropped to the ground. "Given proper leverage, a small man may send a shaft or quarrel farther than a larger man. I have here a rude-fashioned thing of my own—"

THE GRIZZLED armorer was watching interestedly, but Peter Joy and John the Wolf whooped derisively as Robin unstrapped the pack and began to assemble the parts he drew from within. "A crossbow! A devil's windlass, such as the Frenchmen and Genoese use!"

But Wat the Armorer stared at the fitted parts, and then stooped to pick up one of the heavy quarrels. "A six-inch bolt, and a full pound weight! No such arbalest have ever I seen!"

"And two head staves, instead of one!" marveled Hubert the Red. "And neither solid yew nor ash, but strips of horn laid back and front along the yew wood!"

"Roger the Franciscan held that such a compounding gave greater strength and pull than solid yew," said Robin. "Which I have found sooth, since with it I can hurl yon double-weight quarrel twice as forceful and far as any ordinary arbalest. The same power and leverage could have been gained by lengthening the bow stave, but that would have made it unwieldy. So I but doubled the number of staves."

"And thinkest to double the flight of the bolt by doubling the staves?" John the Wolf scoffed. "Can two crossbowmen shoot twice as far, then, as one?"

"If they could string both bows to a single cord," said Robin. "That is what I have tried to fashion—two bow staves with a single string and single windlass between, thus giving double throw to the single quarrel." He glanced along the stream. "Had I but a mark—"

"Peter," said Wat the Armorer, "do thou go down a hundred paces and hang thy targe against yon tree. And do thou, Hubert, stand forth with thy bow and shoot against this devil's windlass."

As Peter Joy slipped off his round archer's shield with its tough bullhide stretched over the stout hickory backing, Robin nodded. "Two targes were better than one, and three were better even than two. Unless thou wouldst not want them spoiled—"

Peter gaped, but Wat the Armorer roared, to send him flying. "Take all three targes, then, and hang them one before the other. And if this Oxford clerk make not a goodly showing, after all his gabbling, we will give his doublet such a dusting as he will not likely forget!"

Stringing his great five-foot bow, the red headed archer moistened his finger to test the windage, then plucked a long goose-feathered shaft from his quiver and notched it to the string. Standing wide-legged and sidewise to the tree, he drew until the bowstring touched his ear and the muscles stood out on his arms and the blue veins on his forehead. Then with a twang and a hiss the loosed arrow flew. It was like a shaft of light, singing sure and true to the targe. And as it thudded almost into the center boss of the hide-covered shield and stood there quivering. Peter Joy's shout came ringing back.

"A full-drawn shaft! Through the first shield, and barbed deep into the hickory beyond the hide of the second!"

Hubert the Red stood down, with a little chuckle of contentment. "Match that if thou canst, clerk, with thy Oxford windlass!"

CHAPTER IV

ON GUARD, FREEMAN

BUT ROBIN, WITH the arbalest staves beneath his feet and the windlass to his stomach, was already cranking the two ratchets that stood out from the windlass on either side.

Disengaging the windlass, he raised the crossbow, grooved a quarrel in its place against the taut string. Then with arbalest leveled and left elbow steadied, he sighted for a bare instant. At the trip of the trigger, the double staves straightened with a mighty twang. So swift was the bolt itself that no eye could follow it, but the men's eardrums sang with its hornet flight, ending with a shattering crash. The foremost shield leaped and fell from the tree, and the two remaining ones hung trembling. And Peter Joy's shout this time was one of utter disbelief.

"Through the three—through the whole three! Not only through the shields, but the bolt is buried flash into the tree itself!"

"The targes! Fetch the targes!" roared the armorer.

And when they were brought, John the Wolf and Hubert stared with crestfallen faces. For not only were the rawhide covers pierced, but the hickory behind was riven and shattered until it hung in splinters, so that they would be no more good for any man.

"A week's work, a week's work to make another targe!" groaned Hubert the Red. "And where will I find other hickory of two years' seasoning?"

But Wat the Armorer was turning the splintered wood over in his hand. "Catapults and ballistae I have seen with such power. But they were of such clumsy weight as to need transport by cart and built implacements, for siege. Never before have I seen bolt from hand arbalest that I thought might pierce through shield and pauldron and hauberk of mail—"

"Not even armor of proof may stand against it," said Robin quietly.

"Aye." And suddenly a great light came into the armorer's eyes. "Perhaps the day has come quicker than I had thought. For in their hauberks and byrnies and casques, the barons and their men-at-arms have been able to over-ride ordinary men, unregarding of our pikes and arrows. But a hundred freemen with only these hand arbalests would blast aside even the Butcher's men-at-arms as if their armor of proof were no more than leather jerkins."

He turned suddenly to Robin. "What other things studied thou in books, besides levers and the making of arbalests?"

A twinkle came again into Robin's eyes. "Aristotle and orisons and the lives of the Blessed Martyrs. But there was also the book of William of Deves on ambushments and the ranging of battles—and Sieur Roland de Barbusse on catapults and ballistae and engines of siege. And a most excellent treatise by Sir Walter of Winchester on the intaking of castles and walled towns, as well as sallies and sorties of the defense—"

"By my beard!" ejaculated the armorer. "And they discoursed on such subjects at Oxford?"

"Nay," said Robin, laughing. "The Franciscans were more partial to Aristotle and the orisons. But the books were there to be read, and I thought it shame to waste them."

"And wouldst still seek the armorer's trade in a forest smithy?"

"If Wat the Armorer has place for an apprentice."

For a long moment the armorer studied him intently. Then suddenly he nodded.

"So be it. But no man fashions armor cunningly who knows not its use. I have here two casques and byrnies all welded and riveted, but as yet unproved. Thou and Peter Joy are of a size. If wilt don one casque and hauberk while Peter dons the other—"

As he spoke, the armorer was reaching down two steel casques and shirts of mail from their hooks on the smithy wall. With them he brought forth two long swords, full forged of blade, but as yet with no edge ground.

RECOGNIZING THAT there was more to the armorer's request than mere testing of new armor, Robin stripped to his shirt, pulled on the padded gambeson, and over it the coat of mail, and then the basinet or light helmet. Peter Joy was reaching for the other armor, when John the Wolf suddenly thrust him aside.

"I have a bruised rib yet from the point of his knife when he caught me unawares. Now let us see if he can give bruises when a man is equal armed and wielding just as ready a blade!"

The unsharpened swords, as Robin realized, would not cut through the tempered mail, but they had weight as heavy as a battle mace. A full-swung blow from them would deal a buffet that would search out any defect of chain mail or rivet—and mayhap of the man beneath.

But as John the Wolf prepared to arm, there was a sudden exclamation from the red-headed Hubert. "Hold! Who comes?"

Through the silence had come the sudden neigh of a horse, the thud of trampling hooves. Hubert the Red leaped for the nearest thicket, snatching a shaft from his quiver and fitting it to bowstring. John the Wolf and Peter Joy were at his heels, slipping to cover like so many weasels. When horse and rider rode into sight around the curve of the woodland road, Robin stood with the armorer and the bellows helper.

But the horseman rode alone. And at sight of him, Robin's eyes widened. It was that same pleasant-faced huntsman who had chided the Lord Warden, Hugo de Breen, on to the chase, and so saved Robin from summary hanging.

Seeing that it was but a lone rider, and him unarmed, the three archers now came stepping into the glade again. The newcomer flashed them a glance and then rode past. His attention was only for the armorer.

"Art thou named Wat?" he inquired. "Wat the Armorer?"

"Aye." The smith nodded. "What do ye want of Wat the Armorer?"

"A set of armor complete—from casque to sollerets, from hauberk to pauldrons and jambes. I go shortly to the wars. And I have heard it well said that no man fashions plate of such proof as Wat the Armorer."

The armorer stared at him, scowling. "And thy name?"

If the rider noted the insulting lack of the customary "sir," he made no show of it. "Allan—Sir Allan Mayne," he said quietly.

"The surname smacketh strongly of Norman, and I doubt not that it is spelled with an 'e,' though Allan is better English," growled the armorer. "Art thou Norman?"

"Nay. Call me rather an Englishman, for it is a name I like me much better." The young nobleman tossed a clinking purse toward the smith. "But take thy price from this purse and sack up the armor, for I am in haste to be gone."

But Wat the Armorer let the purse lie where it had fallen. "I make no armor for roof-burning Normans. Get thee to the armorer of thy own castle; let him fashion thee casques and hauberk and camail, and then pay him with blows, as is the Norman wont."

At first the horseman frowned with anger, and then suddenly he burst out laughing. "Ye do me too much honor. Neither castle nor armorer nor even esquire or man-at-arms boast the over-lordship of Allan Mayne. I am the most landless knight in all Christendom, I wot!"

"A knight without castle or man-at-arms?" Wat the Armorer stared, and then scratched at his grizzled head. "In truth that sounds more English than Norman, since the Norman thieves have left us English with naught more than our name. And ye would still buy my armor?"

"If thou wouldst sell it, old forest bear," laughed Sir Allan Mayne. "English shirt to an English back; English sword in an English hand—and devil take the Frenchmen!"

Again the armorer scratched his head. "Almost do I believe thou art true English-born." Suddenly his eyes narrowed. They glinted cunningly. "But I sell no mail that has not stood proof. There is no better proof for armor than the sword blow that smites it. If thou wouldst test the armor I make, here is casque and hauberk and gambeson. And here is a freeborn English-man to swap buffets with you!" And he gestured toward the amazed Robin.

IT WAS a pointed test, for none of the domineering Norman blood would exchange blows, save in battle, with men of lower birth or outside the order of chivalry. However, Sir Allan Mayne swung down from his horse without a word, reached for gambe-son and hauberk. With his half-armor on he reached for the blunt-edged sword that Wat held out, and for the first time he looked toward Robin who was already similarly prepared.

"Thou hadst better don shield and paulron as well," he said carelessly, "to make the odds fairer. For I have fought in both Flanders and Guienne—"

"No," said Robin stoutly. "I am already armed as thyself."

But the Armorer called out impatiently. "Ready? Then lay on!"

With the word, both Robin and Sir Allan Mayne sprang into action. The knight's sword, hissing in its sweep, slashed out a cut that would have sent sparks flying from Robin's helmet had it landed. But the sparks flew instead from the hilt guard of Robin's own blade as it rose in swift parry. And the riposte came so swiftly that Sir Allan did well to cover with his own blade in time.

Back and forth the two slashed and parried, till the blades rang like hammer on anvil, and the staring archers shouted with excitement. For though the knight had the greater strength and experience Robin had the speed and agility of youth. What blows he did not parry, he dodged, bending and leaping until the grass around was all trampled in a circle. At length they both paused panting, the sweat beads standing out on their foreheads and cheeks.

"Thou wieldest a good sword, freeman," said the knight, between breaths.

"And thou a heavy one!" returned Robin, panting with effort.

But again Wat the Armorer roared the signal. "Lay on!"

Sir Allan, however, was better used to fighting a-horse than on foot. It might have been this that led him into momentary error. All at once his sword glanced off from a high sixte parry. And before he could recover guard, Robin's own blade, sweeping around in fierce moulinet, dealt him such a great buffet on the casque that it rang like a bell. Under that stroke, Sir Allan Mayne crumpled and stretched his full length on the beaten sward.

IN AN instant Robin had dropped sword and sprung forward. Anxiously he jerked loose the points fastening the casque to the hauberk, and threw the basinet aside.

But though there was a great bruise atop his forehead, Sir Allan was not unconscious. Grunting, he drew himself to a sitting position, shaking his head.

"Methinks I am lucky that this happened not in battle in Guienne," he said ruefully, "for then I would have had my throat sliced like a hare's while I lay blinking. But as it is, I have lost both horse and armor, for such are the rules of tournament and tilt—"

"Nay," said Robin, panting, "it was but a friendly passage for the testing of the armor, as asked by Wat—"

"Nay, and still nay again," said the armorer, chuckling. "It was as much for the testing of the men as the armor. And a test I like me very well. For I have gained me an apprentice who will know the use of armor as well as the fashioning of it. And an Englishman has gained him mail for the wars—if he will take it as a gift and not as purchase."

"Gift?" The knight stood to his feet, staring. But it was Hubert, the giant red-haired archer, who broke in with the next word.

"Before giving thy armor so freely, old woods boar, thou had best ask thy Englishman why he rides so friendly in the hunting party of the Butcher de Brenn!"

Startled, the knight turned toward him. Hot words were on his lips. But it was Robin who spoke first. "With the hunting party of de Brenn, perhaps—but not so friendly. For he called off the Butcher when he was all but sending me to the gibbet to join Lory of the Longbow!"

He had removed his own helmet, and now Sir Allan's eyes ran over his face, even to the ear still bloodied from de Brenn's lash. "So thou are that one, eh? Methought you had gone on with the trader's wagons, especially after the warning I gave you for thy sister."

"Trader? Sister?" Wat the Armorer looked from one to another, puzzled. The red-haired archer quickly told him of what had happened on the Salisbury road.

"They were hurrying toward Rye," said Robin, "but they had driven off onto the wrong road. Mayhap by now they have found the right road."

But Sir Allen Mayne looked troubled. "Hugo de Brenn did not even pause for the killing of the stag, but turned in haste back to his castle of Bewly again. I like it not." He turned toward Wat the Armorer. "If thou wilt choose me speedily a casque and hauberk and other armings to fit my inches, and take the reckoning from that purse, I will ride after the merchant. Even Hugo de Brenn would hesitate to make a foray upon a train escorted by a friend of Woodstock's."

"Woodstock? I know not the name," said Wat, frowning. "But he must be of exceeding estate and authority if his very name would give pause to the Butcher's greed. Here is your purse, however—and the armor is yours for the wearing. No man who is guard against Butcher de Brenn can pay money here."

He was choosing all the fittings that went to arm a knight cap-a-pie—when another alarum broke the forest stillness. It was the noise of a man shouting and stumbling along the woodland road.

CHAPTER V

WIND THE HORN THRICE

IT WAS THE fat-bellied merchant. Only now his rich Flanders mercery was torn and muddy from plunging through wildwood and swamp. He was wringing his hands as he came in sight. Then, seeing the party at the smithy, he cried out again, and stumbled forward, to fall at the very feet of Sir Allan Mayne.

"Rescue! Rescue!" he gasped in broken, queer-accented words. "Outlaws—robbers—they have fallen upon me! Help, gentle sir, for the sake of St. Christopher! Oh, my wagons, my wagons—my daughter—"

Rudely Sir Allan jerked him upright, shook the senses back into him. "Hold thy noise, fat belly! Where have they fallen upon you—these robbers? Who has stolen thy carts, thy daughter?"

"At the road crossing—the last road branching before the fringing of the forest!" wailed the unhappy merchant. "Armed chevaliers—men-at-arms! A round dozen of them, in full mail. What men I know not, though I heard someone of the carters shout out the name of one Hugo de Brenn before he ran—"

"De Brenn! Making forays on merchants, kidnapping women

on the king's highway!" Sir Allan Mayne spat the words out with a bitter oath. "And cozening me with sweet words to join his hunt party! With such a man it was well warned to Edward of Woodstock that he had best—" He broke off, snatched for the casque Robin had so recently jerked from his head. "It may be too late. But at least I can ride after and bring de Brenn to personal challenge!"

But Wat the Armorer was reaching down a great cow's-horn that hung on the smithy wall. He set it to his lips, blew three prodigious notes. And after a moment, three more.

"There is yet time, perchance," he said, "if the carts are as heavy-laden and slow as you say, merchant. For the forest road to Bewly is soft and mired in places."

Sir Allan was staring at him in wonder. "That horn, that thrice winding of the horn?"

"Listen!"

Ringing back through the forest glades, almost like an echo from the north came a repetition of the three blasts. Then another horn sounded, but this time from the south. From all parts of the New Forest they came now, some loud, some so far away as to be faint, almost beyond hearing.

"The masterless men!" said Wat the Armorer. "Masterless, but fleet of foot, strong of arm, and straight of eye! Before we reach the curving of the road where it leaves the forest for Bewly, there will be a full two score or more! And not even Butcher de Brenn in all his plate of proof can laugh at the masterless men."

HURRIEDLY LACING the last points of his armor, Sir Allan Mayne leaped onto his horse, snatched the sharp sword the bellows helper stretched out to him. "Up behind me, then, Wat, thou grizzled bear of the forest! Thy legs are too old to run with younger men."

"My legs are stronger than that horse you stride!" retorted Wat, and slinging the horn by a thong from his shoulder, he strode at rapid pace into the forest. Jerking the dazed merchant onto the horse behind him, the knight followed, while the three archers, with bows in hand and quivers a-shoulder, dog-trotted after. Robin, delaying only long enough to throw off the heavy hauberk of meshed steel-links, picked up his double-staved arbalest and pouch of quarrels, and hurried on their heels.

Not a half-mile had they trotted, before out of the greenwood the forest men came trickling to join them. By ones and twos they came, the most armed only with yew bows and quiver and hunter's knife. And every little while the grizzled armorer would wind his horn, three blasts each time.

"Three blasts for the Bewly road—four for Southampton Water, and five for the western edge," Peter Joy explained to Robin. "Two blasts, quick repeated, for scattering when the Warden's foresters are on the prowl."

By the time they came toward the thinning of the woods, there were almost the full two score of masterless men that Wat had promised. And it gave Robin amazement that, wild and hard as they appeared, the forest men seemed to obey the armorer as leader without question.

Then at last they came to marshy ground on either side, and made their way only by reason of a higher open ridge that ran between. The tinkle of a slow-flowing stream came to Robin's ears.

"Bewly Water," said Peter Joy. "It spreads and gathers here in the low ground, before pitching itself down toward Bewly town and the sea."

Then they were out of the marsh and at the cutting of the roadway. Wat the Armorer stepped to the roadside, parted the brush and looked through it. He waved his hand.

And it was full time. For already the sweet-toned bells of Bewly Abbey were beating vespers, and the night-shadows crowded deeper and faster over the forest road. To his left Robin heard the noise of cartwheels and horses approaching. They were out of sight around the road curve as yet, but the creak of the heavy cartwheels was plain, the crack of the carters' whips, the coarse shouts. A woman's voice cried out, and was drowned out in jeering laughter.

ROBIN HEELED his arbalest and wound the windlass, glancing about him the while. Peter Joy was at his shoulder; Wat the Armorer stood tiptoe peering through the brush; Sir Allan Mayne swung his long sword as he sat taut-lipped on his horse from which the merchant had been dumped. But of the two score other forest men, there was not a one in sight. They had sunk unseen into the thickets and the bracken.

And then the cavalcade of horsemen and carts came into sight, creeping along the purple-shadowed road. In the van rode three full-mailed men-at-arms, swords on pommel, glaring to left and right. Behind them came the sumter mules, still laden, and then the carts, with three other men-at-arms on either side. Lastly, bringing up the rear, came three more men, armed cap-a-pie, and amid them, bound atop a sumter mule, rode the girl. Her false hair mat had been ripped away so that her own long tresses tumbled raven-black. Her face was white and pinched, but at every jostle of her mount she spat out bitter words at the armed man who rode beside her. It was his voice that had jeered before. And listening to it now, Robin was sure that this was Hugo de Brenn.

Still Wat the Armorer waited. The last two wagons and the horsemen herding them were almost abreast when the armorer swung the horn to his lips. Its mighty blast ripped the forest stillness.

Instantly mules were shying, horses plunging, and men cursing with surprise, then with pain and anger. And well they might. For the forest brakes on both sides of the road seemed all at once a-boil. Bow strings twanged, and arrows thicker than swarming bees hummed and beat on shield and casque and chain hauberk. Other forest men, as agile as squirrels, were dodging and twisting, slashing at horses' tendons and bellies from underneath. Still others, racing for the sumter mules, were jerking them around and off the road, plummeting from sight in the blackening thickets.

But though jolted and reeling from that arrow hammering, the men-at-arms were proof against all but the most cunningly aimed shaft. Once they had recovered from their surprise, the mounted men jerked their horses around, slashed about on all sides with their long Norman swords. All save two or three whose mounts, hamstrung or fatally stabbed from beneath, shrieked and fell kicking to spill their riders.

CHAPTER VI

RESCUE FOR RANSOM

ROBIN HAD NOT waited to glimpse all that, however. At the first tumult he had leaped into the road, racing toward that sumter mule where the bound girl rode amid her three captors. Behind him he heard Sir Allan's shout, the trampling of his horse's hooves.

That reckless moment might well have been Robin's last. For the horseman who was riding side-guard at that point was swinging about even as he plunged into the open. The mounted man gave a shout, raised his sword, hurled his horse upon Robin. Robin threw up his arbalest, finger to trigger.

Lucky it was for Robin that a shaft struck the animal at that instant. It reared in air, kicking and screaming, and the slashing sword missed his bare head by inches. But Robin's finger, slipping on the trigger, tripped the string; and the quarrel, instead of piercing the rider, drove deep into the horse's belly. The animal came down all a-spraddle, already kicking in its death throes and pitching its rider over its head.

Weighted by his heavy armor, he lay there, as anchored and helpless as a turtle upon its back. Then a forest man leaped on the downed man's chest. It was John the Wolf, the skinning knife in his hand stabbing and slashing. The gaunt archer cursed as the knife point glanced from plate and link. Fiercely he began slashing around the helmet base.

But Robin had no time to see how that fared, either, for another scream from the girl called him on. He saw her sumter mule close at hand, but upon him at that moment spurred one of the three men-at-arms who had guarded her. Robin ducked underneath the horse's belly, and heard behind him the clash of steel and Sir Allan's shout as he engaged the man-at-arms.

Robin was at the girl's side now, reaching for her mule's halter. Her sudden scream brought his head about in time to save him. There almost upon him was Hugo de Brenn. Already the Butcher's blade was raised aloft, poised for the downward stroke.

There was no quarrel in Robin's arbalest groove, nor time to insert one. Dodging, Robin threw up the crossbow to intervene between skull and blow. The parry saved him, for the blade slashed down and past, shearing the bow-staves clean so that they fell loose from the stock and hung a-dangle from the ends of the bow strings.

Dropping the useless crossbow, Robin caught at the horseman's saddle and leg. With a leap he was up and astride the horse behind the rider, binding his arms with a desperate clutch. At the same time his right foot, cunningly crooked under the stirrup, twisted and heaved. De Brenn went plunging to the ground, with Robin atop.

The fall must have dazed de Brenn; he lay as limp as a sack. In that moment Robin knew that he had but to pry the visor open with his knife point, thrust deep, and de Brenn would never mount horse again. But Robin leaped to his feet and caught at the halter of the sumter mule once more. He whirled it around, girl and all, and jerked it into the cover of the forest edge.

He all but stumbled over the merchant Algelt, shouting prayers as if they could have been heard. "Cease thy yelping!" ordered Robin, panting. "Thy daughter is safe—she is even here!"

But Algelt looked once at the girl, and continued his yells:

"The carts! The two heaviest carts! Save the two last carts if ye cannot save all!"

Robin's lips curled with disgust that the man could think of his goods when his daughter was still in bonds. But from the roadway Hubert's voice shouted back: "The wagons! The two rearmost carts! Give me a hand, Peter—John, old Wolf! The fat merchant says that it is in these that he hoards his gold!"

"Then into the forest with them! In with cart and horse!" yelped back Peter Joy. "A ransom—we will hold the old potbelly to fair ransom for his gold! Here, John! A hand with this cart!"

TO ROBIN'S amazement, with a rumble and crash, the rearmost cart came off the road and straight through the bracken, steered deftly by Hubert. After it came the second cart, urged on by Peter Joy and John the Wolf. Wat the Armorer's voice rose in a shout. "Two more carts! and leave the rest here! It is time we scattered!"

From the road the sounds of the mêlée suddenly diminished, ceased almost altogether. Only the curses and groans of the horsemen rang loud. Robin found himself leading the mule with the girl atop, her bonds now slashed, and following close behind the second large cart. Ahead he could hear Hubert and John the Wolf already squabbling over shares of what the carts might contain. Other archers came filtering through the thickets, leading captured sumter mules with their burdens. Just ahead of Robin Algelt stumbled and groaned, still crying out at the loss that had befallen him. Behind rode Sir Allan, with Wat striding at his stirrup.

Suddenly at a narrow point between mire holes where the swamps hugged the little ridge on either side, Wat called a halt. He cut the throats of the horses pulling the third and fourth carts that they had saved, and left them lying jumbled, barring the way.

"That will hold them back until daylight, at least," he said. "And by daylight we will be far away, and past all finding!"

He put his horn to his lips, blew two short blasts, and then repeated them. To the sides and rear came the answering blasts of the masterless men as they sped away.

Once again the march through the forest began. But this time it was in darkness, and moreover there were the two laden carts and the dozen sumter mules as well. But Red Hubert and the other forest men seemed to wind their way amid thickets and swamp as surely by dark as by brightest day.

Steadily they drove the cart mules on, while Robin stumbled and tripped and a dozen times was off path into the mire. He was so near to death from weariness he did not realize that the girl atop the mule was aiding him to keep from falling.

He hardly knew when the ground began to slope upward, the slippery mire to turn to solid earth underfoot. Thickets and brush gave way to a dry clearing. The creaking of the carts ceased, and there rose instead the mumble of many voices. Torches gleamed on all sides, and warm firelight beat upon his face.

But of what came thereafter, Robin knew nothing. A single tuft of grass had tripped him. In his weariness the ground was softer than the finest bed. He stretched his limbs on it gratefully and, spent with exhaustion, slept where he lay.

CHAPTER VII

BOMBARD

WHEN ROBIN STIRRED next it was fair morning, and the sun was drenching his body with pleasant warmth. The crackle of burning wood came to his ears, and there was a smell that could only be roasting venison.

Rubbing his eyes, he sat up and stared about.

He lay in an acre clearing, with dense thickets hedging it about. But in the center, a cook-fire crackled and flamed, while men held venison and fish and hares on spits to roast, and still others roamed about at various tasks.

A voice laughed at Robin's shoulder: "Ho! So the body is not a body at all, but only sleeping!"

It was Hubert, the red-headed archer, and with him Peter Joy, chuckling, and even John the Wolf's gaunt face was smiling.

Ashamed, Robin struggled to his feet stiffly. Wat the Armorer thrust a smoking piece of venison at him on a spit. "Eat, lad. An armorer's 'prentice needs all his strength to clout the red-hot iron!"

It was then that Robin saw Sir Allan brushing down his horse with a rude brush made of broken branches. A merry face with red, laughing lips and bright eyes, showed for a moment in the slit cover of the near cart and then was gone, but the sound of sweet laughter lingered after. Then it all came back to Robin, and he stared about anew.

Wat the Armorer read the expression in his eyes. "Nay, lad, ye will have no sight of Butcher de Brenn or his men here. In the near three hundred years since the Normans landed, naught but Englishmen have set foot on this spot."

"So ye give me cozen as an Englishman and not as Norman, eh?" It was Sir Allan Mayne, come from caring for his warhorse, a great piece of venison in his hand on which he munched with satisfaction. "It is a name I like as well as the stout armor you gave me last eve."

"And a name you proved with stout blows against those same Normans," Wat nodded approvingly. "Had you not proved it so stoutly, you would never have set eyes on this clearing."

The knight's eyes were laughing. "I can well believe that. A dozen times I would have been mired to my stirrups had not your forest men led me back onto the good ground again. How you ever brought the laden carts through the swamps, and in the night at that—"

"Who would know the forest, if not the forest men?" returned the armorer. But there was a look of satisfaction around his firm mouth. "On the highways and in the fields, the Butcher's men-at-arms may ride unbeaten. But in these fens none but freeborn forest men come except with our leave."

"Not even the King's men?" Sir Allan's voice was sharp.

"Not even the King's men," answered the armorer stoutly.

And looking about him at the easy carriage of the forest men, and remembering the tortuous trip through the cunning swamp paths, Robin could well believe that. But a thought occurred to him, brought back by almost forgotten words.

"What if the Lord Warden calls out the levies, sweeps the forest with a thousand well-armed men? He must be biting his nails and raging at last night's ambushment."

"Let him rage," said the armorer carelessly. "If he seeks to follow the way we came he will be mired crupper-deep a hundred times before he reaches here. And if his men-at-arms keep to the open glades, we will rap their hauberks with so many arrows they will be sore of rib and glad to get them gone the way they came."

But Robin's mind was still troubled. "What if his foresters lay hold on some forest man, and put him to the torture to make him reveal the way to this clearing?"

"They could tear him to bits, and his lips would still be silent," Wat replied. "The forest men are all freeborn Englishmen—not castle villeins cringing to the lash."

"AT OXFORD," said Robin slowly, "I read a copy of the Great Charter signed a hundred years agone by King John at Runnymead. By it is guaranteed that no freeborn man may be prisoned or done to death without trial by jury. Nor amerced of goods by taxes to which he has not subscribed—"

"A thing as worthless as the goathide on which it is writ," said Hubert scoffingly. "Certain I am that Lory of the Longbow was not given any trial other than that of the gibbet chain. And the King himself—"

"You speak treason!" said Sir Allan Mayne sharply. "The King is an Englishman even as ourselves, and a just man. And his son, the Prince, even though but a boy, is even more just. I know because—"

"How then does he allow de Brenn to commit robbery and murder and kidnapping of women on his own highway?" demanded Hubert angrily. "Yet did we not witness all this with our own eyes?"

"The King's domains are wide and far, both in England and in France," returned the knight. "Not even to his eyes and ears can come knowledge of all that happens in his realm. And I doubt me not that were he informed of what de Brenn does, he would be as sharp of judgment as you yourself, archer!"

Then he turned to Robin. "You speak of having read Magna Carta, of which even I know only by hearsay. I have curiosity to know your name, especially after the great buffet you gave me not twenty-hours agone."

"My name is Robin—Robin Santerre," said Robin, coloring. "I read the Charter at Oxford where I was a student, though I can lay claim to but little knowledge."

"Aye—only knowledge of the use of arms and the making of such devil's arbalests as no man hath ever seen before," laughed Red Hubert. "But where is the devil's windlass that outdid my strongest bow and made matchwood of my stoutest targe?"

"Ruined—cut in two by de Brenn's sword," said Robin gloomily. "It was stout yew, and the best of tempered horn, I misdoubt me that it will take some weeks to fashion another."

But Sir Allan was still regarding him with curiosity. "Santerre? Robin Santerre?" He translated the French surname into Anglo-Saxon. "Robin Lackland. We should be brothers at the least, since I am also a knight without acres or castles to my name. And whence came you to Oxford?"

"From Scotland, though I have but small memory of it since I went to Oxford as a stripling," said Robin. "My father had a small holding on the border, but he died at the battle of Halidon Hill, and I sold the holding for the expenses of my clerkship in the Scottish College at Oxford."

"You have a good right arm, as I can testify, even if you have no lands or wealth," said the knight, smiling. "What more does any man require? For these be years when a fighting heart and a good swordarm can carve both honor and estate from the battlefields. In truth that is the hope that bears me up. And even now the king—"

BUT AT that moment they were interrupted by a forester who came running into the clear, his hose muddy and his face streaming with sweat. He came straightway toward Wat the Armorer, shouting out as he ran:

"De Brenn—the Lord Warden! I watched, even as you ordered, Wat, and the Warden's castle is a bustle with activity! Men gearing on their armor—stablemen harnessing the horses—archers and bowmen looking to their weapons and bolts! There are scores of them, hundreds of them!"

"De Brenn at Bewly Castle?" The armorer's face was instantly alert. "Mayhap he is even foolish enough to think he can sweep the forest with men in full armor—"

"Not only the castle, but on every road and highway!" panted the messenger. "By the scores, singly and in troops, they are gathering. The call must have been sent out; he must be gathering the levies!"

But suddenly Sir Allan laughed. "Nay, it is not de Brenn who is rousing the levies, to make an onslaught on the forest men. It is for the war. And it is the King himself who has sent out the call to arms."

"The King? War?" The armorer repeated the words with both surprise and no little doubt.

"Aye. It is that for which I sought your stout armor," said the knight. "Ere I left London the King's messengers were hurrying to every knight and baron in the realm, assembling the King's forces. War hath been declared between England and France."

"And the Frenchmen come to invade us here at the Solent and in the Hampshires?" Red Hubert's brows grew dark. "By my bow, if any Frenchman lays foot to English ground, to harry and burn, he will find himself so full of feathered shafts that he will seem a fowl readied for the plucking."

"Nay, not Frenchmen invading England," Sir Allan told him. "It is we who will invade France. The King of France has seized Guienne, which is lawful fief of our own King Edward, and so we must cross to chase the Frenchmen out again."

"But Guienne—is that not in France?" demanded the armorer.

"Yes. But it is possession of our English King, come down with Normandy by inheritance from William the Conqueror."

The armorer shook his head. "What have we English to do with Guienne or any other part of France? I can make no sense of these wars and bickerings. Let the French stay in France, and we English in England."

"Aye. But where then would we landless Englishmen win our lands and wealth if there were no wars and we took them not from the French?" said Sir Allan, his eyes gleaming. "There are rich towns and cities in France, to be plundered by the Englishman who is stout enough. Even an archer there, with fortune, may win wealth enough to secure him his ease for the rest of his days."

"Even an archer, say you?" John the Wolf's ears pricked up. "How then does one get to this Guienne? Is it on the highway beyond London then, and toward Scotland?"

"Nay, it is over the water, in France—across the Channel, which the Frenchmen call the *Manche*," answered the knight, laughing. "That is why the levies are gathering at Bewly, and Romney and Rye. For in those harbors we will take ship to cross to France. Prince Edward, the king's eldest son, is already on the way to make ready the ships and the levies, and the King himself will follow."

"The Prince come to Rye and Bewly? Then he is a fool," said Wat the Armorer sourly, "to lay his head in the trap. For I remember me that twenty years agone de Brenn's father, the old Warden of Bewly, was hand in glove with Mortimer and the French Isabella. And his son Hugo is no better. If the young

Prince Edward comes trustingly to Bewly and lays his head in the trap—"

"How do you mean—trap?"

"What else? Butcher de Brenn could win great ransom for the king's own son, did he seize him and turn him over to the French. He could stop the war and win himself all of Guienne and Normandy in exchange, at the very least!"

SIR ALLAN MAYNE'S brows frowned, and a dark gleam came into his eyes. "By my halidon, there is sooth in what you say! For I do not trust this Hugo de Brenn myself. I must go in haste to warn the Prince." He looked around at the archers. "If any stout yeomen here would like service with a knight who has no holdings but who will swear to lead where honor and wealth may be had, I would welcome such to come with me."

Then, to Robin: "And you, Robin Lackland, I love thee well for the stout buffet you gave me yesterday. And gladly would I have at my side the arm and man that gave it."

But Robin shook his head. "The cutting of men's throats in battle is a bloody business for which I care not a whit. It is the fashioning of metals, the science of levers and forces that interest me—"

"Then there is room for such in the king's artillery—the making and laying of ballistae and catapults and engines of siege—"

But at that moment there was a sound of grunts and groans and stumbling steps and from the nearest cart stumbled the merchant, Jacob Algelt. Hanging to his daughter's arms, he stood and rubbed the stiffness from his limbs. It was evident that his age was too great for the arduous happenings he had experienced in the past twenty-four hours.

At sight of him John the Wolf gave a round oath. "Ransom in France is a pleasant thing, and something to give thought to. But we are forgetting the ransom in hand. Didst not say the merchant's gold was in these two great carts that we saved from de Brenn last night, Hubert? And are we not entitled to fair ransom out of the gold that we saved?"

"Rightly spoken, Old Wolf!" exclaimed Red Hubert. "Trust thy nose to smell out money wherever it may be. Give us a hand then and let us look at this gold."

Despite the old merchant's shouts and protests they leaped inside the carts, slashed off the canvas covers, and began to throw about the contents with great noise and bickering. Then Hubert's voice rose in surprise and disappointment.

"There is no gold here! Naught but two long-shaped bells of metal for the carillon of some minster or abbey! And stone balls for bowling, and sacks of fine crushed charcoal which we could find at any charcoal burner's hut!"

"And the same here!" cried John the Wolf, scowling down out of the other cart. He glanced at the Flemish merchant. "Where is the gold? For thy lies, we would do well to throw thee back to the Butcher!"

"Nay, not gold, not gold!" gasped the old merchant. "I said not that it was gold. I said save these two carts, for that they were of great value."

"Great value? Value in stone balls and charcoal?" John the Wolf cursed. Suddenly he began to hurl them out of the cart, so that the balls thudded about the old man's feet and the charcoal covered him until he was black. "Take them then, old liar!"

ROBIN HAD picked up one of the balls, studied it. He peered into the cart at the long, bell-shaped things of dark metal that lay within. Then, stooping, he thrust his hand into one of the sacks, took some of the charcoal powder into his hand, sniffed at it and touched it to his lips. Startled, he turned keen eyes on Algelt.

"Not only charcoal, but brimstone and sulphur! Is not this serpentine—wildfire?"

"Serpentine!" The old merchant blinked his eyes. "How didst thou know?"

"In his treatise in the library at Oxford, Roger the Franciscan did give the rules for the compounding of charcoal, sulphur and brimstone to make wildfire. In truth I did make shift to compound something of it myself, to the singeing of my own hair and eyebrows."

Robin sifted the powder in his hands again. "There seemeth less than the proportion of sulphur and brimstone, but doubtless it was shaken to the bottom of the charcoal by the jolting of the cart. But what of these stone balls? And surely those great metal tubes, by the thickness of their sides and by their shapes, are no bells for any carillon."

For a long moment the merchant stared at him. Then he nodded reluctantly. "No. They are bombards. And the balls are the missiles to be cast from them by the firing of the gunpowder."

"Bombards!" Sir Allan echoed the word amazedly.

"Aye. It is as I said," responded the old merchant slowly. "These bombards and their balls and powder are more value than were all the merceries and goods in all the rest of the carts and packs. For with these bombards a ball may be hurled further and straighter than the missile of any catapult or ballista, no matter how huge. With them one may batter down walls, breach cities, or blast through shield, haubergeon, and hauberk of the stoutest armor made."

He ceased speaking, his old eyes traveling from one to another. They fell as he noted the derisive grins spreading on the archers' faces, the look of disbelief even on the countenance of Sir Allan Mayne. The Flanders merchant clenched his hands.

"It was even thus when I tried to approach the Court in London. I offered your King the wherewith to blast apart any wall or army in France. For ten thousand *livres* I would have hired him the bombards and the missiles and even provided the bombardiers to serve them. But the King would not see me. And when I tried to bespeak the Prince, I was forestalled there also. By a great, dark-faced man with a broken nose and scarred cheek who bade me begone to hell and take my bombards with me."

"That would be Sir Murray Wilton, the Prince's henchman," said Sir Allan, nodding. "I have fought alongside the old warhorse in Flanders and elsewhere. And he would not give you heed?"

"Not even though I begged him to arrange a test for my bombards against his strongest catapults and ballistae," said the old merchant mournfully.

"And scant wonder," said the knight, nodding. "Catapults and ballistae, a man may believe, for he may see the workings of the beams and ropes. But he would be daft who believed that with fire and charcoal powder and a tube, a man could hurl a missile through a wall or a man in full armor." He turned to Robin. "Is that not sooth?"

But Robin was thoughtful. "Roger the Franciscan wrote naught of using the powder in tubes to hurl missiles. But he wrote that fearful indeed was the force released by the burning, so that no pot or cannister might hold it. And Roger Bacon, the Franciscan, wrote that many strange discoveries would come to pass that we living men wot not of."

"ROGER BACON, the Black Monk!"

At the name, the archers stumbled back horrified, and even Sir Allan Mayne hurriedly crossed himself. For though Roger Bacon had been a Franciscan—a Gray Friar—report had damned his name through all Christendom as a Black Monk, a man in league with Satan. For had he not written of boats that would move without either oars nor sails, and that men themselves would fly in air like birds?

"I can well believe, merchant," said Robin, "that these same bombards may do what you say they will. What are your plans, and where were you taking them when captured by the Lord Warden?"

Jacob Algelt's lips quivered, he looked about him with fright. "To—to the King of France. I had spent many *livres*—all my fortune—in the casting and the compounding of the powder. I had to recover my loss from someone. If the King of England would not hire my bombards, mayhap the King of France would."

"And help the Frenchmen slash us to pieces with these devil's tubes and powders?" Red Hubert let out an oath. "That were treason indeed! Lay hand to him, John—Peter! We will into the fire with him and his powders, and no doubt be the better Christians for it as well!"

Before the merchant could move, the archers had closed in on him with black looks and words. Nor did Sir Allan make move to halt them.

"Mayhap that is a good thought, archer," said he. "Such devil's weapons were well enough to use on paynims and unbelievers. But the French are believers even as ourselves. And to blast a Christian apart with such foul means is not becoming to an Englishman."

The girl gave a scream, endeavored to throw herself between, but strong arms held her back and helpless. Wat the Armorer made protest, but was as quickly silenced. Screaming and kicking, the Flanders merchant was hoisted up, borne on the shoulders of stout forest men toward the fire.

Robin looked around helplessly, but there was no weapon in sight that might avail against the archers. And that they meant to throw the old man into the flames was well evident. For as all men knew, only fire could purge the black magic from a man who had made a compact with Satan.

Closer they carried Algelt to the fire, their faces grimly set.

Again the girl screamed. And suddenly Robin spun about. Dipping his two hands into the nearest sack, he filled them to heaping with the black-grained powder. Then he raced after the archers.

They were already at the fireside, pressing their captive to the flames. Bursting past them, Robin hurled the full contents of his two hands onto the red embers.

In an instant there was a hissing *whoosh*. Smoke and flame billowed and spurted, ashes and great chunks of flaming embers were hurled afar. The smoke cloud billowed about the archers, swallowing them in its acrid fumes. So that with shouts of fright they broke and scattered, coughing from the smoke and ashes, and beating at the embers that were charring flesh and doublets.

Robin too had been caught in the quick-spurting flare; his own hair and brows were singed and his eyelids dusted with stinging ashes. However, he brushed at them for only a moment, before falling to with his hands to beat out the red spots that were charring the merchant's clothing in a dozen places.

Old Algelt's howls were prompted more by fright than by pain; but most of all by the helpless rage of a man who knows that he has been wronged. Robin himself was silently cursing these fools who understood science only as devil's work. The smart of his burns was no worse than the impatience he felt; and it was not easy to hold his peace.

IT WAS Wat the Armorer, however, who pushed forward first, even bolder than Sir Allan Mayne. He lashed at the coughing forest men with bitter anger. "How now, dolts, knaves! Hast so soon forgot the oath ye sware, to do in anything as I bid—the oath to hold me leader of all the masterless men?"

Hubert and John the Wolf cursed and rubbed at their stinging eyes. "Aye, Wat. But naught was said about necromancy and black magic from Flanders."

"So ye would have held Robin's arbalest to be black magic too, in that it would outshoot any ordinary bow, had ye not sense to understand its fashioning," retorted the armorer. "Go soak thy heads, dullards, and may the soaking give ye wit to understand this charcoal powder too! Stand back from the old merchant! Leave him unscathed and get thee gone!"

"But the very smoke and fury of this brimstone is proof that it is devil's doing—"

"Get thee gone, I said! Or wouldst that I should cast this entire sack into the fire and crisp every man in this whole clearing?" Suddenly they saw then that the armorer clutched in his hands the opened bag from which the other powder had come.

And from the sternness of his face as he held the bag forth, they saw that he was full purposed to do as he had threatened.

"Nay! Nay!" Hubert stepped back, and the other forest men gave way along with him. "Hold thy hand from that devil's compound, old forest boar. Thou art still leader, and we masterless men will do thy bidding—ill as it may be that we let this Flanders necromancer go free from his scotching. Mark me: the man's accursed."

Still mumbling, they moved away. Running forward, the girl caught at her father and led him back to the wagons. Robin turned to Sir Allan.

"You spoke of it being foul work to use bombards against the French," he said. "But what difference if a Christian be slain with catapult or bombard? Death comes equally in either case. So it seems to me far better that we use the bombards ourselves than let them go to fall into the hands of the French. Also I have a curiosity to learn more of these bombards."

Wat nodded shrewdly.

"If they are in truth stronger than a catapult to smite through mailed armor," said the old armorer, "it may well be that here is the thing that will make a freeborn forester the equal even of a highborn knight. A hundred yeomen with such bombards would be even stouter armed than if they carried those double-staved arbalests you showed us yesterday."

Sir Allan looked from one to the other of them with blackened brows, and it was plain that the knight was not over-suited with their words. But at last he stood back, as if washing his hands of it all.

"Bombards or no bombards, I must be gone. If de Brenn has treachery in mind, I must seek out Edward of Woodstock at once, that he may be warned away from Bewly."

Perhaps it was the mention of Bewly that made Robin suddenly remember what the knight had said not long ago— something about a trap prepared by the king's enemies. And with this memory flashed the picture of a brilliant cavalcade around the forest point; a slender, richly-clad boy whose brows grew troubled at sight of a gibbet.

"Edward of Woodstock!" Robin looked at Sir Allan sharply. "Is this Edward then a youth of some sixteen, slight built and of exceeding fairness? And accompanied perchance by a dark man with a much scarred face, and a dozen men-at-arms as well?"

"Aye. That would be Edward of Woodstock, and the scarred man would be Sir Murray Wilton. Thou hast seen them then?"

Robin nodded. "At the crossroads gibbet on the Salisbury Road yesterday, just after you rode through the wagons in the chase. They asked the way to Bewly town, and if there were inns there."

"Bewly!" Sir Allan whirled to his horse. "Then I must needs hasten! Perhaps it is already too late, and de Brenn already hath seized the Prince!"

"The Prince!"

"Aye. Edward of Woodstock, the oldest son of the King. The Prince of Wales—though by reason of his dark armor, some there are who call him the Black Prince!"

CHAPTER VIII

THE KING'S HIGHWAY

SIR ALLAN DID not ride alone to Bewly, however, for Robin had a curiosity to see the town also, and a need to buy new hose to replace his own bramble-torn stockings.

Whereupon Wat the Armorer called up Hubert and Peter and John the Wolf and bade them take bow and quiver and accompany the two.

"Poke our noses into the Butcher's trap?" growled Hubert the Red. "And to save a rascally prince who would as soon gibbet me for this very venison we ate, as his Lord Warden, Butcher de Brenn?"

*Robin drove the ball home into the
carefully-aimed bombard*

"King or prince, it matters no whit," retorted the armorer. "But if he be the Butcher's enemy, that is reason enough for honest Englishmen to call him friend."

Sir Allan's face darkened. "Your logic is as weak as your armor is good, armorer. It matters much that we have a just Prince, for without some rightful leader how can a country endure? Even your masterless men, for reason that they might fight better for the common good, chose you as leader—"

"Aye," said Wat stolidly. "And I suit them not, they will as quick unchoose me. But we have no choice in who shall be king or baron over us. However, the barons are worse than king or prince, because there are more of them. When we have got rid of the Butcher and his fellow barons, it will be time enough to think to king and prince."

"Which is treason enough in the very uttering to bring thee to the gibbet, if not to the very stake!" exclaimed the knight angrily.

"That may well be," answered the armorer, unmoved. "But it

may be also that we Englishmen may send a king himself to the gibbet sometime, if we like not his ways. Leaders we must have, as thou hast said. But they will be leaders of our choice, or we will get others we like better."

"Nay, let us keep this Black Prince or whatever he be," interrupted John the Wolf impatiently. "If he will lead us to where we may get many *livres* in loot and ransom, that is leader enough for me."

Sir Allan mounted his horse, with his armor sacked on his saddle before him for greater comfort. But Robin chose to march afoot, with the three archers, only choosing a keen sword and round archer's shield and steel-hooped cap for protection.

Through the fens they marched, and by daylight now they made far swifter progress than the night before. So that in three scant hours they came to the very spot where they had ambushed the Butcher's men-at-arms the evening before.

Here Sir Allan tied his mount in the forest screen and changed from his costly garments to mere archer's jerkin and hose which he had fetched along.

"If de Brenn is indeed up to treason, I would rather see than be seen," he said.

Robin in his torn garments would pass for any village yeoman. Red Hubert's eyes twinkled.

"If we sight the Butcher or that bull-necked seneschal of his, or even his foresters, we shall take to covert like weasels," he said. "We have taken too many deer, I wot, for our faces to be unknown did we come to close view."

BUT ONCE they had left the forest and came to the main Salisbury Road, they had small fear of being noticed. For the highway was dotted with numerous men and even small parties making their way to Bewly town. Most of them were young men, armed with archer's bow and quiver or steel cap, buckler, and pike or partisan, though occasionally there came one better armed in open basinet and half-mail. Of full-mailed men-at-arms there were few, for these were mostly countrymen, and a full coat of mail cost more than an ordinary man might earn in a lifetime of work.

Too, there came men driving cows and sheep and even herds of pigs toward the town. Whereat Hubert nodded.

"You spake sooth, Sir Knight, when you said the call to arms had gone out. For these in truth must be the levies. And these sheep and cattle for the feeding of the men."

Already above the treetops could be seen the thin spire of Bewly Abbey and even the donjon battlements and towers of Bewly Castle itself. Then they came beyond the last thickets and into sight of Bewly town.

Huddled together beyond the plain lay the clustered houses and walls of the town, while to the right upreared the forbidding towers and curtain walls of the Warden's great castle, standing on a rocky eminence. But the plain itself was covered with tents and rude huts and carts and herds, and countless men moving like ants to an anthill.

Between the forest edge and the plain itself, however, lay the curving stream of Bewly Water, and a timbered bridge where the highway crossed. Toward this they made their way.

When they made to cross, however, they found great chains barring their way. And behind the chains, stoutly armed men who bade them halt.

"One penny apiece for every man on foot, and three pennies for cart or man a-horse," announced the leader, a burly man with heavy beard. His eyes scanned them quickly. "And if there be a Jew among you, even afoot, his toll is three pence also, as equal to a man with a cart or horse."

"Toll!" Sir Allan's eyes flashed and his brows blackened with anger. "Toll for men called to levy by the King's messengers? Is not this the King's highway and the King's bridge?"

"The King's business I know naught of," returned the toll-keeper surlily. "But the baron's business is my care. And the baron hath made rule that no man crosses without paying toll."

The knight's eyes were flashing, and his fingers were tightening on his sword hilt. In another instant Robin feared that his anger would embroil them all in a mêlée. Plucking out his purse, he tossed three coppers quickly to the toll-keeper who thereupon dropped the chains that they might pass.

"Mend thy manners though, varlet," the toll-keeper warned Sir Allan, "or next time you will find yourself in the water and not on the bridge."

The knight's lips were still white with anger when they passed to the other side. But Red Hubert laughed.

"King's highway it may be, but the bridge itself is the Butcher's. For I saw with my own eyes his men herding the villeins from the fields to the work, even with whips and sword blows when they were lazy to move."

"But corvees—forced labor—is forbidden in all England, by the stipulations of that Magna Carta which King John signed," said Robin.

"Mayhap the Butcher does not know how to read," said the archer, chuckling.

Sir Allan's brows were troubled. "Wat the Armorer may prove right at that. For if there be many barons like Hugo de Brenn, then Englishmen could not be blamed who rose against them."

BY NOW they were crossing the plain, and in the midst of all the crowds and confusion. Sheep and cattle were being thrown into great guarded herds in rude enclosures, while the squealing pigs were sequestered in a bend of the stream. Farriers were shoeing horses, carpenters plied hammer and saw, while armorers at anvil and forge by the wayside were repairing armor and fashioning arrowheads and pikes by the hundreds. All the preparations for war and arming men were going on in every direction.

Suddenly Robin paused before a score of men at work about a framework of great beams and timbers. Other finished engines were already ranged in rows, the new-hewn timbers and fresh-twisted ropes yellow in the sun.

"Nay, that master artilleryman knows not his trade," he said. "The spoon for yon catapult is overlight for the length of the throw-beam. Any stone of weight would crack it from the lever-age at the first jerk of the ropes."

But Sir Allan pulled him away. "Time enough for your mathematics when you are the king's man and one of his artillery. But if we find not the Prince before de Brenn discovers him, we may not go to the wars at all."

Again they started along the little road that ran through the center of the camp. There came a jingling of chains and armor, the trample of horses' hooves. Hubert jerked his eyes upward.

"De Brenn—the Butcher himself! Quick, Peter—John—behind this forge!"

But already the horsemen were upon them, a half-dozen of them in full armor.

"Too late!" said Hubert. "Down heads then, boys, and look not up for your lives' sake!"

Standing with heads down, and caps doffed, they waited at the roadside while the little cavalcade swept past. Robin was eaten with irresistible curiosity, however, and could not help but steal a glance.

The foremost rider was de Brenn, the Lord Warden himself. His visor was open, and Robin could see the hawk-nose, the dark features, the roving eyes. Too, there was a purplish bruise on the cheekbone just beneath the right eye. And Robin, remembering how he had pitched the man sprawling from his saddle the night before, could not but feel a thrill of pleasure. Then the black roving eyes swept around, rested upon him.

Robin's heart stood still. For the horseman was at short sword's length away, and he himself as helpless against full armor as though he stood naked.

However, the baron, not recognizing him, merely slashed at him carelessly with his riding whip as he rode past, to reprove him for standing so close crowded to the roadside. And Red Hubert gave a grunt of relief.

"Lucky that he had not his head forester with him. For he

would know this red hatch of mine if it hid among a hundred others."

"Put thy energy more to walking and less to talking, archer," said Sir Allan. "He comes from the town. And I will not rest easy as to his visit there until I have seen the Prince unscathed."

CHAPTER IX

TREASON TOWER

SO CHOKED WAS the road, however, with carts and material and constantly crossing men, that they were still within the camp boundaries when again the jingling of armed horsemen assailed their ears. This time it came from behind, and they had but to step aside and wait while the horsemen swept past. Three score there were, this time, and Red Hubert let out an oath.

"That was closer escape still! My red hairs will stand for a week so that my cap will seem like a roof on stilts. Didst note the red-necked rascal that rode in the van, Peter? Brendon the Bull, the Lord Warden's seneschal—or I never drew shaft!"

"De Brenn's seneschal?" Sir Allan's tone was worried. "And at full speed. I like it not. There is foul work afoot here, I fear."

Threading the camp, they crossed across a little meadow, and came to the skirts of the town.

Bewly, being a chartered town, had likewise been a walled town, as befitted its importance. But its walls had been breached in the civil wars of twenty years earlier, and not since repaired. Where once the great gates had barred the way, now there stood but crumbled masonry and a great yawning hole through which they passed unchallenged.

Inside they found themselves immediately in the narrow streets of the town itself. Crooked, winding, crowded by the stone house-walls on either side, they were so narrow that two carts would have been put to it to pass abreast. At crazy angles they branched and crossed, so that the whole town was like a maze in which burghers jostled with travelers and tradesmen. Soldiers scraped their halberds against the wall stones, shouting out in rough good humor at the shopkeepers or the pretty town maids who pretended to draw back with timid eyes from the rough banter.

"We must make haste—it already draws nigh to sunset," said Sir Allan. "We will inquire at the inns first."

Although they inquired at each hostelry and inn they saw along the street, they learned no news of those they sought.

"A dozen men-at-arms, with a scar-faced leader, and a young knight of fair skin and hair? No, none such came this way. None but rascally pikemen and archers who are worse than a murrain upon us!"

Deeper and deeper they pushed into the town, and came finally to an inn, larger than the others, on a corner, with a great painted ensign swinging over its doors that announced it as *The White Swan*. But the landlord of the White Swan only shook his head at their questioning.

"None are here but a dozen thieving soldiers from the up-shires who are drinking and eating me out of house and home," he grumbled. "They eat a *livre's* worth for every penny they pay. You can hear them anow, quarreling at their dice!"

Even as he spoke, the taproom door opened, and a burly leathernclad fellow pushed through, a brimming ale pot in his hand.

"Where skulks that niggardly landlord?" he bellowed. "Come forth and we will wring thy fat neck for thee! This is small beer, and we ordered full heady ale—"

Then all at once he halted in mid speech and stared, unnoticing of the beer that spilled from his canted pot. "Sir Allan Mayne! Sir Allan—or I never bussed a French maid!"

"Jarold—thou stout rascal!" Sir Allan's eyes widened. "What dost thou here? I thought thou wouldst have been gibbeted in Guienne this long time since!"

CHUCKLING, THE soldier doffed his cap, his weathered face agrin. "Not gibbeted yet, though time enough there is yet. We have come down from Kent, twelve of us that were all of the old company. When loot and pillage are in the air, only a scurvy villein will stand to his plow. But I little recked to run onto the old captain of our company!"

The knight smiled at the evident welcome in the soldier's voice, forgetting his own appearance for the moment. "When we disbanded, as I remember, you had plans for a farm, and a wife, and a life of ease. What of the farm? And what of the great horde of *deniers* you had from the pillaging of Angoulais?"

"Gone this twelve-month!" Jarold snapped his fingers. "*Deniers* and farms were not intended for soldiers—or so the dice said. But where there were *deniers* once, there may be *deniers* again." Then for the first time his glance fell to the rough jerkin of the knight. "What ho, Sir Allan? Hast been attainted of treason and deprived of knighthood and the right to gentle garments and armored quarterings?"

"Nay." Sir Allan stammered with embarrassment. "Nay. It is but that I—"

But the soldier was gabbling on, unnoticing. "Attainted of treason or no, it matters naught. For I still have memory of a time at the taking of that same Angoulais when you cut down a scurvy Frenchman who was all for thrusting me through from behind when my back was turned. Only half armor we have, and rough woolen not fitting to thy rank. But what we have is yours, and that without asking."

"Nay, keep thy mail and woolens," said Sir Allan, smiling. "But news I would be glad to accept, if you have knowledge of what I seek. Hast seen aught of a noble party, some dozen or more, with a young knight of exceeding fair countenance, and an older one of brave scars. The scarred one you would know, for it was that same Sir Murray Wilton who led at the taking of Angoulais."

But Jarold shook his head. "Naught of Sir Murray or those

others have I seen. But a little time past another party did come this way. Some three score men-at-arms, with a thick-necked man in the lead, but I gave them little heed."

"Three score men-it-arms, led by a thick-necked man?" Sir Allan's lips tightened. "And which way did they go?"

"Down the street, toward the hall with the tall keep," said the soldier carelessly. "And methought thereafter I heard noise of armed bickering—a mêlée—but I gave it little reck. The only mêlées that are worth our while are those with good *deniers* for those who win."

But already Sir Allan was turned and hurrying for the door, drawing Robin and the archers with him while Jarold and his fellow soldiers stood staring after them.

DOWN THE narrow street but a hundred paces, the thoroughfare curved sharply. And then it debouched into an open space, evidently the town square. There was a tall wall encompassing what was undoubtedly the town hall of Bewly, since a round keep of solid masonry reared sixty foot above it.

Here it was that the chief burghers and masters of the guilds met, to transact their business and make their laws for the governing of the town. But like all town halls of the time, it was a fortress as well, since the burghers were often at odds with the seigneurs of the castle and other barons.

But the gates were not open, as ordinarily they would be in times of peace. Instead the great portcullis was down, its massive bars forbidding in the late light. And beyond the portcullis the solid oak of the great doors stood, a closed barrier.

Too, now Robin noted that the shopkeepers along the streets facing the hall were busily closing their shutters, and barring their shop doors—sign in itself that some untoward disturbance was happening.

Sir Allan, however, led the way straight toward the portcullis and oaken doors. As they came near, a gruff voice called out from the slitted loophole in the round gate towers. "Hold! What seek you here, in the town hall?"

"Sir Murray Wilton and a party who came this way," answered
Sir Allan quickly. "I have message for them, and someone gave
me word they came this way."

There was a moment's silence, and then the voice answered
more curtly than before. "None there is of that name here. These
are the bailiff and the sergeants of the town. Ten rascals of the
camp have committed a robbery and a murder and we have
taken them and are giving them trial. We are locked in, that
none of their rascally companions of the levies may try rescue."

"We are no rascals from the levies' camp," retorted Sir Allan
angrily. "We have messages of importance, and if we cannot find
Sir Murray Wilton, then we must give them to the mayor and
the head burghers. Open up!"

"Get thee gone! There will be no rescue here! And you remain,
you will hang from the keep gibbet along with your thievish
companions! Get thee gone, I say! Bowman, make ready a quarrel!"

And with the words came the unmistakable click of an arbalest quarrel slipped into groove.

But with it also came another sound, from within the gates,
and apparently at the masonry of the keep that towered within.
That sound was a great knocking and banging, as if heavy
timbers battered at stout doors. Then there was the thud of
heavy missiles falling. Curses and groans came up. Then at the
very top of the keep tower Robin caught a glimpse of movement. And thin but clear came a defiant shout: "St. George! St.
George for England!"

"Quick! Away from that arbalest, and around the corner!"
gasped Sir Allan, whirling even as he spoke. The five of them
raced along the wall, keeping so close in under it that any
bowmen would have difficulty training shaft or quarrel fairly
upon them.

AT THE first corner, where the wall of the town hall turned,
there loomed a narrow street, for the open square lay only in
front of the main gates. Down this street, between the wall and

the houses that crowded not a dozen paces away, Sir Allan led. He paused for a moment to draw breath.

"It is as I feared. I would know Sir Murray's war-cry in hell itself. The Prince and Sir Murray, distrusting of the Lord Warden, sought shelter in the town instead of the castle. And being equally distrustful of inns, they demanded lodging in the town hall itself, as being stronger and more royal of quarter. Learning it, de Brenn sent a party under his seneschal to seize and kidnap them."

"I thought I recognized the voice of Brendon the Bull at that loophole," said Hubert. "But why then did not Brendon drag his prisoners back to the castle, if he had them caught? They were surer held there than here in the town."

Sir Allan spoke impatiently.

"De Brenn's men have not caught them yet. Sir Murray is too wise an old fox to be caught napping. He had the Prince and his whole party quartered in the keep. And at first sign of attack, he barred the doors. It was de Brenn's men trying to break them down, that battering that we heard."

"Then we have naught to worry about," said Hubert, shrugging his shoulders. "They can hold the keep against Brendon even as Brendon can hold the outer wall and towers against us. And ere long, if it be the Prince himself, as you say, the King's men will be here in force to catch the kidnappers instead."

But Sir Allan shook his head. "The King may not know until too late. The keep is probably not provisioned against siege in time of peace. And without provisions they could not hold out more than another day."

"Then we have but to scatter among the levies in the camp, and gather men to rescue the Prince," suggested Robin eagerly. "Surely they would not side with de Brenn against the Prince!"

Again the knight shook his head, made a hopeless gesture.

"And who would we be, for them to believe?" asked Sir Allan. "Two unknowns in leather jerkins, and three others who are masterless men. Whereas all the levies are of this shire, and de

Brenn's men—or at least well feared of de Brenn. He need only say that it is a quarrel among the burghers, and they would have no part of it. No, there is no help there."

He stood for a moment, thinking. Then he lifted his head.

"Jarold! Jarold and his eleven! They are stout fighters all, and they would know and believe me." Then his voice suddenly dropped. "But what could a mere dozen do—against three score, behind stout walls at that? And without catapult or ballista to breach wall or gate."

"As for the men," said Red Hubert suddenly, "there are more than a dozen to call upon. There are nearer two hundred! Peter Joy, do you race to Wat, and bid him to assemble the masterless men. All the masterless men in the forest! And then do you bring them here at haste!"

"Take my horse—take my horse, and spare him not!" cried the knight with renewed fire. "Wait! We will go with thee, that far. I have need of casque and full armor."

"And, Peter," said Robin, "tell Wat to bring the carts as well. The carts and all that is in them! And fetch the Flanders merchant with them, if you have to drag him by the neck!"

Peter nodded, and was gone.

CHAPTER X

BATTLE-DAWN

CROUCHED IN THE half-light of the guttering cresset, Robin shivered with suspense, for his young nerves were not yet tempered to that tensity that comes before battle. But around him Sir Allan and Jarold and his seasoned men-at-arms sat at ease and talked carelessly of past wars and sieges, and even more of victories and loot to come.

On either side the smoky light threw gaunt shadows of looms and shuttles against the walls, for this was the Lane of the Weavers, and this room the front of a weaver's shop. Sir Allan had singled it out because its door faced directly opposite the postern door in the side wall around the town hall.

Through the cracked door Robin could see even now, not twenty feet across the narrow lane, the stout iron-strapped door of the postern gate, with the squat guard towers on either side. And beyond it, seeming to rear almost overhead, the sheer walls of the keep itself, now dark and silent against the starlit sky.

No sound of battering or even clank of armor and curses of men at strife came now from the court inside the wall nor in the tall keep itself. But Robin knew that inside the postern towers keen-eyed bowmen stood with ready shafts and quarrels, while mail-clad men stalked the court itself and made ready for the grim dawn.

The lack of noise Sir Allan explained. "Even if impatient to lay hand on the Prince, they have scant wish to break into the keep at night. Sir Murray is an old warrior, and a foxy one. Even with his dozen men he could lay such traps on the keep's stairs and stages as not even de Brenn's sixty men would care to risk."

Jarold's eyes flickered and he thumb-tested the edge of his sword which he was leisurely honing on a stone. "A stout blade and a sharp one. A short battle and a merry one. Even so we sat—remember, Sir Allan?—the night before Angoulais, waiting for the sun to rise."

Beside him lay his basinet, byrnie and shield, laid aside for the ease of his bones. The other eleven men-at-arms, recruited from the White Swan at a single word from Sir Allan, sat around in the same careless manner. Even the knight had laid his mail aside, delaying to don it only when the time for action came.

Only the weaver and his three apprentices, whispering at the back, jumped at each sudden noise or movement, betraying tenseness equal to Robin's. And scant wonder. Peaceful townsmen, their first inkling of what was to befall had come when they had timidly opened the door to Sir Allan's thundering knock.

"What seek ye here?" The elderly weaver had cracked the door to make his quavering question. "We be but peaceful weavers and plain men; we have naught to interest—"

But Sir Allan had hushed his question by pushing rudely in and past him, Jarold's men-at-arms trooping at his heels. "We have no intent to harm thee, master weaver. We do but require the loan of thy shop for a little time. That and the silence of you and your apprentices. If, however, any of you seek to break past or set up the hue-and-cry—" He did not finish. There was no need. At sight of the knight's grim face and the sharp swords of the men-at-arms, the weavers had fallen back and kept their peace, albeit watching with fright, from their corner at every moment.

The bells of Bewly Abbey had long since rung the call to midnight prayers, and now the night silence seemed to crowd closer than ever. And still no news came from Peter Joy.

Sir Allan grew more nervous.

EVEN WITH the knight's horse, however, Robin knew that it would take Peter considerable time to gallop the distance to the clearing in the forest swamps. And it would take even longer time for the return, what with the slower carts and the necessary wait for the gathering of the masterless men. Even though Wat the Armorer sent the carts on ahead while he rallied the forest men with his great horn.

Stepping to the door, Allan drew it open a little, looked out.

The stars had changed place in the heavens, but still the keep and towers and wall opposite loomed dead and silent. Robin's eyes followed that wall thirty paces to the right to where it turned at a corner tower to stretch its stout bulwark along the public square. There, where the great main gate and portcullis faced the square, Red Hubert had been left posted to bring word of any sortie. John the Wolf stood watch at the street mouth opening into the square, to guide the forest men when they should come.

Then in the distant stillness, Robin heard the slow creak of cartwheels. They rumbled over the rutted ground, came into sight. There were two dark splotches—two carts, with horses. But no stream of men came trooping after.

Robin stood back from the door. "Two carts—" he said. "They are just turning down this way. But there are no men, seemingly, other than the drivers."

"Keep the door cracked but an inch," ordered Sir Allan. He began jerking on his armor, as did Jarold and the men-at-arms. "And stand ready to drop the great bar. These wagons may be a trap. De Brenn is a fox, and may have got wind of us. I trust him not."

Rumbling along the narrow Lane of the Weavers, the cart-wheels now sounded louder, nearer. They came opposite the door, and stopped.

Through the crack of the door Sir Allan called out, pitching his voice creaky and high, amazingly like that of the old weaver. "Is that the cart with the looms? The looms my brother Wat in Salisbury gave word he was sending me?"

"Looms? From Salisbury?" John the Wolf's voice answered amazedly. "No—" Then suddenly his words broke off, with a low chuckle. "Aye, the looms! But tell thy Brother Wat in Salisbury that, next time, he chooses other wagons than the carts of John the carter! So heavy the looms are, that they strain the axle. And what with the roads crowded with levies and armed knaves, we were forced to travel by night instead of the good honest daylight. Open the door and take thy scurvy looms!"

"Fetch them in thyself, that is what carters are for!" retorted Sir Allan. Then, in a low voice to those in the shop: "Stand out of the light, out of sight of the doorway, that no glint of arms may show."

And Robin remembered that de Brenn's watchmen in the towers at the postern gate opposite would undoubtedly be watching with keen eyes anything that came or went in the lane, even two sluggish carts.

But Sir Allan was speaking again, his squeaky voice now

impatient. "Bring the looms in, dolt! Bring the looms in! And have a care how you mistreat them!"

THERE WAS the thud of cart gates dropped, stout skids being laid. Then a loud scraping noise, with the grunts and grumbling of men straining with heavy burdens. And in through the doorway staggered John the Wolf, a heavy sack on his shoulder. After him came other men, panting and pulling at rude-built sledges on which were the first of the heavy bombard tubes that Robin had seen at the clearing.

"Ho, master-weaver! Here is the first loom!" called John the Wolf, putting his sack down. "The second will follow in a moment. And all the sacks of shuttles and such other geegaws. Not only that, but here is thy niece that must ride along also to visit with her uncle.... Here, give an honest carter a buss, lass!"

As the slender, skirted figure came past him, John the Wolf suddenly snatched an embrace and a hurried kiss, which she as promptly repaid by a great slap that fair set his head to ringing. Then she came tripping on into the room, so that the light fell upon her. And Robin was struck with such amazement that he had no heed at all for her father, the pot-bellied old merchant of Bruges, who came limping after.

For the girl was now dressed in neat clothing, plain but fitting to any maiden of a craftsman's family. She wore no coif, and her raven locks glinted and rippled in the cresset light, but no blacker nor more sparkling than her eyes. Her lips were as red as cherries, and her piquant face was aglow with excitement. Robin thought he had never seen, nor hoped to see, any maid so lovely.

But her father was groaning and complaining with the cramp of the cart seat, until Sir Allan hushed him rudely lest his foreign accents be too evident to the ears across the street.

As the other bombard was dragged in on its sled, and the last of a dozen sacks that Robin knew must contain the balls and powder was stacked on the floor, Sir Allan tossed John the Wolf a couple of coins.

"Here. Here is my wage, carter! And if you care to trust your carts and wagons to thy drivers, and linger for a bit of sup, you are welcome."

"Aye, that will I, and right heartily." Stepping to the door, John the Wolf spoke a few words, and the horses clumped away down the street again with the carts creaking after them. Swiftly then Sir Allan closed and barred the door. He looked at John the Wolf.

"What of Wat and what of his masterless men that Peter Joy took word for him to fetch?"

"He should be here now. He *is* here now!" John the Wolf grinned, held up his finger for silence. "Listen!"

Then on the flat roof above the shop attic they heard the thump of feet, the low mumbling of voices.

Sir Allan looked up questioningly.

"Wat halted them at the turn of the street, just out of sight of the hall gates," said John the Wolf. "Then set them clambering up, and so on along the rooftops. On every housetop along this lane there will be crouched a half dozen archers, as strong of arm and keen of eye as ever sank a shaft in stag's ribs. Behind the copings and roof ridges they will let loose so many fine-drawn shafts that not a tower loophole or slit will be safe from them, come daybreak—much less the top of yon opposite wall itself."

EVEN AS he spoke, there was a creaking noise on the roof top, where the trap door was set for drenching the roofs in case of fire. The trap itself opened and, glancing up the stairway, Robin saw the clambering legs and then the shoulders and face of Wat the Armorer swinging down through the narrow opening. Grunting from his exertions, the armorer found footing and came the rest of the way down to join them.

"With the dawn we will have the Butcher's men like rats in a trap," he said, looking around with satisfaction. "That is, if these bombards can breach that postern gate as this Flemisher hath claimed."

"Not if they open the main gates and ride away through

those," said Sir Allan. "With all of us attacking along this gate and wall—"

But the Armorer spat. "Not with every street mouth blocked with carts and timbers that we fetched along with us as we came through the levies' camp. Nor will they ride far into the square even, since Hubert is even now stretching stout chains and ropes there, just a little way out from the wall gates, that will throw any horse and rider that seeks to break through. A full two hundred men the Forest has sent this night."

Then his shaggy brows lowered. "And ill it will go with me, if this Black Prince we rescue prove to be not the just prince ye have named him, but only such another over-riding lord as the Butcher of Bewly."

"As to that, wait and thou shalt see for thyself," answered the knight, smiling.

Robin was thoughtful. "If de Brenn sent his seneschal to make the seizure, it is no sign that he sleeps himself. What if he has his castle forces all ready, waiting to see if the seneschal succeeds alone? Then at first sound of our own attack, he would come to crush us from the rear."

Sir Allan nodded. "De Brenn hath left the actual seizure of the Prince to his seneschal, like the fox he is, so that he may disclaim any part in it if his plot goes wrong. But certain he would be to attack us with his men from the castle, once he learns it is only forest men he has to deal with. So we needs must win our victory quickly, it we are to win at all."

During this time Jacob Algelt had been hobbling around, the girl with him, checking on each bombard, each sack of balls or powder. Now from another sack he had brought with him, he drew forth a round, long-handled ladle, a pointed rod as long and thin as a skewer, and a tiny charcoal brazier. Raking the ashes aside in the weaver's chimney, he uncovered the embers and dropped a few of them into the brazier. Then, adding several lumps of charcoal to it, he blew until the new charcoal began to glow. He thrust the pointed rod deep into the coals.

"That is to thrust down the touch-hole and set fire to the powder, when the bombard is charged and laid for the firing," he said.

Robin stepped to the nearest bombard where it lay on its sled, held solid by its flanges against the sled timbers.

"But how is the bombard charged?" he asked, noting that the little round touch-hole was at the closed end of the bombard tube and furthest from the open end.

It was the girl who explained, in her liquid voice with its soft accents.

"The powder is scooped in with this ladle, and then pressed solid against the touch-hole with this wooden ram you see there. Rude wads of matted rushes are pushed in next. Then the ball is charged into the bombard, and likewise pressed down. When the heated rod is thrust down the touch-hole it fires the powder, and so looses the ball."

John the Wolf's lips twisted in a jeer. "But how does one take aim with this great, bulky tube? An archer can shift his aim with but a twist of wrist and bow, and he can set his eye along the shaft to mark the path of flight. But who can—"

"The bombard shoots at no such tiny marks as a target clout at the butts." The girl's eyes flashed. "All that it needs is that the ball strike fair against yonder huge door, even, and it will make a breach—given time."

"Then the long bow is better than any bombard," said the archer triumphantly. "For at this distance I can sift a barbed arrow ten times running even through such a small space as those loophole slits yonder."

"Wait and see for yourself," retorted the girl, repeating almost the very words that Sir Allan had spoken earlier to the armorer.

Opening the door at a crack, Sir Allan looked out once again at the sky.

"The stars fade; the eastern sky is already streaking gray with the dawn. If thou wouldst prove with these bombards what thou claim, merchant, it were well that thou make ready."

CHAPTER XI

DEVIL'S TUBES

ROBIN WAS CURIOUS to see how the bombard would be charged, for it lay almost flat. But Jacob Algelt brought forth a number of stout wooden wedges which he had John the Wolf hammer underneath the front timbers of the sledge. And thus he forced up the front of the sledge and the muzzle of the bombard with it, until the tube stood at a steep slant. When it had been loaded in the manner described by the girl, the wedges were knocked out again, allowing the bombard to sink once more to almost horizontal.

Now the door into the lane was swung open.

Already the dawn gray was creeping over the sky, but in the narrow lane and, still more, inside the weaver's shop, the shadows still hung heavy. But Robin, standing behind and at the side of the bombard, could see the postern door in the wall opposite. And looking along the bombard, he saw that it pointed toward the guard tower at the side of the door, and not at the door itself.

"To the left!" he cried. "It is not aimed aright. To the left—it will have to be swung more to the left!"

"A bombardier! By St. Christopher, a bombardier in the blood!" exclaimed the Flanders merchant, standing back to look. "To the left it must go! Lay hold, archers! To the left; swivel it more to the left!"

Before they could lay shoulder to it, however, from inside the opposite wall and in the direction of the tall keep, came a sudden crashing noise. It was as though a great ram had been pounded there, and close on the pounding came a shattering crash, as of breaking beams and metal. And with it a sudden shout of triumph, then the wild clamor and clangor of men fighting.

Sir Allan gave a start. "The keep—they have broken into

the keep! Doubtless during the night they prepared a battering ram, and had it all ready. De Brenn's men have broken into
the keep; they are even now fighting to take the Prince! Make
haste, merchant!"

And indeed even above the noise of sword on armor, the
shouts of battle inside the wall, there came loud and clear the
dauntless war-cry they had heard from the keep battlement the
eve before. "St. George! St. George for England!"

"The old warhorse, Sir Murray himself! They will do stout
fighting before they win past his blade to reach the Prince, I
warrant you!" In his excitement Sir Allan raised his own voice
in an answering shout. "Stand fast, Sir Murray! We are coming!
Stand—"

The rest of his shout was drowned out in such an ear-cracking
thunder as Robin had never heard the like before. For, snatching
the glowing skewer from the coals, Jacob Algelt had plunged its
redhot point deep down the touch-hole and into the powder.

Almost instantly the whole bombard and its sled seemed to
leap in air. And while its muzzle vomited flame and thunder, the
bombard itself with its sled hurtled backward so fast that John
the Wolf, almost in its path, was hurled sidewise, spinning like
a ten-pin. Nor did the sled and bombard stop until they came
up with a crash against the back wall of the shop.

In an instant the whole room was filled with a strangling
smoke. Jarold and his men-at-arms staggered back, choking.
Even Sir Allan stood in stunned amazement.

It was Wat who found his tongue first. "Open the trap door
onto the roof!" he cried. "It is smoke no worse then a clogged
chimney. Open the roof trap that the draft may suck it through
and out!"

When this was done the smoke, already crowding upward
toward the roof, thinned down below so that Robin could see.

JAROLD AND his men-at-arms were crossing themselves, the
weaver and his apprentices staring with mouths and eyes wide

with fright. But the girl was picking up the still glowing skewer from where it had been blown by the blast.

Then Sir Allan, recalled to senses by the thrill of battle, leaped to the door and peered out.

"A hit!" he shouted. "A fair hit! See, the postern door is crushed! Close to the bottom, and on the right side—see how the splinters gape?"

And looking, Robin was amazed. For, two feet up from the bottom and a foot inside the edge, a great dent showed. The stone ball, striking one of the iron cross straps there, had broken it clean, crashed into the door behind so that the heavy oak had split until the white splinters showed even in the gloom.

With the thunder and the crash, the sound of the fighting inside the wall had suddenly ceased. De Brenn's men cried out in surprise and fright. Then from the wall top and the loopholes of the guard towers rose loud curses of anger. And seeing the smoke vomiting from the open shop door, without even know-ing the cause of it but reckoning rightly that it had to do with this unexpected attack, bows were bent and crossbows loosed. And the shafts and quarrels came humming like bees into the open shop door, mostly to thud harmlessly into floor or walls, though one man-at-arms next to Jarold cursed and caught at his leg where it was naked below his coat of mail.

But only for a moment did those arrows and bolts sing. Then from the roof above and all along the lane came a shout as the forest men rose and loosed shaft. So thick the arrows flew, and so close aimed, that the bowmen on the wall and at the loop-holes in the towers were driven back and down for the moment.

"The door! Close the door!" shouted Sir Allan, and immedi-ately Jarold had leaped and slammed the shop door shut.

Then John the Wolf yelped like a gray wolf itself, and flung himself on the discharged bombard. "Another shot—another ball!" he shouted. "Devil's tube or no, it will crash the door around the butchers' ears! Ho, Wat! Here!"

Without waiting, in his eagerness he seized the ladle, dipped it deep into the powder sack. He ran toward the bombard's still smoking muzzle, swung his arm.

"Nay, nay, John! Stand back!" cried Robin. But too late. The ladle dumped its contents into the bombard muzzle.

Instantly came again the burst of smoke and flame, as the spilling powder lighted from the still burning grains in the bombard muzzle. They singed the hair from the archer's wrist and forearm, even his eyebrows as he leaned down. And the ladle, hurled from his hand by the rush of the expanding gases, flew across the room and banged ringingly against the front wall.

"Fool!" cried the Flanders merchant angrily. "Know not enough to wait until the last grains have burned out? Not that bombard—this other one! It is cold already. Drag it into place and charge it, while the first one cools!"

Even as he had ordered, Jarold's men-at-arms swung over the second bombard on its sled, wedged its muzzle up. Robin by now had retrieved the ladle.

"Thou art a wise lad," approved the merchant. "Bombardier thou shalt be, for my limbs and bones are over-aged for such work. Two ladles of even content, and then the ball."

As soon as the second bombard was loaded, Sir Allan swung open the door again. This time Robin sighted the weapon until its muzzle trained true. Again Jacob Algelt thrust the firing skewer home, and this time all had sense to stand well back from it, both at muzzle and at breech.

Sir Allan yelped with eagerness. "Another hit, directly above the first! Not even Hubert could aim arrow more truly! A sure bombardier indeed, Robin! See, the split has widened! Another half-dozen hits in the same place, and the gate will be breached."

"And not too much time at that," said Wat the Armorer, lending ear to the renewed noise of fighting going on inside the wall. "They are wasting no time at the keep. If they can capture thy Prince before we breach the gate, Sir Knight—"

"Then we will have failed, for they will hold him fair hostage against any rescue we may attempt." Sir Allan Mayne's voice was worried. "Canst hurry, merchant?"

BY NOW the first bombard had cooled to such extent that it could be swabbed out by a lint cloth wrapped around the bead of the rammer rod. Dragging it back into place, it was recharged with powder and ball. But this time as they began knocking the elevating wedges from its forward end, Robin bade them open the door first. He crouched to look along the bombard as well as he could, waving them to swivel its end around as he squinted.

"If this bombard had a notch cut in the back flange with a sight point at the front, both trued to the line of the bore," he grumbled, "it would make for surer sighting. Wat, leave one set of wedges still underneath the sledge. It will elevate the tube, and mayhap land the next ball just above the last one."

Again the bombard recoiled as its powder charge exploded. And this time Sir Allan's voice was triumphant. "It must have cracked the bar that holds the door behind! See how it sags inward, the whole door! Another ball quickly and in the same place if thou canst!" He turned to Jarold and the men-at-arms. "Don casques, and out swords! Be ready to charge if the door is breached!"

Not one shot, but two, it took, however, before the whole door split with a mighty crash, and swung half-sagging on its weakened hinges. Without waiting even for the smoke to clear, Sir Allan was through the door and charging across the narrow lane, sword raised and voice lifted in battle cry. "St. George! St. George for England!"

Behind him, pell-mell, dashed Jarold and his men-at-arms. John the Wolf was notching arrow to bowstring as he ran. Wat the Armorer, a great ax in his fist, was trying to keep pace when Robin raced by him as if he were standing still, and burst through the shattered postern door almost at Sir Allan's shoulder.

Together they struck the barrier, drove it inward with the force of their rush. Figures loomed before them, barring their way. But with a mighty sweep of Sir Allan's sword and a thrust and slash from Robin's, they burst through, and into the open courtyard beyond. Behind them poured Jarold and his men-at-arms, with archers streaming down off their roofs and following after as fast as they found footing.

And well it was they had come when they did, as they saw at one glance.

Crouching on the gangways just beneath the parapets that ran around the outer wall, where they had taken cover from the archers' fire, a score of de Brenn's men stood, dazed at the breaching of the postern. But the major portion of de Brenn's forces were clustered in and around the shattered entrance of the keep itself, trying ever to force their way in and up. And from inside the keep itself, from its stairways and landings, rose the clang of swords and axes, the shouts and groans of warriors, testifying that the defenders were being forced back and upward.

"A St. George!" shouted Sir Allan, turning that way without pause. "An Allan for a St. George!"

"St. George!" came back the shout from somewhere within, though it rang distressed and hollow. "A St. George—for England!"

But not scatheless had the rescue party come through the breach and across the open court. For now that their backs were unguarded to bolts and shafts from the wall, de Brenn's men there and in the gate towers could shoot down upon them. One of Jarold's men dropped, the blood pouring from his mouth, an arrow driven half through his neck. Another reeled as a quarrel bolt hammered at his steel helm. Robin himself felt a shaft hiss past so close that the goose-feathers all but tickled his neck. Then he and Sir Allan and Wat struck the mass at the keep entrance almost together.

ARMED IN full mail, with his sword swinging like a scythe, Sir Allan hewed a passage forward, oblivious of the blows aimed at him from right and left. But Robin, with only his round archer's shield and light steel cap, was hard put to it to guard himself with his shield and sword alone. He found himself matched with a burly man-at-arms, wielding a morning star, or battle mace with star-pointed ball. Robin's own litheness saved him, however, for he ducked underneath the ball, and jabbed upward with his shortened sword-point as he crouched, so that it drove deep into the groin beneath the chain mail, dropping his enemy.

But directly behind him was another, and younger, better trained. With him Robin exchanged blow for blow, hammering at hauberk and helm, while he himself caught the return strokes on his stout archer's shield. A lucky stroke from his own blade found a weakened rivet in the other's headpiece, tore the visor loose and left it hanging. The man gave back, and Robin pressed him close.

And so pressing him, almost came to his own downfall. For he had forgotten the first man he had dropped, until he fairly stumbled over the still kicking body. He tripped, went to his knees, the shield almost flying from his arm. He gripped it again, thrust it upward, but knowing even then it was too late. For he saw the glitter of triumph in his opponent's eyes, the start of the downward sweep that would cleave him to the waist.

But the sweep never more than began. Suddenly the face that glared at him from the broken visor disappeared in a gush of crimson. Fair and true a barbed arrow bad found that visor opening, driven through nose and skull. And John the Wolf's howl came from behind Robin as the man-at-arms toppled and he himself scrambled to his feet to avoid the plunging body.

Now Wat was beside him, and Sir Allan raging only a half-step ahead. Like a wedge they split their way through. And Robin was amazed at the mighty strokes of the armorer's axe, shearing through shield and pauldron, while on his own targe Wat caught blows that would have felled a lesser man. Wat was upholding his own armorer's rule, that he best fashions arms who also knows their use.

Against their surge, aided by Jarold's men and the rain of arrows which the archers behind let fly at every opening, de Brenn's men faltered, tried to slip past and flee. Only a half-dozen now remained in sight, halfway up the stairs leading to the keep landing above. One of them was the giant bull-necked man whom Hubert had told them was Brendon, the seneschal.

The seneschal and his half dozen were pressing desperately upon two defenders who held the landing stage at the top of the steps. One of them was a tall man, rawboned, and swinging a powerful battle ax. But the one who held the stairs beside him was slender. His armor, casque and shield were jet black, except for the golden quarterings on the shield, and he wore a rich surcoat, embroidered with figures.

"Sir Murray! Sire!" cried Sir Allan Mayne, slashing toward them. "Late—but in time!"

The voice of the slender fighter answered from the stairs. "Nay, ye come in good time. But leave me this bull-bodied man—I claim him for mine own sword!"

However, Brendon, the seneschal, had at last realized that something was amiss below. Turning, he stared down. And then with a shout he plunged downward, leading the desperate attempt to cut the way through and out.

FAIR IN the middle of the stairs Sir Allan met him. And though the tall man on the landing above could have clove the seneschal's headpiece with one sweep of his ax, he merely stood and stayed his hand.

Sword against shield, they stood and battered each other until the entire place rang with the clanging of their blows. But powerful as he was, and with the added advantage of being three steps higher, Brendon could not beat down the knight's blade. It was his own sword instead that was suddenly all but hammered from his hand. And before he could raise it again, Sir Allan had swung his own blade in a mighty sweep that gathered force and speed until it fairly hummed. Between hauberk and helm it bit, in the tiny space where the seneschal's mail shirt came not quite to the casque plate. It drove deep through flesh and tendon and bone, until the helmeted head hung to the side, the blood spurted in gushes, and the man himself crumpled like a half-emptied sack of wheat.

With his fall, those of his pack who were left dropped their weapons and cried for quarter. A sudden silence seemed to fall over the place, broken only by the hoarse panting of the victors and the groans of the dying.

CHAPTER XII

HAIL THE BLACK PRINCE

STEP BY STEP the two defenders of the landing, the tall man and the slender, came down from the place they had held so well. They opened their visors, to drink deeper of the morning air.

"Sir Allan Mayne—or I never heard that war-cry on the battlefields in Guienne!" said the older man. The sweat beads stood out on his scarred face. "Ye are well come. In another hour it had been too late. Of our whole party, only we two are left."

But the younger man, whose face was as fair as his armor was black, frowned. "Yet it was an ill service ye did me, Sir Allan. We would have preferred to deal with this last one with our own sword." He pushed at the dead man's helmet with his spurred solleret, "He seemed the leader of the band who assailed our royal person. Open me his visor, that we may see the traitor's face."

When Wat the Armorer lifted the visor, it was the heavy-jowled face of Brendon the Bull that stared unseeing from the casque.

"The seneschal of our Lord Warden of Bewly Castle?" The Prince's eyes frowned. "How now? Is this treason full plotted? And if this be the seneschal, where is the Warden de Brenn, his master?"

It was the voice of Red Hubert that answered that. "He comes even now! The Butcher comes, at the head of a huge array of horsemen! They are pressing thither down the street, upturning the barricades as they come!"

"Then I fear me it is finished—all except the last fight we shall make on earth." Sir Allan wiped his sword blade, turned to Sir Murray Wilton. "How now, old warhorse? Shall we show this traitor de Brenn such a last stand as shall be told about even in Guienne? With the Prince in the keep turret, and the archers posted around, you and I will hold these stairs as long as flesh can endure."

"Nay, the Prince will not hide in the turret, but will keep these landings along with you and Sir Murray," returned the slender warrior coolly. "But perchance it is not finished yet. Perchance the Lord Warden comes to our royal rescue, and not to do us hurt."

"Not de Brenn!" said Sir Allan crisply. "He is traitor as well as butcher. If he comes, he comes for no good."

"Then call your archers into the keep," answered the Prince. "And if thou shouldst send a messenger on a fleet horse up the Salisbury Road, he may still bring help in time. For our trusted Earl of Arundel with a goodly force was to follow us after but two days' time, and even now should be drawing near."

Sir Allan turned to the armorer. "Then send Peter Joy a-gallop again, and up the Salisbury Road! And the rest of thy men, give order to them that they come inside the keep. We may not hold the circuit of the outer walls, but this stout keep itself we will hold while we may."

As Wat sent messengers flying, however, Robin caught at Sir Allan. "The bombards! If we fetched them inside with us, and trained one on the postern and the other on the main gate, we might do de Brenn such damage as will make him pause."

"By my halidon, you are right!" cried the knight. "I had forgot the bombards! Fetch them quickly inside then, and all the store of powder and ball!"

A SCORE of archers swarmed across the lane, laid hand to the sledges with such good will that they seemed to fly across the space almost of their own accord. And with them came not only the old Flanders merchant, Algelt, but his daughter as well. Into the keep entrance the bombards were drawn, and there so laid that the muzzle of one covered the broken postern while the other was trained on the opening of the main gate. Algelt supervised the laying of one bombard; Robin directed the other; and the girl stood between, nursing the firing skewer in its brazier of glowing coals.

Word came from the archers who had been placed as outposts, bringing news of the progress of the oncoming force. "They are halfway adown the street…. They are now come to the White Swan…. They are tearing up the barricades at the ending of the street itself."

Calmly talking to his gentlemen as to the arrangement of the defence, the Prince had yet time to regard the bombards with interest.

"And say you, Sir Allan, that with half dozen discharges they did breach the strong postern door—and that from within the narrow confines of a weaver's shop? It doth sound most incredible!"

"Not only breached the postern, but from space so confined it would not have lent room for half the swing of even a catapult," responded the knight. "It would have seemed incredible, Sire, had I not seen it with mine own eyes."

The Flanders merchant looked up, his old eyes blinking.

"Long effort I made in London, Sire, to see thee and make test of my bombards against any catapult or ballista. But this scarred watch-dog at thy side, he barred the way and bade me take my bombards back to hell whence they came—"

At that the old knight mopped his face and shuffled his feet with embarrassment, but the Prince laughed. "A faithful watch-dog, though perhaps too gruff in the bark. It would seem to me, Sir Murray, that we have a goodly weapon here that may well help us to overthrow our cousin of France—if God wills that we come through this day safely."

But at that moment from the watchers on the keep turret came the cry: "They come! They come!"

"Then look to your bows, men of the forest!" shouted Wat the Armorer, sending his men flying to loophole and slit. From the walls and gates the outposts were already falling back onto the keep, Robin ran eye again along his bombard to see that it was full trained on the main gate. Jacob Algelt did likewise for the postern, while the girl blew on the brazier until the skewer point spat red sparks.

Now the tramp of many horses was plain to be heard, the clank of armor. The head of the column showed at the main gate, and beyond shone countless waving lances and blades.

"Fire!" suddenly screamed Jacob Algelt, snatching at the redhot skewer in the girl's hand.

But suddenly the Black Prince himself dashed it from his hand. "Hold!" he cried. "Hold! They come in peace, not war! See, their visors are open! And the pennons—all the banners and pennons—they cannot be those of Bewly alone!"

"But assuredly that is de Brenn that rides in the van—"began Sir Allan, only to be drowned out by Sir Murray Wilton:

"Aye, but who rides alongside? Arundel! It is the Earl of Arundel! And the pennons and banners—I see the roses of Loring—the lion of my lord Percy—the silver wings of the Beauchamps!"

"Then it is Arundel who has come up in good time, and no mere traitorous array of Bewly." The Prince let his sword-point lower to the ground. "My good Murray, make note that we do here make pledge to the chapel at Westminster of ten score candles for the high altar, and a great chalice of finest silver, in that God hath preserved us this day."

And with the lowering of his sword-point, such a great sigh of relief went up from the defenders of the keep that it was like a long wave breaking on the sandy shore.

ON ACROSS the court the horsemen rode, to drop lance and draw rein at five paces. Then the Earl of Arundel was down, and running across the space to drop to his knees before the Prince, and after him all the other lords and barons of the force, including the Lord Warden.

"Sire," said the earl, "we have come as quick as we might. But we were delayed—"Then suddenly his eyes fell on the dead men lying beyond, and the pools of blood and the battered entrance doors to the keep, and he sprang up, white-faced. "Sire! What means this—this blood, these dead men?"

"That," said the Black Prince quietly, "I am waiting to hear. From my lord Warden of Bewly here since it is in his barony that treason has made attack upon our person!"

At that de Brenn, his face white and his lips dry, rose from his own knees and made stammering answer. "Treason? Treason? I know not of what you speak, Sire!"

"Then look upon this dead dog who led the pack that attacked us," said the Black Prince, spurning the hacked thing that had been Brendon, the seneschal. "Is not this thine own man, the seneschal of thine own Castle of Bewly?"

Staring at the crimsoned features and unseeing eyes, de Brenn could only lick his lips again and shake his head.

"Treason, Sire—but not of my knowledge. He—he has ever been an unruly dog. Last night he asked permit to ride with men-at-arms into the town here, saying that there was rioting and plundering of shops by masterless men and lawless knaves of the levies. And hearing naught thereafter, only this morning I thought wise to ride and see for myself—and so fell in with my Earl of Arundel."

"And art full sure of thy loyalty?"

"No man lives who hath thy interest more to heart than I, Sire!"

A slight curl came to the Prince's lips. "Such loyalty doth well deserve reward," he said softly. "And what greater reward could loyal baron desire than to fight for his liege in the forefront of battle? Be it even so! Thou shalt go with us to Guienne, in the force of our trusted Arundel here, and under his own eye. And to thee shall be the post of greatest danger, the spear-point of onslaught wherever the battle waxes hottest." He turned to the earl. "Wilt see, my dear Arundel, that Baron de Brenn hath full chance to win the honor that his bravery and loyalty crave?"

By the Lord Warden's start and the way he bit his lips. Robin knew that he read the meaning of the Prince's words. Then in his rage de Brenn gave little heed to caution.

"But these masterless men, Sire—these outlaws of the forest which I see here! They have brake the forest laws, slain the royal deer, even done plunder on the king's highways! And in their forest fens they have flouted all effort to bring them to justice. Would it not be well, now that we have them here fair caught, to stretch so many of them from the gibbet that the countryside will be safe from outlawry while we are in Guienne?"

"**MASTERLESS MEN?** Masterless men?" The Prince looked about him at the grim-faced archers. "I see naught here but our loyal subjects who have shed good blood this day for our person. Naught would more besuit me than to have these same straight-shooting archers with us when we do battle in Guienne."

"Sire." Sir Allan stood forth. "Mayhap these men have no master, but it also occurs to me that I am knight without men. And it please thee, Sire, and please these archers as well, I would well love to lead these forest men in Guienne, believing that much honor and glory may be had thereby."

It was John the Wolf's voice, speaking boldly from the archers' ranks, that made answer before the Prince could reply.

"By my bow, I would gladly choose this bloody-sworded knight to lead me in Guienne or anywhere else! For if he lead as well as he fight, then our pockets will be well-lined with those ransom *deniers* and *livres* he spoke of, ere we return!"

But though the other archers looked equally satisfied, they did not answer forthwith, but looked toward Wat the Armorer.

The armorer shook his grizzled head, and spat. "Follow ye the knight. I am but an armorer, and not a captain of archers. Also, I have curiosity to know more of these bombards here."

"Thou shalt know that too," said the Black Prince, smiling, "if this Flemisher here will renew his offer. How much, Flemisher, for thy bombards and the men to work them?"

"Ten thousand *livres*, Sire—only ten thousand *livres* I ask, for the hire of the bombards and bombardiers to work them," cried Jacob Algelt quickly. But then the cramp caught at him again, and he groaned as he fell to rubbing his leg. "Nay, I could see to them in camp and in the baggage train. But my limbs are over-aged for battle in the field, and also I have a motherless daughter who must bide with me. But if some bombardier captain could be found to take them for me onto the battlefield—" He turned to Robin. "This young man here, he hath shown good knowledge of the bombards."

The Prince looked at Robin with keen, appraising eyes. "Thy name?"

"Robin, Sire. Robin Santerre—" stammered Robin. In that instant he looked full into the girl's eyes, and suddenly it came to him that in those eyes was deeper lure for him than battlefields or bombards or anything else that might come in the provinces of France. If she were going to Guienne also....

But the Prince was speaking again, impatiently. "How now, Robin—wouldst take service with me as bombardier and captain of the king's artillery? In France there is both honor and glory to be had, and no small chance to win estates and knighthood as well."

"I will go gladly with thee, Sire, and with these bombards." And Robin flushed as he saw the girl's eyes sparkle anew, and realized with amazement that as yet he did not even know her name.

"Then so be it." The Prince nodded. "And now, my lords, we had best seek quarters. For it has been a sleepless night, and I am aweary and athirst, and there is much yet to be done toward the assembly of the levies."

One of the newly arrived knights came running then with a flask of wine and a silver cup which he filled and held out to the Prince. Edward of Woodstock, Prince of Wales and heir to the throne of England, took the cup and held it high.

"To your health, gentlemen—and to our good success in France!" Quaffing deep, the Prince threw the emptied cup into the air. "St. George for England! And on to Guienne!"

Instantly the caps of ten score archers were flung into the air. And ten score forest voices took up the cry with a shout so full and deep that it set the echoes rattling from battlement to rooftop.

"St. George for England! On to Guienne!"

ARGONOTES

When you were small, your Aunt Florence must have told you about her friend, now deceased, who read the encyclopedia right through from A to Z. This singular feat probably impressed you at the time, but afterward you decided that it was just one of Aunt Florence's legends. Well, we know a man who is cheerfully plowing through the encyclopedia at the present moment. His name is Roy de S. Horn, and he ought to be in the M's by now.

Mr. Horn started reading the encyclopedia because he thought it would be good for his soul. But before he finished with A he had become so fascinated by the history of artillery that he found himself lugging home innumerable dusty volumes on the subject. Eventually Mr. Horn determined to share his delight over bombards with less fortunate folk, and so he wrote a story called "Men With No Master," the first installment of which appears in this issue of Argosy.

There are going to be more stories about Robin the Bombardier you'll be pleased to hear. Mr. Horn tells us that the whole development of heavy artillery occurred during the Hundred Years War. His idea is to exercise his writer's privilege and to compress that history within the lives of his main characters. So by the time you have finished with

*Robin the Bombardier, you will be wise in the ways of gunpowder.
And you'll have had a thoroughly good time.*

Now Mr. Horn has some interesting things to say about the historical background of "Men With No Master."

I HAVE TRIED to give an accurate picture of the people and social conditions in England at the start of the Hundred Years War. Conditions in the royal forests, of which the New Forest was the most famous, were as stated in my story. The references to Oxford (better known as Oxenford) College are accurate, as well as the amazing researches and predictions of the Franciscan monk, Roger Bacon, who predicted that men would fly in air and that boats would be self-propelled. Because of his scientific researches and deductions, as being contrary to Holy Writ, he was imprisoned for almost the full last twelve years of his life.

Although it is common belief that gunpowder was invented by the Chinese, and some hold that it was early known to the Persians and Turks and even the Greeks, it is an amazing thing that nowhere in their chronicles is there actual proof, such as a formula. It is possible, even probable, that their so-called gunpowder was merely "Greek Fire," combustibles of brimstone, tar, etc, rather than actual explosives. Such "carcasses" were in regular use in sieges from the early days of Rome. Certainly the formula Roger Bacon wrote down for gunpowder is the first known record of the actual formula.

Though Roger Bacon put the formula for gunpowder in writing, its use as a propellent was first practiced in Germany and Flanders. It was from there that cannon—"bombards"—were first introduced into England. And these bombards were privately owned, merely leased under contract to the king or prince.

Anything so mysterious and thunderous smacked so strongly of the Devil that the bombardiers were under suspicion of being black magicians, compacted with Satan. The penalty for black magic was burning at the stake, so that the bombardiers had as much to fear from their own forces as from the enemy.

Considering how even today explosives must be handled with so much care, though their scientific composition and resolution of forces is well known, the early bombardiers must have had a lively time, learning as they did by trial and error, by bitter experience.

In order to follow the early development of artillery more fully, I have chosen a young Oxford student, the forerunner of a modern engineer and scientist, as my hero, giving him the same scientific and deductive mind as Roger Bacon must have had. And through him I hope to trace the developments of early-day artillery, and all the mishaps and discoveries the early bombardiers must have experienced.

The Black Prince was probably the most romantic figure of all chivalry. For the better understanding of the present-day reader I have named him as such, though it was not until several hundred years later that he began to be known in history as "The Black Prince." Until then he was generally called Prince Edward, or Edward of Woodstock.

Roy de S. Horn
New York City

ARCHERS TO THE FRONT

Knights, don the casque, belt on the long sword; and seize the bowstaves, fill the quivers full, you forest men! Tomorrow you cross the Channel, to battle for a hundred years against our cousin of France.

CHAPTER I

BOWMEN AND BOMBARDS

HORSES STAMPING, ARMOR clanking, shield's rattling and lances ringing—it was as if the whole countryside had been sowed with dragons' teeth and now was springing up in armed men. From every highway and crossroad, from every village and forest path they poured. Until the Southampton road was clogged with knights and men-at-arms, and archers from the King's forests jostled elbows with pikemen and even with barelegged "stabbers" from Ireland and Wales.

Not since the Crusades had Merrie England seen such levies as these that Edward III was assembling to war on his cousin Philippe of France.

But in the six heavy carts fighting for a way through the press on the road, there was one at least who had no eye for the brave display. Perched on the head cart, Wat the Armorer scowled and spat.

" 'Tis a fools war! If the Frenchmen were invading England, it would be reason enough to fight. But what business have we English in France that we must e'en cross the water to settle it with sword and ax?"

"Business enough, old Woods-boar!" answered Red Hubert, shifting his giant body to easier position in the cart. "The Frenchmen have stolen our own King's rightful province of Normandy. And now they would steal Guienne as well. If we scotch them not, they will steal all England next." He nudged the archer next to him. "Eh, old Wolf?"

John the Wolf, gaunt and grizzled, paused to squint down
the arrow shaft he was scraping before replying. "Normandy
I cannot eat, and this Guienne sounds no better. But if these
Frenchmen have jewels and gold and rich velvets for the taking,
as Sir Allan Mayne hath told us, it is business enough for me."

"Then you had better stayed with Sir Allan's archers than with
these devil's bombards, if it is pillage and loot you have in mind,
Wolf John," said the slender youth perched on the thick metal
tube in center of the cart. "When these bombards begin to belch
their brimstone and iron upon the Frenchmen, they will fly so
fast that there will be none left for ransom!"

"And that, Peter Joy," remarked the giant Hubert, chuckling,
"is well said. We bombardiers will breach the walls, and the
archers will get the pillage and the loot."

"Nay," snorted the armorer sourly. "The blows and the loot
will be divided as always. The barons and the knights will get
the gold, and we common men the blows!"

"Then why did you so sweetly give up the leading of the

Mace lifted high, the sable Frenchman
charged on the men-at-arms

forest men to serve these same bombards, old Woods-boar?"
demanded Red Hubert.

"Because," said Wat crisply, "if these bombards and devil's
powders can overthrow knights in armor, then there may come
a time when the division will be the other way around—we
honest freeborn men will take the gold and the Devil will take
the knights!"

"And the gibbet will take thee if thy tongue continues to wag
with any baron nigh to hear," said John the Wolf. "And here
comes the Butcher de Brenn now—a murrain upon him!"

CLATTERING DOWN the road at the head of a score of men-
at-arms rode a dark hawk-faced man in full armor, the quarterings of his shield and the fluttering banner on his squire's lance
marking him a full baron. With the flats of their swords his men
beat a pathway through the press on the road, and dark looks
and muttered curses followed them.

"If I had had my stave strung and a good shaft notched, I would well have loved to test that same armor of his," growled John the Wolf, glaring after the baron.

"Nay, even a full-drawn shaft would not pierce a well-made hauberk." It was a new voice that broke in, and with the words the speaker was in the cart at a single bound, regardless of the sword and bossed shield he wore. "Have I not told thee, John, that naught less than a half-pound quarrel, full barbed, and hurled from a crossbow with double staves and pull, would do such work?"

The newcomer was a youth of not more than Peter Joy's own twenty years, but his forehead was high and his eyes deep and thoughtful. However, the smile that crinkled his lips was boyish. "How now, Wat—are the bombards well lashed and riding well?"

"Better than seasonably well, Robin," answered the armorer. "But our fat Flanders merchant has been running back and forth from cart to cart like a hen with one chick, asking now about the serpentine and now about the balls, when it is not the bombards he is weeping over!"

Red Hubert grinned. "Well it is, then, that our merchant hath engaged such stout bombardiers as Robin and John and Peter and myself, to tend them in the wars if here on a peaceful road he takes so much unease."

"Peaceful?" jeered Peter Joy. "There would have been naught of peace to it, if John Wolf had had his longbow strung and arrow to hand, when Butcher de Brenn rode by. John cannot forget the forest warden's deer he has poached, or that the warden still hath a gibbet over-hungry for him."

"It will be different," growled John the Wolf, "when we are in France. Let the Butcher ride bare of back but once, then—"

He hushed, for all at once the cart rounded a curve and come into full sight of Southampton Water. And the sight there was enough to stop any man's mouth full open.

From Romney Marsh all the way to the Test estuary, the harbor was a mass of shipping. Craft of all size lay there at anchor or tied up to the new-built wharves. Sails fluttered and yards and cordage creaked as sailors ran about like squirrels on the decks. Small boats plied the harbor like skimming bugs.

For over a thousand ships were assembled here, levied from the Cinque Ports all the way to London. On those already loaded, pennons and banners flew, to show what knights or barons held their stations there. Others were still receiving their loads of casks and beeves, warhorses and supplies, as well as pikemen and archers, men-at-arms and knights in full armor.

Into this jostle and hubbub the cart forced its way, the other five carts creaking after. And to their inquiries as to where the *Falcon* lay, sweating sailors paused to wave and shout: "Further down. The white cog with the black poop castle. You cannot miss it!"

Then they came to a white ship with great crossed yard and black stern castle, and Wat drew the horses to a stop. "Is this the *Falcon?*"

A huge, ruddy man with flaxen hair, and bare-bodied save for doublet and sandals, ceased bawling to his sailors long enough to answer. "Aye, the *Falcon* it is. And I am Shipmaster Swann of the *Falcon* myself. But this ship is ordered for the King's artillery and not for carters. So get thee hence!"

Robin leaped out, stretched his long legs. "Then this is the ship we seek. For this is the King's artillery in these carts, and I am Robin Santerre, master artilleryman."

STRIDING TO the cart, however, the brawny shipmaster jerked the canvas aside. Then at sight of naught but the long, round metal tubes, he let out a roar. "Artillery? Think you I know not a catapult when I see one? More likely bells for some abbey carillon, these—so take them hence, and speedily, or we will dump them into the water. And thee along with them, young cockerel!"

"None the less these are the king's artillery," retorted Robin, his lips tightening. "One bombard such as these will outmatch

a whole shipload of catapults, or I will eat thy *Falcon* cog, sails
and all! Now, call thy sailors that we may be at the loading!"

But still the cog's captain stood blinking and scowling. "The
King's artillery I have order to load—and naught but the King's
artillery will I load! So get thee hence with thy cart and bells
before I lose temper and souse you e'en as I said."

He made as if to lay hand on Robin. But at his first move,
out of the cart thrust a great freckled hand almost like a ham
for size and brownness. It reached for the sailor's yellow mop of
hair and jerked. And to his utter amaze the ship captain, large
as he was, found himself lifted in air till only his toes dragged
earth. Red Hubert, holding him thus helpless, raised himself
over the cart side until the whole of his huge body had unfolded
itself, joint by joint.

"Souse a bombardier, will ye—and our captain at that?"
Hubert turned an inquiring face toward Robin. "Say but the
word, and we will give this shipmaster a long drink of his own
muddy water, and then load the cog ourselves. Ho, John—Peter!
Out of the cart—and fetch thy staves with thee!"

Out scrambled John the Wolf and Peter Joy, their five-foot
bowstaves stout gripped and the eagerness for brawling in their
faces. Shipmaster Swann gaped wide at them.

"Nay, I want no bowstaves cracked across my pate. Artillery it is—whatever name ye choose to call it." Then, staring at
Hubert's mighty frame, he shook his head incredulously. "Never
have I felt such a clutch, nor thought to feel such, until Gog and
Magog returned to earth!"

"Then will you please unload our carts into your cog?"
demanded Robin sharply.

"Methinks I have but little choice." Suddenly the shipmaster
began to grin. "I have a pilot—an overbearing man, and quarrelsome. A full butt of ale will I give thee, Red-thatch, if thou
wilt draw him into a bicker and use that same strength on his
noggin!"

Red Hubert's eyes sparkled. "For a half butt—a single pot—

even for no ale at all, I am your man. Where waits this pilot who loves to bicker?"

Hurriedly, however, Robin drew him back. "This is no time for brawls. We have the bombards to load aboard, and many casks and sacks."

At the bawl of the shipmaster, many sailors came running, to lay stout timbers and lead out thick blocks and ropes. The archers were amazed then, as, with deft hitches of ropes and tackle rove through a great block on the crossyard above, the casks and bags and even the heavy bombards themselves were started aboard.

In the midst of this such a sudden hubbub arose along the quay that sailors and archers turned to look.

Adown the quay tramped a dozen stout men in half-armor, with a mounted knight at their head. The soldiers were burly men, with weathered faces and steel caps and shields well dented from stout use. The knight, however, wore burnished new mail, and his clean-shaven face looked out pleasantly from beneath his raised visor. Even Sir Allan's warhorse, almost as well shielded as his rider under its flowing trappings of leather and steel, seemed to prance with eagerness.

BUT IT was the serried men tramping ten abreast behind the knight and soldier who drew the eyes and the shouts of the townsmen lining the quay. Clad in leather jerkins, steel caps gleaming, bull-hide shields rattling against the quivers at their backs, and their long bowstaves in their hands, the archers came on, rank by rank. And as they marched they roared out in full-throated chorus the song of the men of the forest:

> *The King he has his royal throne,*
> *The earl his donjon keep;*
> *The abbey monk he counts his beads*
> *Thrice nightly in his sleep!*
> *But the forest men, the forest men,*
> *They need no castle wall,*
> *They would not change their green roof-trees*
> *With any man at all!*

So bend the bow, and loose the shaft!
And let the red deer fall!
The forest men they would not change
With any man at all!

The shipmaster stared. "Verily, they have been at heady ale, these forest men. For less than such a song have men swung high afore now. Let but the King hear such words—"

"And well deserving of the King's gibbet!" broke in a rasping voice behind them. "Aye, drawn and quartered, if they burn not at the stake!"

He of the rasping voice was large, brawny-muscled, and wore sailor's garb, but his black-browed countenance was darker than any sailor's around. His full lips were twisted back, and arrogance rode his harsh words.

Robin swept him with a quick glance, sensing that this was that same pilot of whom Master Swann had spoken as a quarrelsome man.

"That may be, but there will be many King's men sore handled in the doing," he said tartly. "For these are the Masterless Men of the New Forest. And as to the hanging or burning, the prince— our own Prince Edward of Woodstock—may have some little word to say. Since it is by his own command they come, full-pardoned of all crime, for his own royal rescue some days since when he was beset by traitors in the town of Bewly."

The pilot at that gave him a dark glance, and bit his lips. But the Masterless Men were now swinging past and dividing up among the ships that lay along the quay. Shields and quivers rattling, voices yelping, they poured over gangplanks and onto decks until the ships seemed packed with their green and gray.

Sir Allan Mayne, with his dozen men-at-arms and a round score of the archers, came toward the *Falcon* cog. At the swaying gangplank and the smell and sight of the lapping underneath, the black warhorse held back, snorting and champing. But at the touch of the rider's golden spurs, he surged ahead and trampled the gangway with ringing hoofs. Behind him poured the men-at-arms and archers.

"Ho, Robin!" called Sir Allan, swinging down from the saddle as he reached the deck and sighted him. "The bombards and powder and balls—you have them aboard?"

"They are—or will be ere nones-time," answerd Robin. "We had not thought to have the pleasure of your company too."

"Perhaps the pleasure will not be all sweet," said the knight, laughing, "for the Lord Warden of Bewly—Baron Hugo de Brenn—will also be here shortly, to have full command of all the fighting men." He swung about. "Ho, Shipmaster. See to this horse of mine, that he has a dry stall and grain in plenty. And also make place for Sir Hugo de Brenn when he boards the ship."

At that Robin frowned, and John the Wolf muttered under his breath. But Red Hubert was too busy swapping great clouts of the back with the burly leader of the men-at-arms.

"Jarold, thou wine-guzzling stealer of villeins' sheep! Is not risk of drowning in this tub of a cog enough ill-chance I must suffer, without thee along to make the Devil's welcome double-sure?"

"Hubert, is it thee, thou great ox?" retorted the soldier, grinning. "Better a sheep-napper than a woods-running poacher from the King's forest!"

"If there be woods in France, we mayhap shall see who does the running—whether it be soldiers or forest men," replied Hubert. "Eh, Tyrel?" And he grinned at the long-shanked leader of the score of archers who had come aboard.

But now Robin was anxious to be at the unloading of the carts again, and even Sir Allan Mayne stamped the deck impatiently.

"Tyrel, put thy archers at the hoisting ropes, and Jarold, do thou the same with thy soldiers of Kent," he ordered. "Ho, Shipmaster! Can make no more haste with these bombards?"

Shipmaster Swann shrugged his shoulders. "If the tackle fails, that bombard will make all too much haste into the hold. It is a heavy thing, and might well burst the cog's timbers if it fall."

However, he took his stand on the forecastle and from there drove the sweating sailors to speed.

All this time the black-browed pilot had stood idle, scowling at the incoming casks and sacks. Sir Allan Mayne touched his shoulder.

"This is no time for idleness. Set thy brawny shoulder to yon cask."

The pilot drew back. "I am no soldier. I am Pierre the pilot. I have naught to do with the ship save under oar or sail."

"Pilot or no, you shall set hand to this loading or else taste the flat of a blade!" snapped the knight fiercely. "If you be no common sailor, then into the hold with you and see to the storing of the artillery that it may not come a-loose to the damage of the ship or the horses!" And Sir Allan's eyes gleamed so hotly that the pilot hurried to turn and descend to the hold out of reach of that heavy Norman sword.

"And, pilot—see to it that the casks and sacks be set in a dry place and away from bottom-water or leakage!" called Robin after him.

SWIFTLY NOW the first of the bombards swung aboard amid lusty grunting of the men at the ropes, and after it the remainder of the casks and sacks containing the powder and ball. From the hindmost cart stepped two figures, who also crossed over the gangplank.

The first was a white-headed, fat-bellied man in the robe of a merchant, his puckered eyes flickering with nervousness as he felt the swaying of the ship. The second, black-haired and red-lipped, was a girl of scarce sixteen. Her small feet ware quick on the planking and her eyes sparkling at the sights around.

The paunchy man was Jacob Algelt, the Flemish merchant and owner of these strange new bombards which he had leased to King Edward for his artillery. And the girl was Katherine, his daughter.

"Strange fighting this French war must be, with women going

to the affray," grumbled John the Wolf as the girl stepped lightly aboard.

"Nay," said Red Hubert alongside, "the Queen herself and her ladies of the royal court will follow soon, as quick as seasonable place may be readied for them. There will be camps as well as fighting, old Wolf. And the girl has knowledge of this Devil's powder greater even than any save her father and our own Robin,"

Sir Allan had stepped to meet them. "The half of the after cabin is curtained off and ready for your use. It is cramped and ill-smelling for a lady, but the crossing should not take long."

Robin Santerre himself stood as if his tongue were tied, even though the girl's shoulder all but touched in the passing. But as her dark eyes threw him a smiling glance, his face reddened and he turned to shout needless commands to the archers who were already straining their utmost.

Wat the Armorer chuckled. "More fright has he of this maiden's eyes than of all the Frenchmen in France. A pot of ale against thy bowstave, Wolf John, that he would not change that one smile from her for all the French ransom you are already counting as in your pouch!"

"Let him keep the smiles, and I will choose the ransom!" replied John the Wolf, growling. "What said Sir Allan—a hundred *livres* for a simple knight and five hundred for a baron of full quartering?"

"Aye, but why wait to get to France?" gibed Peter Joy. "Here comes your baron e'en now, and easy into your hands for the taking!"

John the Wolf and Red Hubert both cursed beneath their breath as the hawk-faced man of the morning's passage on the road spurred his clanking warhorse aboard. For as Lord Warden of the New Forest Baron de Brenn had little love for the forest men, nor they any at all for him. Too oft had they seen their own fellows swinging from the warden's gibbets as poachers, which hard usage they repaid by notching the thumbs of the warden's own foresters so often as they caught them.

Hence there were sly grins and chuckles aboard as the baron's warhorse plunged, wide-eyed, at the swaying gangplank, almost to the unseating of its rider. With a Norman oath the baron sank his spurs deep and so came aboard at a run. His eighty pounds of full armor clanked as he swung scowling down to the half-deck planks. One of the men-at-arms led the caparisoned warhorse below, while Sir Allan greeted the baron and passed with him to the quarters in the stern castle.

CHAPTER 11

CRY PILLAGE

BUT WHEN SIR ALLAN returned alone shortly after, his lips were tight and his brows black. He said nothing, however, even when the pilot, Pierre, went into the stern castle. Nor when, upon his return, the pilot took over the command of the loading on deck, while Shipmaster Swann was sent to take charge of the stowage in the hold.

But Wat the Armorer, who had scant bridle to his tongue, was not slow to speak. "It is a poor leader who so soon changes the orders of his under-officer. Sir Allan's glowers would fire that sterncastle and burn Butcher de Brenn with it, if looks could burn."

If it had been de Brenn's intent to speed the loading, the results were all amiss. For under the pilot, all the loading gear and tackle seemed to come a-snarl. Stout hempen ropes parted, the crossyard hoist went adrift, and thrice the great tackle block on its end jammed its running parts in its cheeks. Three full carts and two of the bombards had been loaded before noon under Master Swann, but the last cart and its bombard still waited unloaded on the quay when dusk began to fall.

At the third jamming of the yardarm block even Robin Santerre bit his lips. Red Hubert swore and looked toward the pilot so fiercely that instead of sending a sailor up to clear the tackle, as on previous occasions, the pilot himself laid hasty hands to the rigging and clambered aloft.

"I had thought these sailors with their ropes and lifts were exceeding clever, until now," growled Wat the Armorer. "But we had done this loading quicker if we had put an hundred stout archers to the burdens and hoisted them aboard by main strength."

Robin shook his head. "It is not the fault of the tackle, not yet of the rope. According to the principle of levers and forces which I studied as laid down at Oxford in the book of Roger the Monk, a rope thrice run through double blocks increases a man's strength by six. It is the poor ordering of the tackle blocks that caused the rope to break."

"Then let me throw this interfering pilot overboard and bring back the shipmaster to attend the loading," said Red Hubert testily. "Else we will not be finished by curfew."

But Robin only shook his head and went below impatiently to examine his precious sacks and casks for the sixth time.

It was Shipmaster Swann, swearing in a darkened corner of the hold, that took him that way.

"The bottom-leakage—that lazy pilot hath not laid the planks above it and the cargo on that at all, as I bade him! See—he laid the casks and sacks right against the bottom planks themselves!"

Running his hands down because he could not see in the gloom, Robin felt the dampness of stinking water.

"A leak? You mean the cog leaks?" he demanded sharply.

"Nay, no more than any boat leaks," said the shipmaster. "Always does a boat take some water in the bottom, which we must bucket out when it grows too great. Which is why we lay these great planks against the bottom ribs themselves to make a dry platform for the cargo above. But here are the planks unlaid, and at least a good part of thy sacks and casks soaked in the bottom water itself. Is there aught in them that will harm from the leakage?"

"No more harm than perhaps a complete waste of all this artillery," said Robin bitterly. "Bombards are not catapults whose timbers work whether wet or dry. The balls have no hurt, for they are of stone and iron. But the serpentine—the brimstone and sulphur and charcoal that are the compounds of the powder—it will be useless until it is throughout dried. And I know not how strongly it will take fire even when dried."

While the shipmaster called to some of the soldiers to make haste and shift the wetted cargo into dryer place, Robin started to clamber out of the hold to have word with the pilot.

And then suddenly—

It was the squealing of the tackle-block overhead, the singing hum of overtaut hemp, as much as Hubert's shout that made him look up.

Almost directly over him, dangling from the cocked yardarm, hung the third and last of the great bombards. It was lurching and dipping, swinging wildly from side to side. From the block itself, far above, came a sudden straining crack. Then rope and block and all, the bombard broke loose and came plunging its full ten hundred-weight of metal into the hold.

WILDLY ROBIN threw himself back and sideways. And even as he leaped from under, he felt the air-rush as the plunging bombard hurtled past. It struck a cross-brace timber, smashed through the stout oak as if it were mere wheat straw, struck an already stowed bombard with a deafening ring of metal, half spun and buried itself with a dull thud against the layer of bags beyond.

His face white and eyes gleaming, and with nerves still a-quiver from that close brush of death, Robin leaped for the short ladderway to the half-deck above. He scrambled out onto the open deck almost at the feet of the dark-faced pilot who took one look at his blazing eyes and stumbled back.

"The lifting block—it broke from the yard!" he cried. "The rope was rotten; there was naught I could do!"

"There was naught you could do to keep the sacks out of the bottom water, either, except to lay the dry timbers underneath as you had order," said Robin tensely. He turned his head. "Peter Joy, do you scramble up this mast and fetch down the parted tackle rope that still hangs to the yard. Mayhap we may find a knife-cut there, rather than only the fraying strands of outworn hemp!"

Peter Joy laid quick hands to the mast. But before he could even begin his climb, the pilot let out a great oath in Norman French. His hand whipped to his girdle, rose again. And the keen edge of the snatched knife stabbed with deadly intent at Robin's breast.

Robin, however, had turned his head aside, but not his eyes. He glimpsed the quick movement, the raised hand. And that hand, falling, found not unresisting flesh but the quick, hard grasp of Robin's own hand. With the pilot's wrist firm clutched, Robin took a half turn, jerked, and the knife went spinning out and into the hold below.

Amazed, the pilot jerked loose, glared. Then with a bellow like a bull he threw his brawny body forward in a charge, seeking to hurl the slender bombardier over the side and into the swirling tide beneath.

But almost in mid-air the pilot seemed to take wing and fly away. Red Hubert, moving with incredible speed for one so huge, had seized the pilot's jerkin in his enormous fist. And Hubert's strength, not applied directly, merely added force and direction to the pilot's plunge. Up, head-high, and on over the cog's side the pilot spun, to land with a half-choked shout full ten feet beyond the cog's fat sides. And with the splash came Hubert's joyful shout.

"Thy ale, Shipmaster Swann! Fetch thy promised butt of ale! For this bickering brawler of thine is gone overside to show these salt-water fishes how to swim!"

Worriedly Robin hastened to the side. But the pilot, sputtering and cursing, had already come up from his unexpected dive and was swimming strongly toward the quay. There he found helping hands and vanished into the crowd.

"The ale is thine, Red-thatch, and double-ale, not small beer!" answered the shipmaster, panting from his climb to the deck. "But it was not full earned, since I was not there to see."

ROBIN, HOWEVER, sent the shipmaster scurrying again with order to hoist all the wet casks, and sacks up on deck again for drying, and to lash the fallen bombard in place. Then as he himself turned to look toward the quay again, he was surprised to feel the touch of fingers on his arm.

It was the Flemish girl, Katherine Algelt.

"It—it almost struck you!" she said, gasping. "I saw it—saw it fall! It would have ground you like a crushed fly had you been underneath."

"An old and rotten rope and a lucky leap in time," answered Robin. He felt a wave of warmth flow to his very ear tips—a warmth that was both pleasant and confusing. The blackness of her eyes was even more dizzying. And so, because he was young and had no knowledge of women, he stammered and gulped his words, "This Norman-speaking pilot, though—he is very careless in his loading. Half the charcoal and serpentine is wetted—"

"If they had talked with good English tongue, instead of swinish Norman French," said John the Wolf behind them sourly, "mayhap we would know what lies behind this all. For I stood outside the aftercastle door when the pilot went in to talk to Butcher de Brenn, and for half the length of an abbot's vespers their words came through the door. But their gulping Norman was too strange for my honest Saxon ears."

"The pilot's name—Pierre—it is Norman, too," said Robin thoughtfully. "However, inasmuch as he is a pilot and needs must know the landmarks of the shores, both English and French, it is but reason that he knows the speech too."

"De Brenn—de Brenn—" the girl was repeating the name

wonderingly. "It seems to me that I have heard that name before. But in Normandy, not England, At the market fair in Cherbourg; my father had business with the mercers there. And there was a Comte de Brenne who held a barony there. I recall it because he amerced us for thrice the tax that was the usual custom."

"It is not strange," said Robin carelessly. "Half the barons in England have holdings in France as well, held from their grandfathers and great-grandfathers before them. Our own King Edward did homage to his uncle, the King of France, for his Duchy of Aguitaine. This Comte de Brenne of Cherbourg might well be cousin or even closer kin to our English Baron de Brenn, and yet be full Frenchman in all else."

"Then why do not these testy cousins do their own bickering, instead of levying honest English archers and franklins into their wars?" grunted Wat the Armorer.

"Pillage! For the good sake of pillage!" retorted John the Wolf. "If we pillage our own lords here, it is the gibbet and the stake. Whereas to pillage a Frenchman is a praiseworthy thing. I care naught for the rights of the quarrel, so long as I can but lay hand on some rich Frenchman to hold to ransom!"

CHAPTER III

NOBLE BANNERS FLYING

WITH THE COMING of dusk, and the last of the cart loads aboard the cog, most of the archers and sailors had taken themselves ashore again to sleep. The girl had returned to her father in the sterncastle. The armorer, with Hubert and Peter Joy and John the Wolf, ate cold loaves and venison from their pouches, and stretched themselves as best they could on the cog's deck. What sailors remained to watch the ship were warming their meat over a tiny charcoal brazier they had set up on deck, having thoroughly sprinkled the deck planks with water to guard against scattering coals.

Standing on the raised forecastle, Robin Santerre gazed about him at the vast cluttering of ships and the bivouac fires ashore, and wondered.

It was strange that he, who had no liking for either war or bloodshed, should be embarked to sail to war on the morrow. As a student at Oxford, he had found more interest in the study of levers and weights and forces than in the martial application of them. The smelting of iron with charcoal to make the fine steel was more important than the hacking of other men's necks with that same steel.

Then in a yellowed parchment of the Franciscan monk, Roger Bacon, he had run across that intriguing formula for the compounding of this strange mixture called "serpentine"— gun powder. Neither the old monk nor Robin, at first, had known that it was gunpowder, or that men would fashion great bombards of metal from which to shoot balls of stone and iron with that same powder.

Robin had learned that only when this Flanders merchant with his pretty daughter had come with these bombards wrought in Flanders, to hire this amazing new species of artillery to King Edward for his wars in France.

It was the thought that here was a new and greater force to be harnessed than man had ever possessed before, that had caught Robin's interest, brought him here. That, and perhaps the equally amazing force that lay in the Flemish girl's sparkling eyes....

Equally powerful, and yet in Robin's mind perhaps even more praiseworthy than his own motives, was the reason that had brought Wat the Armorer in company with him. Perhaps the master armorer of all England, Wat had ceased the making of hauberks and helms because only the barons and knights were rich enough to purchase them. And protected by those same hauberks and helms, the barons and knights over-rode all ordinary Englishmen, taking what they would and paying as oft in blows as in coin

But seeing the power of those new bombards, Wat the Armorer had recognized that there might be a force sufficient to overcome the vast advantage that arrow-proof armor gave. The new engine of war would make a freeborn archer as good as a king. And so, at an age when ordinary men dropped sword or hammer to sit in the sun and play with their grandchildren, Wat the Armorer had joined Robin's little group to serve the bombards. Had joined that he might see the proof in bloody war, that these new engines were as he had hoped.

THE THUDDING of hooves below as Sir Allan's mettlesome charger impatiently kicked at his stall recalled Robin from his mood. He went over to where the drenched bags had been laid for drying. Running his hand into the nearest, he took out a handful of the lumped grains.

Laying a pinch on a dry timber, he picked up a coal from the sailors' brazier. The powder was lifeless. Only a little spot where the grains had not soaked through sputtered for a moment.

With sudden thought, Robin bent to the sack, drew some from the side where the late sun had struck. This burned better. But it was a small raveling from the hempen sack, which had become mixed with the grains, that seized Robin's attention. The hemp, impregnated with the powder, did not leap to flaring flame; neither did it hang fire and smolder slowly as ordinary cordage would char. Instead, a sputtering, sizzling spark ran slowly but measuredly along the hempen strand and yet could not be extinguished easily.

With eyes sparkling Robin twisted another strand from the sack, then another. Hubert and the other bombardiers were around him now, watching interestedly. A couple of the sailors had come up to stare at the strange hissing spark.

All the weariness from the day's toil had gone from Robin now. His breath came quick, his face was eager. He cast a swift look about him.

On the deck a few feet away lay a discarded wine flask, emptied and dropped there by the archers after their meal. The wine fumes were heavy, but the pottery flask was dry.

Taking it up, Robin hurried below, filled it with a double handful of powder from the dry sacks in the hold. Then he returned to the deck and the brazier.

With nervous hands he twisted another powder-granulated strand from the hempen sack. Thrusting the strand into the powder in the flask until only the end protruded, he glanced about again. A gnawed half loaf of bread lay where the flask had been discarded. Tearing a handful out of the softer part inside the crust, he crushed it into a tight ball, pressed it into the flask neck and around the hempen strand.

He held the flask before him.

Red Hubert chuckled. "Think you to fashion bombards out of pottery clay, Robin? Even a small blow with a sword would shatter the flask to bits."

"That," said Robin, "is something I must prove."

Holding the flask in his hand, he thrust the end of the strand against the brazier coals until it began to hiss and spit. Then he raced as far forward along the ship's deck as he could go, laid the smoking flask down, and raced back. He had scarcely reached the others around the brazier again when there came such a rattling crash that the horses below snorted and plunged with fright.

With that roar the flask had shattered like a meteor bursting in the night. The flaring flame lighted the deck and masts, the gaping eyes and mouths of the men. Bits of flying shard rattled as they struck, and Red Hubert cried out and clapped a hand to his thigh. Then the night's blackness curtained down again, and there was only the stink of acrid smoke.

"A murrain on that devil's powder!" roared Hubert. He took his hand away from his thigh, held it to the brazier glow. "Blood! I have been scotched even through this stout leather jerkin.

Did I not say it would shatter—that clay would fashion no bombards?"

"But it shattered! It shattered, and with cutting force!" said Robin, panting. "It was not bombards I had mind to—no, not bombards!"

"The more I see of this mixture, the more certain I am that it is devil's doing," rumbled Hubert. "Had you held it in your hand, had you fired it closer—our hides had all been as full of clay shards as a target butt full of arrows!"

By now feet were running along the quays; voices shouted, sailors called from ship to ship. Even Sir Allan and Baron de Brenn and the girl came dashing out to inquire.

"What hell's noise is this?" demanded de Brenn angrily. "Sir Allan, have you no order over these sailors that they make disturbance to wake the dead?"

"It was but the powder sacks—the powder for the bombards," said Robin cunningly. "It was wetted by mischance, and I but tested a handful with a coal to see if it were dry. I am sorry if I have waked thee—"

"Then see to it that it happens no more!" snapped the baron and, turning, he stamped to his quarters again.

But Sir Allan looked sharply at Robin. "It was no noise of loose powder burning; it was more like the blast of a loosed bombard itself."

"Yet it was no bombard. The bombards are all stout-lashed in the hold," returned Robin, and explained no further.

But he walked forward, gathered such shards of the shattered flask as he could find, touched with his hands the splintered planks where the flask had exploded. He held the shards for a long time, staring unseeingly over the water.

This night meant much to him.

And now the bell in the great lower of Southampton Hall began to ring the *couvre-feu*. From the rambling town came the calls of the watchmen: "Cover your fires! Cover your fires!"

A bellowing horn on the largest ship took up the curfew call, and from ship to ship adown the line the other horns sounded.

From the brazier the sailors plucked a few coals aside and quickly covered them with ashes, to save the fire for the morrow. The rest of the brazier's embers were dumped over the side. Finally the King's great fleet lay in silence.

STANDING ON the cog's forecastle in the bright sunlight of the following morning, Robin Santerre thought never to see a more stirring sight. From every mast and staff fluttered the bright pennons and banners of the warriors of England; steel glittered and sparkled on every deck. Sir Allan Mayne came and stood beside him; the knight read off the 'scutcheons as a monk tells his beads.

"Gold, a chevron gules—see the red chevron on the gold field? The Earl of Stafford keeps that ship. And there is the Earl of Warwick with his fess and six crosslets of gold. The lions of Arundel, the chevrons and ermine of Oxford. Never has there been such a brave gathering in all England. And look upon the devices: the swan of Bohun, the blue boar of Vere, the griffon of the Montagues, the horseshoes of Ferrers!"

Wat the Armorer, who had come up to douse his grizzled head in water, gave a grunt. "A brave show, mayhap, but a flaunting one. Must a man then make a display of silken flags and painted shields to prove himself a true-blooded knight or baron?"

"Nay," said Sir Allan. "The banner or shield is intended to mark the rallying point in battle, by which the men-at-arms may know the whereabouts of their leader. And by the same token, if a knight be craven, his arms will be seen fleeing to the rear and recognized as such to his everlasting shame."

The armorer glowered at the great banner of Baron de Brenn fluttering its scarlet and sable overhead. "Then for the nonce we on this ship have naught to fear. For pigs have no zest for fight, and the boar's head on yon banner is a fitting device for a Butcher!"

A soft voice broke in, pleasant but eager. Katherine Algelt stood there, gazing about with flushed cheeks and glowing eyes.

"But that golden shield on that galley there, with the solitary wedge device of simple red adown its length. Whose would that plain shield be? And see—the banner at the mast has only the head of a blackamoor upon it."

Sir Allan looked, and his voice became soft and reverent. "Wherever those are seen on the fields of France, there will rage the hottest of the battle. For the Saracen head banner and the gold shield with the pile gules are those of Sir John Chandos, and there is no braver man in all Christendom. Only a simple knight he is, even as myself. Yet, had he wished, he could have had ten thousand of the bravest in all England under his banner."

"More even than a baron or an earl?" inquired Wat the Armorer.

"More than even the greatest belted earl in the land—more even than the Earl of Warwick himself."

"Then," said Wat the Armorer, "mayhap there is somewhat to this arms and banner flaunting after all, when a simple knight has greater honor than a belted earl.... But, look to this cog next to us. Is not that a ballista they are lashing upon the forecastle there?"

Robin Santerre looked, and nodded.

UPON THE high forecastle of the adjoining ship men were rearing and securing in position the great timbers and spoon beam of a ballista. From rail to rail they lashed the foundation timbers, and fastened other hawsers to mast and bow.

Then they laid shoulder to the stout windlass bars and tugged. Foot by foot the huge spoon beam came over and back in its arc, and the twisted ropes creaked and groaned under the strain.

Presently the master artilleryman tripped the trigger, and the great beam whipped around and up until it brought up sharp in its checks. The whole ballista rocked and rattled, and the stout cog itself quivered and reeled in the water.

"Do they think to drag cog and all overland to the battle,

or do they think to match yon ship against a sea barbican in France?" scoffed the armorer.

"Not against walls, but against some ship of the Frenchmen if they come to meet us in the *Manche*," replied Sir Allan. "One great stone from that ballista, fair thrown, would shatter a ship's timbers like an eggshell."

"And one of our bombards would make eggshells of both cog and ballista," said Wat the Armorer proudly. "Besides, the ballista must hurl its stone in a long over-sweep which, if the Frenchman came close in, would overshoot and miss. But our bombard, since it shoots straight and true, would be even more potent at close distance."

"Then why not hoist one of our bombards up on our own forecastle?" demanded the girl.

Robin shook his head. "Yon ballista has long foundation timbers which spread its weight over great space. Our bombard is short of body and of great weight. We would need to cut and fit special timbers for the foundation, and mayhap other great posts of oak to strengthen the ship's timbers and deck underneath."

"Then the bombards are of no use save on land," said the armorer gloomily.

"Nay, I said not that. Given time, we could build such timbers as would withstand even the back-throw of the bombard. But there is no time. See, Shipmaster Swann is already come to the deck."

The shipmaster had indeed come onto the raised forecastle and was casting his glance about, both alow and aloft. But mostly it was the sea and the dark rim of the sky above the hilltops that held his gaze. And as he looked he shook his head.

"If the King comes not quickly now, he need make no haste at all," he said slowly. "That dark cloud, low and to the land. See how it gathers, how quickly it eats into the sunlight? Such clouds have I seen before; they bring with them such storm as no shipmaster would face if there be harbor for the seeking."

"Storm?" Sir Allan gave an impatient frown. "You think then that it will come to storm?"

"Aye—and quickly."

"But not too quickly, mayhap," said the girl, turning her head down the shore. "I think the King comes now."

Then along the road and through the town came the fanfare of trumpets, the winding of horns. Drums and tambors rumbled and rolled. And with them came the clanging tramp of feet and steel-shod hooves, until the whole town seemed to shake.

"The King!" exclaimed the shipmaster.

"And our own prince, Edward of Woodstock!" said Sir Allan Mayne.

CHAPTER IV

TO SEA—TO BATTLE

FOR AT THE head of the serried ranks of mounted knights and footmen of the London levies rode Edward the Third, King of England. He was a man of but thirty-three, tawny haired, and brawny of limb.

He bestrode a white jennet, his equerry behind him bearing his armor and another leading his caparisoned charger. Beside the King, and for once in full armor save for his doffed helmet, rode his son and heir, Edward of Woodstock, Prince of Wales, but whom some day men would best know as the Black Prince.

He was a slender youth, not yet sixteen, and his golden hair and fair skin made him appear boyish. Yet he reined his heavy warhorse as expertly as a veteran, and he had the soldier's carriage. Over and above the riders streamed the great royal standard, with its golden leopards on its scarlet field.

Even as those on the cog looked, the Earl of Warwick rode from under his own banner with its six golden crosses and spoke deferentially to the King, pointing toward the ever darkening sky. But the King shook his head and waved an imperious hand, and the array of steel continued to pour down the road and along the quays. The waiting ships seemed to swallow them up, so quickly did they pour into the cogs and galleys.

Even as the royal standard ran to the masthead on the King's ship, a great horn sounded, calling all the captains to council. But a little time later, when the horn sounded again for the breakup of the conference, it was the King's own ship that spread its sail and led the way to sea.

Then the whole harbor broke into motion, as far as the eye could see. Horns sounded and drums rolled, the air was full of the creaking of yards and cordage and the shouting of the sailors. The deep-laden cogs swung out their great sweeps, long oars manned each by a half-dozen men, to work out and clear to where the wind would belly the flapping sails.

Galleasses, with both oars and sail, slid slowly past the burdened cogs. But still swifter, the galleys with their long pointed bows and their myriad oars beating the water like hundred-legged bugs, skimmed past and away, their fore- and aftercastles black with armed men and their waists sparkling with the glint of pointed steel.

Then from the people left behind on the quay came a great shout of farewell, so loud that it echoed even above the noise of ships and oars.

At the bellowing of Shipmaster Swann, the *Falcon* too had swung its nose, wallowing toward the open channel. Two great sweeps forward and two at the stern gave it help, and the grunts of the rowers came measured and loud. Beside the stern steering sweep the pilot, Pierre, hurled his Norman-French oaths at the sailors who tugged at it to steer.

"Ho, our butcher baron comes to add his voice," said Red Hubert, who had found place on the forecastle with Tyrel and his score of archers. He pointed aft to where Baron de Brenn stood beside the pilot.

The speedier ships had by now pulled out ahead and were

skimming and churning their way toward the open water. The *Falcon* and the other cogs, fat-bellied, heavy laden, wallowed along in their wake.

Sir Allan gave a sudden cry. "Our pilot—he is heading away and to the east! Why does he not steer closer to the south, as do the others?"

Indeed the *Falcon,* now that her great sail was taut and pulling, was drawing clear of the pack, and skirting more to the eastward.

"Mayhaps the pilot holds her clear, to avoid ramming other ships," said the armorer.

But Robin's brows were thoughtful. "Sea room is a good thing, and rocks are more deadly than neighboring ships. But it would suit me better if I knew our shipmaster's thoughts on it."

SHIPMASTER SWANN was even then clambering to the high forecastle. His face had a worried twist, and his eyes glanced from the straining sail to the ever increasing cloud. The cog was clear of the inner waters of the harbor now, and feeling the full force of the rousing breeze. White caps were slapping viciously at the wallowing hull, the mast and yard were creaking and groaning, and the whole northwest quarter of the heavens was a lowering black.

"Do we not head over-far to the east, and away from the main fleet?" inquired Sir Allan sharply. "It was my understanding that we were to follow the head ships."

"It suits me ill, too," answered the shipmaster. "The storm swells apace, and there is no safety on a rocky shore. But I have order only over the sailors. The setting of the course is in the hands of the pilot. And mayhap he hath his orders from the Baron de Brenn."

"You have spoken to him, then?" inquired Robin.

"Aye. And his answer was that he steers this course to avoid the mischance of striking rocks on the lee shore. And ahead and in that direction lies the Isle of Wight."

"But before the Isle of Wight comes the pass of the Solent,

and a safe haven there if the storm grow too strong. Is that not true?" demanded Sir Allan.

"You speak sooth, yes. The Solent would give haven to the whole fleet if need arise, and there we could ride out even such a storm as seems in the making."

"But we draw over-far to the east, if we would seek shelter in the Solent, do we not? And if we miss the mouth of the Solent—"

"Then there is naught to do but seek safety in the open Channel, and stay wide of any shores as best we may. For a ship in storm there is safety only in two ways—a safe haven, or else the freedom of the open sea."

That the storm was waxing fast was already more evident by the moment. The wind against the great sail was pressing the cog far over, the hum of the cordage was like a rising wail. Spume from the crested waves was driving like pellets of rain.

Archers and soldiers, stout-hearted enough in battle or on the solid land, were staring at the vicious crests with white and anxious faces. From below came the plunging and snorting of the affrighted warhorses. The straining of the decks and timbers of the whole cog had become by now a tremendous rattling and creaking.

"Look!" suddenly cried the armorer. "The King's ship and the galleys in the van—they are turning. They are turning short to the west, with all effort!"

"The mouth of the Solent lies there!" answered the shipmaster. "The King has seen the fury of the storm. He is leading into the safety of the passage inside the Isle of Wight!"

"And now our pilot and de Brenn must needs follow also," said Sir Allan with relief. "They dare not disobey the King's orders in open sight."

True, after a moment the great steering sweep was put over, and tardily the cog began to turn her head westward.

But now the distance that the *Falcon* had worked away from the fleet and to the east became evident. With its single great square sail and its sluggish hull, the cog made but slow progress westward, but far faster progress southward. Already the steep rocks and headlands of the Isle of Wight were plain in sight, with the surf breaking white at their feet.

"Down! Down from the castles and the high points!" shouted the shipmaster to Tyrel and his archers. He bawled the same message to Jarold and his men-at-arms on the sterncastle. "Down into the ship's waist, lest she be topheavy and not take hold in the water as she should!"

"Would it not be better to send them as much as possible into the hold at the stern?" asked Robin. "It is the higher sterncastle that catches the wind and swings the bow ever away from the Solent mouth. A heavier weight underneath would increase the drag and thus make a balance of the force of wind and sea."

Shipmaster Swann looked his amazement. "How knew you this? I had thought you were but a man of land—not a sailor!"

"The laws of levers and forces are no different on sea than on land," said Robin. "Even as the goose feathers on one end of an arrow balance the weight of the barb on the other, to the making of true flight, so does deep weight in a ship balance the wind on the sail above."

EVEN WITH this change in the disposition of the men, however, the headlands of Wight seemed to be rushing down at them. Double crews of oarsmen were now tugging and panting at the great rowing sweeps. But the open mouth of the Solent into which the rest of the fleet was streaming like frightened pigeons was already abeam and even drawing astern.

"It will be close!" muttered the shipmaster. "Too close! Only St. Christopher could shepherd us into Solent Water now."

"If that single great square sail had been split in two, and one part stretched on a mast far forward and the other well aft," said Robin, "it had been easier to go to the west. For flattened along the length of the ship, one sail would have balanced the other, as the feathers balance the arrow barb."

"But then we would go but sideways, and not ahead—"

"Nay," said Robin. "The cog's deep hull in the water would have prevented sliding sideways; the ship would have been forced on ahead. Had we time I would have well liked to make the test. But without a forward mast—"

He broke off. Onto the now almost empty forecastle had clambered a slight form, willowy, and almost seeming to bend like a young tree under the force of the wind. Katherine Algelt's kirtle was spray wetted and glued to her slender body, and her dark hair was straining in the wind. Despite the reeling of the cog and the hammering of the waves, there was no fear in her face. She clung to a shroud, flushed and in high excitement.

"The wind, it has the sound of a thousand clarions, and the waves are like the beating of great drums!" she exclaimed. "Only the good God in Heaven could fashion such beauty as a storm!"

"You are not afraid?" asked Robin, staring.

"Afraid?" She caught at her streaming mantle and laughed. "At the storm that the good God fashions? Nay!"

"But the good God also fashions sharp rocks," muttered Shipmaster Swann, and then as hastily crossed himself. "Now will I pledge the good St. Christopher a full score of tapers for the altar of Romney Abbey, if these rocks take us not full abeam!"

But even as he spoke, there was a shout from the stern, and many men running. The great steering sweep came around and over, and the *Falcon* ceased its vain struggle toward the Solent mouth. Full before the storm the cog swept, now more swiftly than any slim galley, and straight toward the open Channel. Not half a bowshot away the outthrust of rocks of Wight swept past, so near that the roar of the breakers was thunderous. Like some petrel of the storm with outspread wings the cog drove on, into the open *Manche*.

"Not one score, but two score candles of the purest wax will I burn to St. Christopher!" said the shipmaster with a great sigh. "The *Falcon* is a stout cog and we may well hope to weather the storm in the open Channel now. And the Frenchman is a good pilot—he made past the rocks with not a short cablelength to spare."

"Aye," said Robin Santerre. "Aye. He made it with a good reckoning. Even too good reckoning, mayhap." His eyes were brooding and thoughtful.

CHAPTER V

'WARE BUTCHER DE BRENN

ALL THAT AFTERNOON the cog ran, under the merest rag of sail, for long since the shipmaster had lowered the yard lest the exceeding force of the wind tear even the shortened sail out of its holdings. Even so the *Falcon* drove like a wild thing, curveting and plunging.

The land behind had been lost beyond the spray and scud, and on all sides was only the riot of foaming waters. So fast the ship drove that Robin was afraid they might be hurled across the Channel in the night and shattered on the rocks of France. Having the same worry, Shipmaster Swann held council with the pilot and de Brenn. As a result of which, the cog's head was kept off as far as possible to the west and an open run down the Channel.

But when nightfall came, no one aboard slept. The skies were as black as ink, without any stars to guide, and the cog seemed to be racing in an abysmal void halfway between sea and sky.

But in the last daylight hours before the night closed down, the shipmaster had turned the sailors to work, tightening the ship against the storm. Great hides had been spread over and atop the more delicate cargo, including especially Robin's sacks of serpentine and charcoal. Leathern buckets were brought out, and lines of men set to scooping the bottom water from the hold and passing it hand by hand to the side where the last man hurled it back into the sea.

Through all the night they kept at the labor, the archers and men-at-arms taking turns with the sailors, so that the ship remained dry and safe despite the spray that constantly drenched aboard. But as Shipmaster Swann had boasted, the *Falcon* was a stout cog, and her timbers held against the wrenching of the sea.

"The heavy weight of the bombards low in the bottom also steadies her," pointed out Robin. "They give her balance against the top castles and the mast. But it is well that we did not attempt to make fast one of the bombards atop the castle, like a ship ballista."

Shipmaster Swann shuddered. "It would have carried a-loose ere now, no matter how stout the lashings. And only God's mercy could have saved us then from it crashing down and battering a great hole in the bottom planking."

With the coming of morning, the sky was still gray and sunless, nor was there any land yet in sight. For which all on board devoutly gave thanks with many *aves* and *pater nosters*. The shipmaster remarked that undoubtedly the wind had changed, and hence they were driving down the length of the *Manche*, perhaps almost to the Western Sea itself.

"And what lies there?" demanded Wat the Armorer grimly.

"I know not. On the English side, lies Cornwall and the Lizard, and beyond that even the Land of Eire to which I was once blown. But on the opposite side of the *Manche*, beyond the Gulf of Gascony, lies the land of the Basques, the marches of Spain, and so on even to the countries of the Paynim whom our grandfathers' grandfathers fought against in the great Crusade."

Sir Allen Mayne, who had joined them, looked sober. "These Basques—I have heard tell of them, and it was an ill telling. Men have it that they are as scant of mercy as the Paynim themselves, so that any luckless traveler who falls into their hands does not live for long."

So for another night and still another day the storm held, driving the cog ever into the rolling wastes. Then at last the gale blew itself out, and the cog ceased to groan and rack, and men found chance to lie down and sleep. When morning came, it brought with it the warming sun, and a gentle breeze springing from the west.

THEN A council was held between de Brenn and Sir Allan, to hear the arguments of the shipmaster and the pilot. Robin stood near, listening.

"There is naught to do save steer back toward the east," advised the pilot. "If we hold to the north, where mayhap England lies, it might be that we would miss England altogether, and even Eireland, and thereupon be lost in the great Western Ocean itself. But to the east we should strike land, which may tell us where we are. Thus we can set the course homeward again."

"Then it had best be done speedily," grumbled the shipmaster. "Already the drinking water runs low. There are not three half-butts left for both men and horses, and that stinking."

"To the east, then, with all sail!" ordered the baron. "If we find not land and fresh water ere long, we shall risk the losing not only of our chargers but our lives as well."

So with the sail raised to the full once again, the cog was put toward the east. At last, on the seventh day out of Southampton, they sighted a tall coast, and beyond it the loom of even taller hills.

"What is this, pilot?" demanded Sir Allan sharply. "These hills—you have knowledge of them?"

But the pilot shook his head, "It is a landfall I have never set eye upon."

"Then skirt the coast and steer more to the north for another day," ordered Baron de Brenn. "We have the dregs of the drinking casks to last us one day further yet."

So the *Falcon's* head was held up still more, and all that day they skirted the coast, keeping it plain in sight but steering wider of it at nightfall, lest in the dark they run onto the deadly fangs of some rocky point.

Robin, however, watched on the forecastle where Sir Allan

stood, likewise looking across to the now invisible land with gloomy eyes.

"That land would be Gascony or Normandy, mayhap, and either one worse than the other to make a landing. Undoubtedly the French King has knowledge of our gathered fleet, and his ships and corsairs will be quick to fall upon any lone ship of England."

"Yet we must have water," said Robin. "It would take days yet to beat against this unfavoring wind and so back to England."

"But the Frenchmen will begrudge us their water as much as their land. And with only a score of archers and Jarold's dozen men-at-arms, we might find it a hard landing."

Like two tall shadows out of the night Red Hubert and John the Wolf came up to join them.

"If this pilot knows not the landfall here, as he claims," said Red Hubert, "it is strange how eagerly he talks to the Butcher de Brenn, with great pointing and gesturing to the land side. And strange how the Butcher nods back, and seems so greatly pleased."

"What?" exclaimed Sir Allan. "You saw and heard them thus?"

"Aye. On the sterncastle but now. A friar could have said ten credoes while John Wolf and I spied upon them."

"You spied, you say? But did you hear their words?"

"Heard, but could make naught of them, since they gulped in outlandish Norman-French. But methinks we heard the words 'Gascony' and 'Normandy' amid their gulpings."

"Gascony! Normandy!" Sir Allan whirled on Robin. "What think you of this?"

"THE SAME that I thought, that first day out of Southampton, when this pilot steered so wide from the fleet," said Robin. "I think this pilot is a traitor, fit for hanging. And that he steered so of purpose, that we should miss the Solent and be forced out alone into the Channel."

"But to what gain?" inquired the knight puzzledly.

"To the gain of all these bombards and their store of powder and ball, as well as we few men who know how to discharge them," answered Robin. "If through the pilot's falseness we and the bombards should end up in the hands of the King of France, I doubt not the pilot could ask and receive much gold for the treachery."

"But the pilot has no knowledge of the bombards' power. In truth, had I not seen with my own eyes when they battered down the stout steel bars and oaken doors of Bewly town hall when we rescued the Prince, I would not have believed it myself!"

"And what you saw, de Brenn saw as well, since he came late to that same rescue."

"De Brenn!"

"Aye. Was it not he that assigned the pilot to have charge over the loading and the stowage? Had the powder been all ruined by that bottom water, or had the falling bombard crushed the bottom planks, sinking of the whole cog and cargo, it would have been an ill blow to King Edward's battles. But not nearly so ill a blow as for the King of France to capture the bombards for his own artillery."

Wat the Armorer had come, curious, and now he put in his own word. "The Flemish maid—the daughter of the merchant Algelt—she said somewhat of a Count de Brenn in French Normandy. If they be kin, mayhap there is a reckoning between them."

Sir Allan nodded, frowning. "On our own King Edward's ship there is a Norman Lord, D'Harcourt, who is blood brother to a full *comte* in the French king's army, yet is treasonably come to guide our English army into his own country. If we have treason helping us, it may well be that the French have the same."

"Then let us do a good deed both for our king and for ourselves by drowning this treason forthright," said Red Hubert cheerfully. "The stern is dark, and the ship asleep. Within two winks Wolf John and I can waylay both this Judas pilot and the Butcher himself and cast them overside."

But Robin shook his head. "We have not full proof as yet, and without proof it would be murder. Also we may have more need of them alive than dead. All we may do as honest men is to keep good watch with both eyes and ears."

"A sound saying, if we did but know from what point danger threatens," said the knight. "Of ourselves and Tyrel's archers and Jarold's men-at-arms we are sure. But of the cog's sailors we know naught, save that the shipmaster looks honest."

"Both honest and tight-mouthed," agreed Robin. "We might do well to speak with Master Swann."

The shipmaster, when they summoned him quietly to the forecastle knitted his brows over their irquiry.

"For all but two I can answer, for they have been long in the *Falcon* with me. But there are two new men—Black Arnuf and Adam of Rye—who joined last week to make the full crew. Their honesty I cannot vouch for, but they know well their craft, since smugglers must be good sailormen."

"Smugglers!"

"So I heard rumor. But many good fishermen along the Five Ports hold smuggling to be no evil, since the King's tax brings him unearned profit."

"And whence do the smugglers obtain the goods for their smuggling?" demanded Robin quietly.

"From France and Flanders, mostly, since Eire-land lies too far distant."

"And have you noted these two smugglers of yours in talk with de Brenn or the pilot?"

"Not with de Brenn. But only yesternoon I marked them sharing a flask of wine with the pilot."

When Master Swann had gone away again, Sir Allan drew a deep breath. "It may mean naught, and it may mean much. But none the less, to keep watch on their doings may bring us sounder sleep."

"John Wolf will take the forecastle, I will take the aftercastle, and Peter Joy the hold," said Red Hubert quickly. "So go soundly to thy sleep. Not a one of us but could split a flying pigeon with a shaft, if need be."

"And you and I will take turn by turn, Robin," said Sir Allan. "I will stand watch until the half-night, and then you until the dawn."

But the night passed peacefully enough. The new day came with a warm sun and a pleasant sea and a breeze that swung the cog along at a rippling pace.

WITH THE daybreak the pilot had turned the ship nearer in toward shore, until they skirted it at but four good bowshots' distance. The sailors, meanwhile, had fetched out the brazier and the covered embers they had nursed throughout the storm, and for the first day in many they had the taste of fresh-warmed meat with their flasks of wine.

It was the girl, who first caught sight of the opening in the land.

There between two great ridges of hills had opened a green and gentle valley. The greenness was swiftly accounted for by the sight of a white and tumbling fall of water that plunged down the rocky hillside to join a turbulent stream at the valley mouth.

From the shout aft, they knew that the waterfall and stream had been sighted there also. And after a little time de Brenn came climbing onto the sterncastle to look long and close, and to have much talk with the pilot.

"Water!" exclaimed Wat the Armorer, joining Robin and the girl. "And so clear and swift that it arouses a great fire in my throat at the very sight. Doubtless now Butcher de Brenn will be quick to hoist out the casks and fill them for both men and horses."

But strangely enough the pilot did not steer toward shore. He ordered the sail half-lowered instead, so that the cog barely made headway through the water. And while almost the whole morning dragged, de Brenn continued his careful watch on the shore. Master Swann, who had already made ready the casks and the small boat housed in the waist, began to stride up and down and mumble impatiently.

Sir Allan and Hubert had also come up on the forecastle where they muttered with equal impatience.

"It would seem to me better reckoning to have made a quick dash in to fill the casks, and then away again," said Robin. "Thus the Frenchmen, if there be any there, would have no time to collect and stand in force against our landing."

"De Brenn thinks it better caution to spy out the land well in advance," explained the knight. "He recks that if for another hour we sight neither man nor boat ashore, it will mean certain that there is no habitation there."

"Then squinting through visor slits makes for poorer sight than looking over goose-feathered shafts," growled Red Hubert. "Once and yet again I would have sworn I glimpsed a wisp of smoke, quick snuffed, beyond that first turn of the valley."

"Smoke!" exclaimed Sir Allan. "Then I had best report your glimpsing to de Brenn at once."

But already the sailors were busied at hoisting out the boat and the empty casks. When the knight returned, he was grim.

"De Brenn thinks danger is more like to come from corsair galleys at sea than from land. So he has ordered me and all the archers to stay on board for defense of the castles. Wherefore, since the bombards are all stored below and you have naught to do, you and your bombardiers are to go ashore with a couple of sailors for the oars, to fill the casks."

"We only—without defence of any sort?" demanded Robin in surprise.

"Nay, you take with you Jarold's men-at-arms—a round dozen."

"Now that is a fool's order," said John the Wolf, his lean jaws snapping. "He should have sent archers. For defence against ambushments or sudden raids, one stout archer is worth ten men-at-arms!"

But Robin was frowning. "Two sailors, you say. What two sailors?"

"The two whom Shipmaster Swann forespoke as smugglers— Black Arnuf and Adam of Rye."

"Who as smugglers mayhap know this coast almost as our own," said Robin. All at once his eyes began to widen and to dance. "It is not likely that de Brenn or the pilot would know Tyrel's archers by face, save for Tyrel himself, mayhap? Or that they would have any better knowledge of Jarold's men-at-arms?"

"No," agreed Wat the Armorer, puzzled. "But what has that to do with our landing?"

"This much," said Robin softly. "If a round dozen of Tyrel's archers borrowed sword and basinet and mailed shirt from Jarold's men, they would appear, going ashore, only as so many men-at-arms, would they not? And if by chance and Shipmaster Swann's help, their bowstaves and sheaves of arrows were hidden in the bottom of the small boat—"

"By my bow, you have it!" exclaimed Red Hubert, his face agrin. "And not only Tyrel's bowstaves and shafts in the boat, but mine and Wolf John's and Peter Joy's as well." He jerked his great thumb rudely into John the Wolf's ribs. "My quiver against your baldric, old Wolf, that I speed three shafts to your every two!"

"That may be," said the weazened archer tartly. "But the ransom of my first Frenchman against your bow that I drop as many men with my two shafts as you with your three!"

CHAPTER VI

ARCHERS, BEND BOWS

THUS IT WAS that when the pilot brought the cog close in to short bow-shot from shore, Tyrel's archers in the borrowed mail and casques of Jarold's men-at-arms were rowed ashore, five at a time, by the two smugglers, Arnuf and Adam of Rye. As they landed they formed defense in a little group, pikes advanced and sword to hand and their keen eye searching of the valley beyond the waterfall.

Then Robin and Wat the Armorer, with Hubert and John the Wolf and Peter Joy made up the last boatload, the empty casks towed astern on a hempen line.

Arnuf was a black-browed, sullen man, and Adam of Rye was small and furtive-eyed, moving with a rat-like quickness.

Great was the surprise of these two when, as he stepped out, Red Huber jerked aside the soft cowhide that Maste Swann had stretched in the bottom of the boat, and began lifting out the long bowstaves and goose-feathered shafts. As fast as he lifted them, he passed them to Tyrel's men who came running up and received each his own bowstave and sheaf of arrows. In a trice each archer had taken his coiled bowstring from beneath his steel cap, and had strung his bow. Then with arrows sheathed in their arms, they advanced to and beyond the waterfall.

Black Arnuf stared at the amazing sight of men-at-arms suddenly changed to archers. He glanced at his comrade Adam and then back toward the cog. He raised his arm and seemed half of mind to shout. But that Red Hubert stopped by clutching his windpipe with a grip that had his eyes bulging.

"The casks—the water butts!" said the giant bombardier. "Lay hand to them and make haste to the filling. We five will follow close behind with the others."

His fierce glower and Wat the Armorer's gesture with his keen-bladed knife sent the two sailors hurrying to seize each a cask. Rolling them along over the sloping ground, they brought all the casks to the pool made at the foot of the fall by the cascading water from above.

"And now, Peter Joy," said Robin, "while the casks are filling, do you climb these steep rocks alongside the fall, and call out whatever you may see."

As Peter Joy scrambled up the rocky slope like a goat, Wat the Armorer took charge of the sailors and made quick work of the cask filling. He was pounding in the last bung, when Peter Joy above let out a wild shout.

"They come—they are almost upon us! Two score—five score—and mounted men as well as foot!"

THE ALERT archers needed neither Robin's nor Wat's orders to swing shields to front and crouch low. And well they did, for suddenly from the top of the low shoulder shutting off the upper valley came a whirring, singing noise like a cloud of hornets a-swarm. Feathered shafts hammered on bullhide shields, and crossbow quarrels clanged on casques and steel mail.

One of Tyrel's archers cursed, and tugged at a barbed shaft that had bitten into his thigh, until his neighbor broke the shaft short, and jerked the feathered end free. Then around the bend of the shoulder poured a full two hundred Frenchmen, weapons glittering and voices shouting.

"Two paces! Take two paces distance, each man!" shouted Wat the Armorer, looking appraisingly toward the oncoming horde. "Ground shafts! Loose shafts—and the devil take the laggard!"

At the word, the archers quickly spread into a thin line so that each man had arm space and to spare. Then the sheaf thong was ripped away, and each archer thrust his arrow barbs into the earth beside his left foot so that the nocks stood up waist high and close to hand. They each nocked and drew an arrow full to the ear, regardless of the shafts and quarrels that still buzzed and hummed. Then at a full hundred paces the feathered arrows flew.

And like stricken deer, a dozen of the Frenchmen in the front of the onrushing wave plunged and fell, one man for every shaft. Yet they had not even touched ground before again the bowstrings twanged, and another dozen arrows sped. These French levies made fair targets, and there were those among the forest men who could draw and loose four shafts before the first had fallen to earth.

Side by side, Red Hubert and John the Wolf were bending their bows and exchanging gibes while their arrows flew.

"The tall one with the beard—mark him, John, and then mark this shaft. Through the eye—Ho, said I not so!"

"But you said not which eye!" retorted John the Wolf. "The left eye of the bowman to the left, with the devil's windlass— mark you, the left eye, Hubert! And it is the left eye that takes the shaft!"

Against that deadly rain of arrows the undisciplined French levies, poorly armed and recruited from the countryside, could not stand. For the first time they encountered the amazing archery of England that was to be the wonder of the continent for the next hundred years. Riddled and with half their numbers down, they turned to flee.

Whereupon the two score mail-clad knights and men-at-arms who rode behind them drew their swords. They spurred their horses forward, regardless of living or dead, riding down the fugitives and trampling the dying. Then, their horses bloody of fetlock, they massed for a heavy charge and came on thundering.

"And this," said Red Hubert calmly, "will be different. Arrows will not pierce those shields and closed casques and ringed hauberks. Have a care, old Wolf, or they will split thy pate for thee."

"It will be an ill splitting if I lay hand to their stirrups first," growled Wolf John, fingering his stabbing knife.

But Robin broke in with a quick shout.

"Spread apart! Spread apart, with most archers to the left! Make a lane that they may see us here at the fall and charge for us!"

"Truly you are in haste to get your own pate split, now!" marveled Red Hubert.

But Wat the Armorer cried him down. "The lad is right! Robin is right! For when they ride at us, with right arms raised high to slash, their armpits will be bare of defense. Then those archers who are keen of eye may pierce them through!"

"By my bow, thou wilt be wearing knight's spurs yet!"

exclaimed Red Hubert admiringly. He raised his voice in a mighty shout. "Their armpits! Draw shaft at their armpits!"

NO SOONER had he shouted than the archers in front scattered, forming irregular line again on either side, and backed up the slopes a little way amid the rocks. Seeing this and thinking they had broken in flight, the oncoming French knights raised their battle cry and drove at Robin and the few who remained still at the pool below the fall.

Only when they were within a score of yards did the charging men-at-arms learn the trap that had been laid for them. Then as the bows twanged, in an instant the crowding troop was thrown into a turmoil. Men screamed and groaned, pitched from their mounts or reeled, clinging to their saddles. Riderless steeds were plunging and snorting at the fallen bodies and the smell of blood.

But those in the center, protected by their companions to either side, still came on, though at each instant their number became smaller. One tall Frenchman on a great black horse, with arms as sable as his mount, spurred upon Robin and Wat, in his hand an upraised mace with a star-pointed head. None of the archers at the right seemed able to bring him down.

Robin hurriedly snatched up the shield and sword the wounded archer had dropped, sprang in front of the grizzled armorer. But at that instant Red Hubert's voice called out:

"Left-handed! He has no exposed armpit on this side, old Wolf! So aim at his casque! At his casque, old Wolf, and hold string till I give word. Then both together—*now!*"

Almost as one their taut strings twanged. And almost as one the steel-barbed arrows struck full and fair on the side of the Frenchman's helmet. Even though they could not penetrate the thick plate armor, so terrific was their force high up on the head that they overturned the knight, hurled him from the saddle as if he had been pole-axed. He lay crumpled on the ground, his heavy mace, torn from its wrist-thong in his fall, flew on and thudded harmlessly on Robin's upthrown shield.

At his fall, the remaining horsemen lost heart and fled. There were less than half of those that had charged. John the Wolf was like a leaping cat as he bounded on the fallen Frenchman, jerked open his visor with knife raised to strike. But after one glance at the contorted visage with its blood-streaming lips and nostrils, he rose, sheathed his blade.

"Dead, with his brain fair addled!"

Lowering his shield, Robin took a glance around the stricken field.

"It is finished. Now to the casks, and with them to the boat, before the Frenchmen collect courage to come again!"

Breaking off the battle as quickly as they had begun it, the archers came scrambling back, with only a few gashes and bruises to show for their fighting. They laid hand to the casks, began to roll down toward the boat.

It was only then that Robin perceived the black-browed Arnuf standing as if frozen, a look of fright on his face. The cause of his fear was Peter Joy, standing to his back with a knife-point thrust against his ribs.

"This one made move to flee, so I pricked him with my point to keep him safe." Peter Joy grinned.

"Where is the other one—where is Adam of Rye?" inquired Robin hurriedly.

The rat-like little sailor was nowhere in sight, nor was he among the dead on the field when they made search.

"Methinks I saw him scampering like a rabbit when the charge was at its height," said Red Hubert, scratching his red thatch. "He raced almost underneath the mace of the black Frenchman. And I thought it strange at the time that the Frenchman did not strike him down."

"Then he is gone," said Robin. "So should we too be gone back to the cog, and swiftly."

Into the first boatload he placed the wounded archer and Arnuf, with Hubert to man the other oar, and two of the full casks they tied on behind to tow. Four trips the boat made back and forth before Robin and Wat and three picked men who had remained to the last, reached the cog.

CHAPTER VII

BOAR'S HEAD ON SCARLET

SIR ALLAN WAITED there at the side, and Shipmaster Swann, and de Brenn with a pallor on his face. The water casks had been swung in and stowed, and now the shipmaster was in haste to swing the boat in as well. When it was done, without waiting for orders the shipmaster bawled to the sailors, and the great sail ran up and the steering sweep was put over. Quickly the cog began to pull away from the land.

"An ambush? You fell into an ambuscade?" inquired the knight quickly.

"Come away to the forecastle, and I will tell you," said Robin in low tones.

When he had told, Sir Allan's face grew grim.

"Then it was treason? They were lying in wait for you? You think it was for that, that the pilot kept the cog off shore all morning?"

"It so seems. For not so soon otherwise could they have collected in such force, with horsemen full harnessed."

Sir Allan gave a great oath, laid his hand to his swordhilt.

"Then I will split this pilot now, and have done with treach-ery."

"Too late for that," said Robin. "Look—that is what I feared. Adam of Rye has found his corsairs by now." And he pointed.

Around the point of land astern and to the southeast, three long black ships had poked their bows. Their single sails amid-ships bellied, and rows of oars threshed water on either side. And their forecastles and waists were black with armed men.

"Galleasses—French corsairs. It is well for us that they are not galleys!" said Sir Allan, frowning. "They would catch us over-quickly then."

The bawl of Master Swann told that he had sighted the ships almost as quickly. Men ran on the *Falcon's* decks, getting out the great rowing sweeps. And under full sail and oars the cog fled out to the open northern sea.

Instantly Sir Allan was up and shouting, sending the men-at-arms and the archers to the two castles. The sailors were lugging great stones and bars of iron, carried for that purpose, up onto the high castles to be hurled down upon any who should approach. Mantlets of wood and hides were erected to shield the steersmen and the sailors at their stations.

Shipmaster Swann paused for a moment, to wipe the sweat from his forehead. He glanced back at the three corsairs.

"It will be a long chase, and a close one."

"Mayhap we can give them the slip if we stay ahead till night-fall," said Sir Allan.

"Aye. Not only night, but that gray cloud to the south brings rain as well." Master Swann pointed off to the south where already the sparkling sea had begun to darken.

Within two hours, however, the corsairs were perceptibly closer, and the rain still held off, though the wind had freshened.

"Master Swann," said Robin, "if you had a spare mast and sail, we might even test the matter of that forward balance sail I mentioned once before."

"The sail I have, but not the mast. Howbeit, there is an extra yard for the mainsail, if that would do."

"Fetch it, and a couple of sailors handy at lashing, and we will do what we can," said Robin.

AT THE same time he called Hubert and Peter Joy and sent them to collect as many empty wine flasks as they might find. While the sailors worked at fashioning mast and sail as he directed, he took the half score of flasks that Hubert had brought, and descended to the hold. He was carefully filling each with a double handful of serpentine when he became aware of someone at his side. It was Katherine Algelt.

"You are measuring charges for the bombards in advance?" she inquired eagerly.

Robin shook his head. "Nay, not bombard charges. But something that may do in place of bombards, if need arise."

She stared, and then suddenly she cried: "Now I know! It was one such as this that caused the great noise, that evening in Southampton! The shards of a wine flask—it was those I saw!" And without asking, her deft hands seized a flask and began scooping the powder in.

While she worked, Robin began drawing strands from the hempen sacks, dampening and rolling them in powder, twisting them into cords. When they were rolled and dried in the sun on deck, he threaded them inside the flasks and wadded them tight with crushed bread.

By that time it was coming close to dark, and though the three galleasses were far nearer, they were still almost a mile behind.

"Now by my bow," exclaimed Red Hubert pointing to the leading galleass, "I know yon corsair for a thief as well as a Frenchman! For he has stolen our own Butcher de Brenn's banner to fly at his masthead!"

Robin saw that the corsair's war-flag was indeed in color and appearance almost the same as the scarlet banner that flew from their own cog. He thought he could even make out the sable outlines of a boar's head against the scarlet silk.

"It does indeed look alike to de Brenn's device," he said.

Sir Allan was now coming up with the shipmaster, and had heard Robin's words. He too stared at the flag.

"There might be many, even to the third and fourth degree of cousinship, who have right to wear the boar's-head sable, on gules," he said. "A bend, a charge of rondel or saltire, might well make the difference almost unseen." Yet the knight's eyes were troubled.

However, Master Swann was in haste to make his own report.

"The new sail and spar are finished and all ready for the setting."

"Hold them yet a while. Mayhap we may not need them," said Robin, glancing at the darkening sky.

The shipmaster nodded. "Aye, another hour and it will be night. If we change course then, they may miss us in the dark."

Swiftly then the dark came down, for the sky was by now completely overcast. A rain squall swooped over, pelting the sea and ship. And when it had passed, the corsairs were blotted out in the dark.

FOR STILL another hour the shipmaster held course, however, and then changed almost to right angles. This time the pilot did not dare to order otherwise. The cog ran under oar and sail, until at length Master Swann ordered the sail dropped and the rowing sweeps drawn in. In dead silence the cog lay drifting on the water.

"Hubert," directed Robin, "now do you and John and Peter Joy take station with your bows. And at any sound or any glimpse of light flare, do you loose shaft hard and true."

He himself remained on the forecastle, Sir Allan having taken watch at the stern.

The night seemed filled only with the noises of the wind and sea—the faint hum of the breeze against the bare cordage, the *slap-slap* of waves against the sides.

Then all at once, from the darkness to the right, Robin heard the thresh of oars, the swish of a sharp prow cutting water. From the left, and even closer, came a like sound. Then the bawl of a corsair captain rang in the dark as the galleasses searched the night for their quarry.

Robin listened, all but holding his breath.

In the cog's waist almost beneath him there was the sudden sharp twang of a bow. It was followed by a muffled thud, a half-groan, and then the momentary drum of heels, quickly ceasing. Robin hurried to descend.

There, close beside where the brazier had been left with its embers covered, he found Red Hubert and Peter Joy. At their feet lay a dark figure huddled.

"Arnuf. He will plot no more treason," said Red Hubert simply. "He was blowing at the brazier, holding a hempen flare to it and fanning it to flame, when Peter here loosed shaft. Peter Joy does not miss."

Sir Allan joined them

"It was well done. Now we have naught to watch but the pilot and de Brenn."

"John Wolf has the pilot under eye and shaft where'er he moves," said Red Hubert. "And I will answer for the Butcher, though he keeps close in his stern quarters till now."

For a little while yet they stood, listening. And the two unseen galleasses on either side drew ahead and away, until even the threshing of their oars was stilled.

"Now we may sleep sweeter," said Sir Allan, breathing deep. "Do you take the first half-night watch, Robin, and I will stand guard then till dawn."

Again the rain squalls came pelting down as Robin stood wide-eyed on the forecastle. But there was no more sound of the galleasses. He began to think of the girl below, and remembering how raven black was her hair, and the flash of her eyes like sheet lightning in a summer sky. He was amazed how soon it was that Sir Allan stood beside him, and bade him stretch his limbs and sleep for the second half of the night.

ROBIN HAD scarce so much as fallen asleep, it seemed, before he felt hands shaking him. It was Red Hubert.

"Sir Allan sends word to come quickly onto the forecastle. The dawn comes—but with it comes something else too!"

On the forecastle Robin found not only Sir Allan, but Shipmaster Swann and Wat the Armorer, talking in worried tones.

"If in truth we do go to the southeast as this archer claims," said the shipmaster, "then the pilot or someone has changed the order of the course since last evening. For we need to go to the northwest, rather than southerly, to reach England."

"If it was not the morning star I saw through a break in the clouds, then I am blind!" retorted Hubert. "And since the morning star stays always close beside the sun, it comes always in the direction of the sunrise. But when I glimpsed it, it was here even to the left of the cog's head."

"Listen!" exclaimed the knight suddenly. "Is that not the sound of waves on rock that I hear to the right?"

"Aye!" said the shipmaster with even greater excitement. "But no more so than the sound of waves on rock that I hear to the left as well!"

"And if that is not a dog's first bark to the morning, then am I deaf as well as blind!" cried out Red Hubert.

Clear in the thinning night came the unmistakable bark of a dog, and this sound was straight ahead.

"We are almost upon the shore!" Shipmaster Swann turned and raced aft, bawling at the top of his voice. "To the deck, sailors! Awake, and to the ropes!"

Now Sir Allan was shouting, and from fore- and aftercastle came the answering shouts of the archers and men-at-arms who had held station through the night there. De Brenn's voice spoke from the darkened stern quarters, and from the steering sweep the pilot made a muffled response.

Then almost like a curtain rolled back, the low clouds and scud scattered in the east, and the dawn light came struggling through, revealing the surrounding view.

On either side ran out rocky points, and the *Falcon* had crept between them and deep into the little bay beyond. But it was not sight of these that caused Robin's stare. It was the tall gray walls, the turreted keep, the clustered rooftops of a spreading city that loomed directly ahead and all the way to the right. Along the quays and to the left lay masts and ships of all sorts, on whose decks already horns were blowing and sailors shouting. From the stronghold walls and from the town itself other horns were blowing, bells ringing, and drums beating. Had the lone *Falcon* been King Edward's fleet itself, the alarm could not have been greater.

Master Swann's voice rose in a shout of panic.

"Cherbourg! Cherbourg—see the shipping and the castle walls? And with the wind from the sea we are fair caught almost beneath them!"

"Nay! In the trap, but not caught yet!" answered Robin. "Now is time to spread and test that new sail you fashioned but last night. Forward—set it forward, and haul the sail as taut to the bow as you may. And the same with the great main sail, drawing it toward the stern and not across-ship!"

Desperation rather than belief sent the shipmaster running. There was a sudden brawl at the stern, and then Red Hubert came dragging the pilot, Pierre, from the steering sweep, holding him clear of deck. He was kicking and spitting like a caught cat.

"Onto the forecastle with the traitor—and set a man to guard him well!" ordered Sir Allan grimly. "And we win clear, I will hang him from the masthead with my own hands!"

CHAPTER VIII

A FLASK OF POWDER FOR FRANCE

THE COG'S FORWARD progress had ceased now and with the steering sweep put over and the rowing sweeps threshing, she was slowly coming around. But she hung there, while Master Swann and his seamen struggled to set the sails and masts as Robin had instructed.

De Brenn had climbed to the sterncastle now in full armor,

and the cog became strangely hushed except for the slight clinking of metal as men donned byrnies and casques, and the strum of bowstrings when the archers tested their tautness.

With a shout Shipmaster Swann finished his work and set the new sail to the wind, even as from the top of the tall sea wall there sounded a brazen horn, drawing Robin's eyes that way.

On top of the wall huddled figures moved about a contrivance of timbers and beams, Robin saw the long spoon beam wound back. There was a moment's pause, and then the rumbling clatter and jerk of the great siege engine. The spoon beam flew through its full arc, and from it at the top of its swing soared a whirling boulder. So slowly it came in its long swoop that the eye could follow the turnings of its jagged sides. With a mighty splash the ballista missile, almost half the height of a man, and of four men's weight, dropped into the harbor, short of the *Falcon*.

"Good luck to us that it missed," growled Wat the Armorer, beside Robin. "An one of those flying mountains strike us fair, it will make such a hole as all the harbor will not fill up!"

Even as he spoke, the ballista rattled again. And this time the hurtling stone fell so close that it splashed the cog's sides in falling.

"Steer close into the wind and as close under yon castle wall as you may!" shouted Robin to the shipmaster. "So close that the ballista will overshoot us!"

Instantly the shipmaster was running aft. With steering sweep outswung and rowing sweeps threshing and the newly set sails flat and drawing, the *Falcon* turned recklessly in toward the gray castle wall that upreared from the very water's edge. The fourth stone struck the cog's bow a glancing blow that nevertheless shook it to its keel, but thereafter the missiles passed harmlessly overhead. The artillerymen at the siege engine vainly tried to depress their aim.

Now, however, there was a stir among the mass of shipping, and half a dozen long prows thrust forth. Two of them were galleys, packed with men, and the other four were galleasses. Seeing which Red Hubert let out an oath.

"By my halidon, it is the same Frenchmen as of last night. See the boar's head on yon third ship?"

There was no doubt now that the Frenchmen flew a red banner with a black boar's head upon it.

But the galleys were coming on apace, their banked oars beating the water, their castles packed with fighing men.

"Ho, Tyrel!" shouted Red Hubert to the captain of the archers on the stern castle. "Do you take the steersmen of that right galley, and we here will take the left! And waste no shafts!" Then turning to Peter Joy and John the Wolf beside him, "I will take the front man on the steering sweep, Peter the next, and you, old Wolf, the third."

On came the two galleys, drawing nearer together and pointing their bows inward. It was a favorite maneuver—to ram the opponent's stern oars and then sweep alongside for the boarding attack. So sure were they of their prey that their crews set up a shout of triumph.

THEN FROM the cog's fore- and aftercastles came such a stream of arrows as changed their triumph instantly into dismay. With their first discharge, though the distance was almost two hundred yards, Hubert and Peter Joy and John the Wolf had found their marks.

Spitted, the three Frenchmen at the galley's steering sweep loosed their hold and dropped kicking and screaming to the deck. Almost as fatal had been Tyrel's marksmen. Of the three steersmen on the right galley one still remained afoot, though sore wounded. His sagging weight pushed the sweep so that that galley veered around. Within six oar strokes it crashed into its companion, with a great shattering of oars. Then the two galleys, helpless and disabled, began to drift under the English bows.

The archers from the New Forest did not fail to take advantage of that mishap. As fast as they could draw and notch arrow, they sent the shafts speeding. They swept the galley castles clean, and then raked oarsmen and fighting men.

But the English cog was by no means free of danger. From the bowmen on the galleys, as well as those on the other ships now coming up fast, came a flood of missiles that seemed to darken the sky. A sailor alongside the cog's mast staggered, with feathers buried almost to his chest, and caught for a moment at the ropes; then he crumpled and fell. One of the archers beside Robin coughed oddly and sat down, the blood bubbling from around the crossbow quarrel that had pierced his throat. Another quarrel took Robin full on the steel headpiece so that his ears rang and his brain reeled.

Nor were the French ships the only threat. For so close had the English ship come under the sea wall of the castle now, that the bowmen there had found the range. They began raking the cog.

"An we could gain clear of yon castle wall, we would find stronger breeze there, and might even yet win clear," grumbled Shipmaster Swann, eyeing the slack sails gloomily.

"But not without bloody brawling yet," answered Wat the Armorer, scowling. He pointed astern to where the four galleasses were coming fast.

The archers could not spoil the steering as they had done with the galleys, for the great square sails of the galleasses shut off all sight of the steersmen behind. With their numerous oars they were gaining on the cog at every stroke. The galleass with the boar's head banner was in the van, with another just a scant stroke to the side and behind. From the left quarter and the right they drove at the cog, their bows already packed with yelling boarders, waiting but for the impact to leap.

Already Sir Allan was leading half the force of men-at-arms to one threatened waist, while Jarold led as many to the opposite side. The archers on both castles continued to sweep the packed Frenchmen with their whirring shafts.

"Now if we had but the bombards loaded, and could fire

through the cog's side as we fired through the door of the weaver's shop in Bewley," said Wat the Armorer, "we could make short work of these Frenchmen. Six shots each at the water's edge would shatter them."

"Not yet, but some day, mayhap," said Robin. "Howsoever, there are other things than bombards."

Scrambling from the forecastle, he hurried toward the deck where he had laid his readied flasks the night before.

When he reached the brazier, he found someone else there before him. Regardless of the flying arrows and clanging quarrels on all sides, Katherine Algelt knelt beside the brazier. She had scooped the ashes away and was blowing the embers to redness, while against them she held the frayed end of a bit of hempen rope. Quickly the rope end took fire; a smoking red spark began to travel down its length.

"Away from the deck, and into the hold!" cried Robin. "This is no place for a woman! Into the hold, quick, before a flying quarrel finds thee!"

Her face was pale, but her lips were tight and her eyes obstinate as she made answer. "The brazier—it is too unhandy to carry to the threatened side. But this rope end, it will serve as well. And there are the flasks, too, to carry."

"Nay, get below—and swiftly—"

The rest of Robin's words were cut off. With a rending crash the leading galleass rammed the cog from the left quarter, and almost instantly the other Frenchmen followed on the right. Stout as were the cog's timbers, she reeled and quivered from stem to stern with the shock of the impacts.

Instantly the cog's sides were buried under a mass of leaping boarders.

BUT THERE to meet them were Sir Allan and the men-at-arms. The knight's sword was like a long-bladed ax that rose and fell, and with each blow it cut down a boarder. From the cog's castles, too, the sailors were now hurling down their heavy stones and bars of iron, each missile carrying down half a dozen boarders when it struck.

What boarders avoided the slashing swords and axes or the sailors' missiles, the archers searched out with their unerring shafts, driving barbed points deep between steel cap and shield. The Frenchmen fell into the water, back onto their own decks, even down into the cog's hold.

Twice the cog's defenders beat the Frenchmen back, but still the boarders came. And even the strong arms and stout hearts of these English fighting men could not keep up the battering forever. A man-at-arms went down, and then another. And through the gap Frenchmen were pouring.

It was then that Robin touched the glowing rope end to the powder-ingrained cord sticking from a flask neck. He held it for a moment to make sure the hemp caught and sputtered; then he threw it. It arced just over the boarders' heads, fell into the packed mass of men on the galleass's decks. With a shattering crash it exploded, spurting out flames and a great billow of smoke. And full into the smoke cloud Robin hurled another lighted flask, and then a third.

From the Frenchmen's deck screams arose and shouts of fear. Faces and limbs cut, their jerkins and gambesons flaming and charred from the burning powder grains, the Frenchmen broke and scattered. Pell-mell they fled, hurling each other aside, trampling the fallen, crying prayers to the Virgin for protection from this devil's fire.

Sir Allan's men-at-arms, taking courage, turned upon the half-dozen that had gained footing on the cog and cut them down or drove them headlong into the sea. To complete the rout, Robin hurled yet other twain of lighted flasks into the galleass's waist, to explode among the benches there and drive the rowers in panic from their seats.

But now cries for help from the *Falcon's* other side told that Jarold and his men were sore pressed. Not only had Frenchmen found foothold there, but they were driving Jarold's soldiers back, step by step. And over the cog's side scrambled more and more boarders.

Shouting his battle cry, Sir Allan turned that way, his men at his heels. They struck the surprised Frenchmen and split their ranks wide apart, so sudden was their rush. Jarold's men joined quickly in the counter-attack. That whole side of the cog became a mêlée of flashing swords and axes, stabbing pikes, panting warriors and groaning men.

Robin discovered that only one flask remained of the armload he had first gathered up. But as he blew on the glowing hemp, he became aware of Katherine Algelt close beside him, her two arms hugging the rest of the flasks to her breast.

"Quick!" she cried. "I will hold them."

Robin lighted and hurled his powder-filled flasks, first at the boarders at the rail, and then upon the galleass's deck and bow.

It was not until he had hurled his fourth flaming missile, that the boarders from the second galleass break and flee. Safe on their own decks, they frantically thrust out with their oars and threshed away as if the Devil himself were after them.

In the sudden quiet the shipmaster's voice rang out loud and triumphant. "They draw—the sails draw! We are clear of the wall and pulling ahead!"

In truth, the castle with its gray sea wall was slipping astern. The cog's two sails, flattened fore and aft, were drawing her almost into the wind itself, against which the two remaining galleasses could make but grudging headway.

ALL AT once there was a cry from the forecastle, and the trample of running feet, then the flash of a human body soaring far out from the castle top and into the sea in a clean dive.

Even with the splash came Wat's angry voice. "The pilot! He has knifed his guard, and taken to the water!"

Jerking his visor open to gulp the fresh sea air into his panting lungs, Sir Allan grunted in disgust. "Now he will get clear away! And there will be no one left to question!"

But Red Hubert's voice, drifting down from the castle over-head, made answer.

"Clear of the cog, but not safe away. Not so long as John Wolf and I have shafts to draw…. Old Wolf, mark him the next time he comes up! And I will mark him the second."

Almost at once the blue water broke into white a full thirty feet out from the cog's side. The fleeing pilot showed his head for but an instant before he gulped breath and dove deep again. He came up a second time, but still neither archer loosed shaft.

When the swimmer's arm broke water the next time, Red Hubert and John the Wolf were both ready. Their bows were full bent, their eyes squinting down the long shafts. And though the dark head of the pilot barely appeared, the two bowstrings twanged together. Swift as light the two shafts flew. Where they struck, the water was in an instant all aboil, at first white, and then reddened. Half out of water, the stricken pilot reared, like a hooked fish, and then fell back threshing. After a moment the threshing ceased. And there was no more sign of the swimmer.

"Now we will have naught but our word against de Brenn's," said Sir Allan sourly. "And so naught to prove his treason."

"It matters little. We have the bombards, and all safe," said Robin.

"Not if those Frenchmen still have aught to say about it," grunted Shipmaster Swann, pointing back toward the port. "Here come galleys now—not galleasses nor cogs. And not even with these new-fashioned sails of thine, Robin, can we hope to outdistance their hundred oars."

Full half a dozen long galleys had showed beyond the turn of the castle walls. That the cog was their quarry was evident by the swift change of course they made when they sighted her.

Wearily Sir Allan leaned on his long sword and looked about. His helm was dented, and his gauntlets bloodstained to the wrists.

"It has been a good fight, as should be, since it is to be our last. We cannot hope to defeat six galleys with the injuries we have already taken."

But Katherine Algelt, who had climbed high on the forecastle, looking about, suddenly let out a cry, pointing ahead. "Look! Ships, ships—a thousand ships!"

Ahead where the open Channel stretched its shining sleeve toward England, the horizon seemed a veritable forest of masts and sails. From right to left they stretched, galleys, cogs, and all manner of craft, with their oars threshing and their sails bellying and bright colored banners fluttering from every masthead.

Fighting men stood and cheered.

It could be naught but King Edward's fleet, come out at last from its storm-bound anchorage in the Solent.

The galleys of the Frenchmen sighted the great fleet at once, for they put about at great speed and retreated toward Cherbourg.

But Robin's eyes, looking after them, were neither amazed nor triumphant. They crinkled queerly at their corners.

"Since the Frenchman were so eager to get sight of these bombards," said he, "it were shame if we disappoint them when next we meet. And so methinks I had best go below to see that the seams have not opened and the serpentine, mayhap, soaked once more in bottom water!"

BOWMAN'S BANNER

Robin the Bombardier has gone to the wars! With stout archers at his side and the Devil's Fire in his care, young Robin shall win a new sort of warrior's glory on the plains of Normandy

CHAPTER I

PILLAGE IN NORMANDY

TO THE PEASANTS of Normandy, in that July of 1346, it must have seemed that the curse of heaven had fallen upon them. For out of the north Edward III of England had swept with a full thousand ships until the Channel seemed white with oars and sails.

Almost under the walls of Cherbourg he had flaunted his standards, swept around Cape La Hogue, and then descended with full force on the hapless fishing village of St. Vaast de la Hogue. Anchored or drawn up on the beach, the ships had disgorged five thousand English knights and men-at-arms, ten thousand archers, and four thousand wild Irish and Welsh "stabbers."

Now while the sailors unloaded warhorses, beeves, pigs, and other provisions, and the engineers, or *gynours,* unloaded their siege trains of catapults and ballistae, the archers and mounted men scattered over the land like devouring locusts, pillaging and looting, and burning all that they did not take away.

But not all the archers were so employed. In a glade ashore, their bowstaves and quivers laid aside, Red Hubert and Peter Joy and John the Wolf tugged and swore as, under the direction of Wat the Armorer and Robin Santerre, they hoisted and lashed great oaken bed-timbers atop the axles of three stout carts.

"A murrain upon these bombards! And a murrain upon me for ever volunteering for a bombardier!" John the Wolf dashed away the sweat that dripped from his lean temples down over his

On the French knight's shoulders leaped Wolf John,
savagely carrying his prisoner to the ground

gaunt cheeks. "The men-at-arms and the archers from the New Forest and Kent still have stripped the land of the last hen and pig while we are still wrestling with these bombards and carts!"

"Hear the Old Wolf howl!" laughed Red Hubert, slapping his hand atop one of the fat bombard muzzles, "Not two days landed, and already hungry for a Frenchman to seize and hold to ransom!"

"And why not?" snapped the gaunt archer. "Did not our leader of the New Forest men, Sir Allan Mayne, say that to him who laid a prisoner to heel was due the ransom? And that a simple knight would ransom for an hundred *livres* or better, and a full baron for even five hundred? But how can a man find Frenchmen to ransom when he is caught up in this mass of carts and tubes and devil's powder?"

Peter Joy laughed, but Wat the Armorer shook his grizzled head. "Few knights and barons will they find in these fishing villages. Naught but fishermen and villeins as poor as ourselves.

It is an accurst war that plunders a poor French fisherman or yeoman of his last fishing net or fowl."

"But there was plunder at Valogues and Saint Come and Carenteau! And this very moment the King and the Black Prince with their men-at-arms are making assault on Cherbourg. Surely in a town so great as Cherbourg, there will be French knights and barons—"

"And as surely they will be firm barricaded behind the stout walls of the fortress," said Robin Santerre.

He was fair-faced and fair-haired, with a forehead both high and wide. But though he was no older than Peter Joy's own twenty years, he was captain of the King of England's bombardiers and as such bore the rank of master artilleryman. "And even such a stout archer as yourself might get his fingers burned trying to waylay a full-armed French knight behind a stout barricade."

"That, doubtless, is why our lord warden, Butcher de Brenn, is riding by now, instead of fighting in the hot mêlée at Cherbourg," said Wat, pointing.

IN FULL coat of mail, so heavy that even the sturdy warhorse panted beneath the weight of it and the rider's huge body, rode the most hated man in all south England. Certainly the most hated by John the Wolf and the other archers from the New Forest.

For as lord warden of the New Forest, Baron Hugo de Brenn had punished with heavy hand all poachers of the royal deer to such extent that between him and the masterless men of the forest had risen an eternal feud. Though now the forest men marched in the same army they did not abate the feud one whit. And least of all John the Wolf.

"For once he rides with his visor open!" Wolf John reached around for his discarded bow and quiver, and then bit off a savage oath. "A mark I could hit in half-dusk at an hundred yards—and me with my bowstave unstrung!"

Red Hubert laughed with silent mirth while Wolf John glowered and the hawk-nosed baron spurred past, his black eyes gleaming with hate at the men beside the bombards.

Nor was his hate directed only at the bombardiers. It fell with equal fury on the cast-metal tubes, the kegs and sacks of gunpowder and the balls.

For five hundred years knights in their full mail had been able to over-ride and cut down with impunity the lesser armed footmen and local levies. But Baron Hugo de Brenn had seen these amazing new bombards hurl balls that bit through great steel bars and thick oaken doors. And seeing, he had understood that against those balls even his stoutest armor would have protected him no more than had he ridden naked.

"Mayhap you are luckier than you know, Old Wolf, that your bowstave was unstrung," grunted Wat the Armorer. "For see, here comes the Butcher's esquire and half-score of his men-at-arms. One ill-drawn shaft, and you would have been left dangling your heels from a high gibbet instead of hunting through Normandy for a French lord to ransom!"

Nevertheless, when the mounted men had ridden on in the direction of Cherbourg, Wolf John's first move was to string his bowstave and set the ready weapon carefully alongside his quiver of arrows. Robin Santerre nodded approvingly, and glanced around at the trees and brush thickly bordering the glade.

"It is well that we all made ready. Those thickets would make easy range for French bows or arbalests. And a Frenchman who has just had his roof-tree burned would have no more love for us than for the pillagers who burned it."

Instantly Red Hubert and Peter Joy likewise strung their bows, and laid their shafts ready to hand. Wat the Armorer and Robin already wore half-shirts of mail and had but to see that their shields and light steel caps were at their fingertips.

"Ah-h, Cherbourg must have fallen!" suddenly exclaimed Peter Joy. "For here come riders trooping back. And see—the Butcher returns with them!"

Into the eastern end of the glade, not four score paces away, had suddenly debouched a little troup of riders. But at sight of the shield blazonings and the great standard overhead, Robin let out a gasp.

"The King—and the Black Prince himself! The Earl of Warwick's crosslets, and the gold and red shield of Sir John Chandos! Butcher de Brenn is the least among them!"

"And not the most favored, either," said John the Wolf with considerable satisfaction. "By the King's loud words and black scowl, he is tongue-lashing the Butcher for his delay—" He suddenly broke off. "By my bow! What was that?"

CHAPTER II

ARCHERY FOR THE KING

INSTINCTIVELY THE FIVE bombardiers had shrunk toward earth as there came a whistling hiss almost directly past their ears. From behind them came almost simultaneously a sharp twang, and then after that a ringing clang amid the party of horsemen. With startled shouts the riders suddenly drew their swords and, setting spurs to their horses, drove down with thundering hooves.

But instead of sweeping past and charging into the thicket for the ambusher, as Robin had expected, they rode directly down upon the bombards. In an instant the bombardiers were hemmed inside a circle of naked blades, while Baron de Brenn rubbed at his helm cheek-piece and roared with anger.

"Seize me these traitors! Seize the villeins and to the gibbet with them! A hand's breadth to the left, and the shaft would have been in my eye!"

Half a dozen squires swung clanking from their saddles, swords drawn. John the Wolf and Peter Joy snatched at their longbows and quivers, but Robin stepped between. His words were respectful but they were addressed to the King.

"Sire, meseems there is some mischance here. If you seek the marksman who sped yonder shaft, you would do better to search yon thicket. We are but your bombardiers, fashioning carts to bear their weight."

But de Brenn let out another roar. "A lie to match the treason, Sire! You heard the shaft, saw the murder intent! See, their bows and quivers are ready, and close at hand! Would they have need of strung bows in the fashioning of carts? I gave warning ere we left England that these were masterless men and outlaws. And had they aimed shaft at your royal person instead of at my own head—"

At that the King's brows clouded. Edward III was as scant of temper as he was reckless of courage. "That was well said. We will make a lesson of them—"

But Sir John Chandos respectfully put in a word. And though he was but a simple knight, his lion fame as a soldier was so great that half the belted earls of all England would have gladly ridden under his banner. Now Sir John's soldier eyes glanced shrewdly back at the glade entrance, then toward the thicket, and once more toward the bombardiers.

"Sire, am I be permitted to say so, an over-quick decision here might bring injustice and hence tarnish your knightly honor, which God forbid. If these bombardiers can bring proof—"

"What proof can they bring?" The King spoke angrily, and then as quickly cut short his words and nodded. "Let them speak further, then, and bring their proof before us for judgment."

At that Robin was troubled, but John the Wolf grunted.

"Proof, Sire? The proof itself is in the fact that the shaft glanced from the helm instead of striking home! Had I at the age of ten, even, missed so wide a mark as an open visor, my father would have dusted my doublet 'til my hide rattled inside. And Red Hubert and Peter Joy here are no less sure. If the Baron de Brenn would see a test—"

"A test! Aye, there is the soldier's proof!" Sir John Chandos' eyes gleamed and the scarred face beneath his raised visor lighted up. For Sir John Chandos was never so happy as when engaged in battle or watching a martial spectacle. He turned to his solitary squire. "Do thou, Peyton, ride back and set thy casque upon the spot where the arrow struck. And leave the visor open when you ride back."

Then he turned to John the Wolf. "A single shaft shall you loose. And if that shaft pierce not the visor opening fairly, then you shall dangle from the nearest tree. And not only you, but all your comrades as well."

THE SQUIRE turned his horse and was already riding away, when John the Wolf spoke again. And his words were full of scorn.

"Though I dangle on the gibbet, I will not shame my father by loosing shaft at so huge a mark. But if you would see proof of how an archer of England shoots—" He glanced around the glade in the opposite direction. "The spot on yon twisted oak where a branch has rotted and fallen away—the ring left in the bark—that is fair mark for a forest man."

At that even Robin's eyes opened wide. For the oak was a full hundred and more paces away, and the ring itself scarce a penny size and almost invisible, marked only by the discoloring of the bark. The King mumbled incredulously, but Sir John Chandos' nod was quick and grim.

"You have chosen your own mark, archer. Now step forth and shoot. An you miss it more than a hand's breadth, you swing from that same oak—all five of you!"

But it was Peter Joy who stepped forward first, his yew bow in hand and a goose-feathered shaft plucked from his quiver.

"Since my own skin is at stake, I claim the right to shoot as well."

"And that too is a fair claim," agreed Sir John Chandos, "though it will not save this old wolf's skin if he misses. Stand forth, then, and shoot."

Wetting his finger first to test the slight breeze, Peter Joy notched his shaft. Then standing sidewise, with keen eyes narrowed over the shaft and lips tight pressed, he bent the bow until the muscles ridged above his jawbones. With a sudden twang and hiss the arrow sped. And then from the squire who had ridden down and dismounted beside the oak came a startled shout.

"Not a finger's breadth! Not a finger's breadth between shaft and knot!"

"Aye. I thought you allowed over thinly for the wind," said Red Hubert, and stood forth in turn.

But instead of wetting his finger, he plucked a wisp of withered grass and tossed it in air, to watch carefully as it floated down, before notching his own shaft. This time, with the thud of the barbed point, the squire shouted with even more amazement. "An even thinner finger's breadth! But to the left, this one, and not to the right!"

The Black Prince, a youth of scant sixteen with fair complexion in startling contrast to the sable armor that gave him his name, was aglow with excitement, and even the King's stern face had relaxed. But Sir John Chandos still sat his saddle, unmoved.

"The word of a Chandos is never changed. You still have your own skin to save, old wolf."

Grumbling, John the Wolf drew from his quiver the first shaft that came to hand. "I came to France to seek a ransom, but I had no thought my own skin was the first to be ransomed!"

Then without even testing the wind, and with posture so careless the arrow seemed shot at random, he bent and loosed the bow with a single motion.

Yet even as the arrow struck and quivered, the onlookers needed no shout from the waiting squire to know the result. For straight between the two previous shafts the barb had sped, and now its gray goose-feathers blurred with the others, the arrow having struck precisely between them.

SIR CHANDOS let out an exclamation. "A fair test, and full proof for the seeing! Ye must seek your ambusher elsewhere, de Brenn! For had a single one of these three archers drawn shaft at you with murderous intent, as you made claim, you would not be riding with us now."

"Aye," said the King. "And leave your purse with them when you ride on, my lord de Brenn, for the injustice which we near committed for your sake. England could ill have spared such three marksmen as these."

Then he turned to the lean-jawed archer. "How are you called among your fellows, archer? I would know the name of one who comes to do such stout service for us in France—"

"As to my name," said John the Wolf grinning, "it is John the Wolf. But I had no thought of kings when I came to the wars."

"No thought of ourself? Then why—"

"For ransom," answered Wolf John, blinking. "Sir Allan Mayne hath said that an Englishman, even an archer, who catches a French knight or baron alive may hold him to ransom. And that the ransom should be from an hundred to five hundred *livres*, which I could well use."

Sir John Chandos' face was blackening, but all at once the King let out a great laugh. "Nay, Sir John, hold thy hand. You fight for honor or glory, but this archer is even as honest as ourself. We fight for the crown of France and for our captured provinces of Normandy and Guienne, but this archer fights for five hundred French *livres*. There is no great difference." He turned to Peter Joy. "And why came you to France?"

"Because Red Hubert came," said Peter Joy.

Without waiting to be asked, Red Hubert tugged at his red thatch of hair and blurted out, "And I came to be with my friend Wat, here."

Thereupon King Edward turned his keen eyes on the grizzled armorer. "These three have proved themselves the best archers in all England. What claim have you, then, above other forest men?"

"I am an armorer," answered Wat the Armorer tersely. "The best armorer in all England, if not in all Christendom!"

"The best armorer in all England!" The smile died from the

King's lips. "Nay, now that is a claim for which you can make no proof. For our own armorer is the best armorer in England."

"Then the armorer's trade is fallen into sore strait since I laid down my hammer," retorted the grizzled armorer.

He cast another glance at the squire riding close behind the King, at whom he had looked several times before. For on his saddle pommel the squire bore a great casque with the royal leopards of England on its crest—the King's own helmet doffed for comfort. "I would take a look at this sample of the royal armorer's fashioning."

Before the squire could protest, he had reached out and taken it into his great gnarled hands. Thrice he turned it over, running his fingers over it the while. Then before anyone could stay him, he drew the keen sword from his scabbard and smote the visor pivot with a single sharp stroke. The sound of the blow was drowned by an indignant roar from Sir John Chandos and then the King's startled cry.

For the single steel rivet which held the visor to the temple piece and on which it pivoted, had popped out and away, leaving the whole left side of the visor dangling.

"THERE," SAID Wat the Armorer, "is a poorly set rivet that might well have caused a man's death in battle. For it was thinly hammered and therefore loose, as could be seen at a glance. Two score lashes, well laid on his back, might teach your armorer care and make him a better armorer, Sire."

"And two score lashes he shall have!" King Edward was frowning, and he turned fiercely upon Robin. "And what brought you to France?"

"These bombards, Sire—and an over curiosity as to the strange force that doth seem to lie in this gunpowder." Robin patted the cast tube of the nearest bombard. "In the writings of Roger the Franciscan at Oxford, concerning levers and fulcrums and forces, there was somewhat also of the compounding of sulphur and charcoal and brimstone into a forceful powder called serpentine.

"But when the Flanders merchant, Joseph Algelt of Bruges, held forth that this same serpentine, fired in a bombard tube, would hurl weighty balls with ten-fold the force of a ballista, I was eager to come and see with mine own eyes."

"So these are those same bombards of which I have heard tell." The King looked about him with both curiosity and satisfaction. "Our well loved son and prince hath done well to hire them to our service, then, if they be more powerful than any catapult or ballista."

"Mayhap a good service to the cause of victory, but an ill service to knighthood and chivalry," said Sir John Chandos gloomily. "For if these bombards and their devil's powder have such power as you say, then the time may come when a brave knight on horseback may not overthrow even a churlish villein in leather jerkin behind these same bombards. Where then may a gentle-blooded man seek honor and renown, if there be no champions among the enemy to measure swords with, but only devil's tubes and powders?"

King Edward laughed. "Spoken like a true knight, good Chandos. Doubtless there will be many stout champions among the knights of our cousin Philip of France, however, from whom you still may win much honor. Especially since these bombards will have station among our catapults and other engines of siege."

"And yet, Sire, that is not the proper usage for these bombards, to my reckoning," said Robin Santerre respectfully. "Catapults and ballistae are engines of placement. Whereas on these stout carts we are fashioning, these bombards may ravel with the horsemen and so take station in the very front lines of battles. And I make no doubt that there they could hurl such balls into the charging troops of the French that neither horse nor man could withstand them."

"Said I not so?" grumbled Sir John Chandos. "Had I the say, I would cast bombards and ball and powder into the sea, and then hang these bombardiers. After which we could meet the French in mêlée with sword and ax and lance, to the great pleasure and honor of both parties!"

But the King was regarding Robin keenly. "If you march separately from the guarded siege train, what will prevent the French chevaliers from riding you down and slaying you in a sudden onslaught, and making capture of bombards and all? With naught but sword and shield and half-mail and these archers' arrows, you could not hope to withstand mounted men in full armor."

"In the excellent treatise of William of Deves concerning ambushments and ranging of battles, which I read at Oxford," replied Robin, "he held that equal arms was the best defense against any force—knights against knights, foot against foot, and archers against other bowmen.

"Hence, to defend against sudden raids and onslaughts from French men-at-arms, we should have convoy of equal men-at-arms. Half a hundred archers and a score of knights and men-at-arms should prove ample defense against any sudden raid or ambushment."

"By my halidon, the youth speaks like a seasoned warrior, and not a simple bombardier!" marveled the King. "You had best look to your reputation, Sir John. Nonetheless he speaks sooth, and I would not have our bombards fall prey to our cousin of France until we have at least made test of them in battle or siege.

"Do you then, my lord de Brenn, take a score of your best mounted men-at-arms and ride convoy on these bombards, and see that three score archers march with them as well. And now that the town of Cherbourg has fallen, we had best haste to our nones-meat."

He turned his horse's head away. But Sir John Chandos made the boldness of staying him. "This thicket and the French bowman skulking within—would we not do well to beat him out and make an end to him?"

The King shook his head. "Nay. Let the Frenchman live to flee homeward. We have perchance already burned his roof-tree.

A single shaft in exchange for a burned roof is but fair enough, since no blood was spilled."

With armor jangling and hooves pounding, the whole cavalcade spurred away.

CHAPTER III

TRUMPET THE CHALLENGE

WAT THE ARMORER gazed after them with a sour grimace. "Setting Butcher de Brenn to guard us is as much protection as setting a wolf to guard sheep. For from his scowl, the Butcher would more cheerfully cut us down than slay any Frenchman."

But Red Hubert was looking toward the thicket with his nostrils sniffing. "If any Frenchman loosed that shaft, then I know not the twang of good English yew nor the hiss of our own Hampshire goose-feathers. Do you, Peter and Wolf John, search the bracken from that side while I steal into it from this."

In an instant the three archers were scattered, slinking into the brushy copse as stealthily as gray wolves. After but a few moments there was a sudden threshing and outcry, and Peter and John the Wolf came stumbling out, dragging between them a snarling man in forester's jerkin and doublet.

Red Hubert let out a snort of surprise. "How now, Will o' the Fens! When there is sack and pillage afoot, what keeps you away from the other pillagers? An I remember aright, you were ever a lout more given to thieving than risking of your skin alone! Does Sir Allan Mayne know that you have left his company?"

"To the devil with Sir Allan! And to the devil with all knights and barons!" snarled the trapped man. He hammered his bow violently on the ground. "Had not this yew played me false, I would have brought the Butcher to ground like a spitted deer!"

Wat the Armorer thrust himself forward. "You were ever an evil man, Will, and over-given to revenge. What unusual rankle has led you to skulk and loose a murder shaft? For waylaying is murder, even though it be the Butcher de Brenn!"

"What rankle, say you? The gibbeting of my own cousin, Lory of the Longbow, which I saw the Butcher do on his New Forest gibbet, for no more than the poaching of a deer and a brace of hares! If that was not murder—"

"And now you lie, Will o' the Fens!" broke in Red Hubert rudely. "Your tongue flies as far from the truth as your shaft did from its mark. For I know you lost no love on your cousin Lory. More like, it was that matter of the dozen lashes o' the back the lord warden's men gave you for stealing of the Widow Landy's cow. For the honor of us forest men, I wot you need a lesson…. Peter! Hubert! Lay the lout to heel!"

With willing hands, and instantly, the two archers laid hold of the trapped man and threw him to earth where they held him strongly despite all his struggles. Taking the prisoner's bow, Red Hubert slashed the string with one slice of his knife. Then he laid the stout yew across the prisoner's buttocks for a round dozen stripes, until Will o' the Fens writhed and cursed and howled.

At the end of the whipping, Red Hubert cast the bowstave away. "Those lashes are not for missing the Butcher, but for loosing the shaft in such manner that we five honest men all but swung from the gibbet for your deed." Then to Peter and John the Wolf: "Let him a-loose. He will loose no more shafts this day."

Jerking him upright, Peter Joy gave the howling man a great clout on the ear. "And that is for my own skin which you laid in peril!"

John the Wolf followed the blow with a mighty kick which sent Will o' the Fens flying on his way. "And that is for loosing shaft at a mark that is my own meat! For I have marked the Butcher for my own reckoning, and a blight upon the man who comes between!"

But Robin Santerre's eyes were thoughtful as he gazed after the fleeing man. "Now that was an ill deed which might well cause us bitter rue. Already we have the Baron de Brenn riding guard for us, which is danger greater than the French. And now we make an added enemy of one who shoots from covert rather than the open."

John the Wolf spat scornfully. "An ever he comes nigh, the smarting of his skin will so shake him that any shaft he looses will fly full wide."

He turned back to the bombard carts. "Hubert, thou great ox, lay hold to this timber. The quicker our bombards are loaded and on the march, the quicker mayhap I will meet that Frenchman whose skin is worth five hundred *livres'* ransom."

WITH CHERBOURG fallen save for its fortress into which the governor had withdrawn and so stoutly defended its walls that Edward thought its taking not worth the cost, there was nothing to stop the English. So in three columns the English advanced, like a three-tined spear driving deep into the vitals of Normandy, while from those columns parties of archers and men-at-arms spread out on all sides, pillaging and looting.

In between the left and center columns Robin marched with his bombards, keeping ever near the van. Whereupon Wat the Armorer shook his head, for the columns here were miles apart.

"There is room enough and to spare, for a goodly force of Frenchmen to slip between. And it would be an ill day for us if they broke suddenly upon us from these thickets and glades."

Robin pointed to where de Brenn with his men-at-arms rode ahead on one side while the half-hundred archers marched on the other. "It would take more than an ordinary force to deal us great harm. And help from the columns would not be too long in coming."

Red Hubert eyed the escort with glowering brows. "If those had been Jarold's men-at-arms from Kent, or Tyrel's archers from Sir Allan Mayne's company of masterless men, I would say you spake sooth. But I put no trust in the Butcher or the Butcher's men."

Now the army turned eastward and took St. Lo and Torleval in the province of Caux, the men-at-arms riding over and cutting down with ease the poorly armed levies from the towns. As the smoke of burning St. Lo rose to a sky already darkened by the ashes of Barfleur and Cherbourg and Carenteau, Wat the Armorer shook his grizzled head.

"This slaying of half-naked French villeins and the burning of their fields and roofs is but an ill way of making war, or winning crowns. Mayhap the day will come when common men will have some say as to whom or for what they fight. For certain it is now that these poor peasants have naught to say as to who shall be king of France."

"That may be. But they would pillage and sack our English towns with equal pleasure, if they had crossed the Channel and not us," retorted John the Wolf. "As for me I care not who is king of France, unless I should capture him to hold for ransom." He smacked his lips at the very thought of it.

With the approach to Caen, however, the archer's face became even more avid. For Caen was the leading city of the province, and word had come that the Count d'Eu, one of the constables of France, was gathering a considerable force there of both horsemen and bowmen from Genoa.

"Now we shall see how these Genoese crossbows stand up against our English longbows," said Red Hubert with satisfaction. "I will wager thee my quiver against your baldric, Old Wolf, that we outshoot them three to one."

"Keep your wager," snorted the gaunt archer. "It is not Genoese bowmen I shall look for, but some noble of good value among their chevaliers."

"Then here come enough nobles to fill ten ships with ransom, if they were but Frenchmen," said Peter Joy, looking over his shoulder.

THERE RIDING at an angle toward the head of the march was almost the same cavalcade that had surrounded the bombards in the glade in Normandy. Evidently King Edward was riding in person to see to his lines of march.

They were not a score of paces away as they came abreast. Then Robin heard the silvery fanfare of a trumpet from ahead, at which there was a sudden shout amid the King's cortege and they all drew their horses up short.

Looking ahead toward where Caen lay, Robin saw to his amazement two solitary horsemen riding forward. One of them on a full-caparisoned charger was a giant knight in full armor, even to the lance and the closed visor. His shield was all silver except for a fesse, or single band of red horizontally across the field. The same silver and red showed upon his casque crest.

But the man who rode beside upon a small white jennet was completely unarmed. His tunic and mantle were of the finest silk, dyed in the same scarlet and silver. In place of a lance he bore a long trumpet with a silver and scarlet banner hanging from it. This trumpet he now placed to his lips, and blew another fanfare, after which both riders pulled up their mounts.

"By my bow!" exclaimed John the Wolf. "These Frenchman fight strangely, if they send mountebanks to the battle. For naught but a mountebank could dress in such fashion!"

At that instant from beside King Edward rode out a horseman garbed with equal brilliance, and he answered the first trumpet with fanfare of his own.

"Not mountebanks, dolt!" rumbled Red Hubert. "Hast never heard of heralds, then?"

At the blast from the English ranks, the knight in silver and scarlet had opened his visor so that the full sunlight beat in on his countenance. Then he sat waiting while his own herald advanced halfway toward the English and began to speak in a loud clear voice.

"Hear ye! Hear ye! Hear ye! My master, the gracious Count d'Eu, proclaims to all the world that his liege lord, Philip of France, is the only true and rightful king of France. And if there be any true English knight here of equal blood who holds to the contrary, my master doth challenge him here and now to prove his claim in single combat with lance and sword, and to the *outrance!*"

At that Sir John Chandos spurred his horse a few paces to the front and called out eagerly. "I am but a simple knight, Sir John Chandos. But no man can say I have not been true knight. And I beseech you to go tell your master that I would deem it great honor if he would choose to grant me a meeting on those terms which he just proclaimed."

"Chandos—Chandos—I know not the name," answered the French herald. "Have you blood then to match a d'Eu? For my master is not only count of Eu, but also viscount of Hogue, marquis of Quercy and lord of the southern marches!"

Sir John Chandos shook his head gloomily, but his voice was still hopeful. "Nay, I claim no such baronies as those. But my name and lineage is an ancient one, and I trust that your gentle master would find no dishonor in matching swords with a Chandos."

The Earl of Warwick now rode out, his golden crosslets gleaming on his red shield. "Tell your master to close his visor and make ready for the course. Beauchamp of Warwick will meet him, and the earldom of Warwick is the equal of any barony in France!"

"But are you a constable of England?" persisted the herald. "For my lord, the Count d'Eu, is also a constable of France, champion of champions. It would ill befit his station to cross lances with a lesser knight."

The Black Prince, who had been holding his horse in with quivering hand, rode out at that, and his boyish face, framed by his raised visor, was flushed with anger. "Ask your master, then," he shouted, "if he would think it disgrace to meet Edward of Woodstock, Prince of Wales and heir to the throne of England?"

But before reply could come, the earls of Warwick and Stafford, at a nod from the king, laid hold of the Prince's reins and perforce detained him. King Edward's voice itself lifted then until it rolled across the space like a clarion.

"Tell your master, the Count d'Eu, that by grievous mischance our own constable, the Earl of Northampton, is ill of a fever, but will gladly meet him when he is ahorse once more.

"And bear word also to your master's liege lord, Philip of France, that we ourselves, Edward III, King of England and Wales, Duke of Normandy and Aquitaine, do challenge him to single combat for the Crown of France at any time and place he choose!"

CHAPTER IV

TO YOUR ARMS

ALL THIS TIME John the Wolf had been listening to the exchange of words in bewilderment, for it had been carried on in French.

"What says the Frenchman?" he inquired. "Christian hey may be, like ourselves, but certain it is they speak more like swine than Christians. And our Norman kings and barons are but little better. Scarce one word of their gulpings could I make sense of."

Robin interpreted into the more common Saxon-English the gist of what had passed. Red Hubert jerked a new bowstring from his steel cap where he carried it to keep it dry, and began to string his bowstave. He was mumbling:

"A champion of French champions, is he? Then with one shaft I may save good English lives, and mayhap a battle as well. An I not put my first shaft even-centered through his visor opening at this distance, I will never again call myself archer!"

But Robin Santerre struck his hand down. "Nay, he is but come to challenge in knightly fashion. Put down thy bow!"

"Challenge? Then is it not to battle? Is he not a Frenchman and an enemy? Then why should we not loose shaft at him now, as well as in battle later?"

"Not when he comes under truce, with a herald," replied

Robin. "For by the custom of chivalry, a foeman may ride safely into and out of our camp again if he come under truce of herald. And it would be great dishonor to us did he come to harm."

Red Hubert shook his red-thatched head. "Then this chivalry is a custom of fools. We have the Frenchman under easy bowshot, and yet we must even let him ride away to spit us with his lance, mayhap, some other day."

"Aye, hold thy hand, thou ox, and let him live until that next time then," broke in John the Wolf. "An you let him live, he may yet fall into our hands alive to the profit of a goodly ransom. But shoot him, and there goes five hundred goodly *livres!* For how can a dead man pay ransom?"

By the time they had finished with their bickering, the two Frenchmen had turned and galloped back whence they had come. And the King's party, having finished their reconnaissance, likewise turned about and rode once more to the rear. The bombardiers goaded the horses that were harnessed to the heavy bombard carts, and once more they took up their march.

YET THAT very afternoon, Red Hubert's forebodings seemed like to come to pass. For as they were creaking at half-bowshot distance past a thick wood, Robin's watchful eye caught the sudden glint of steel.

"The French!" he cried, snatching at his sword and shield. "The French—in yonder thicket! Wat... Peter... Hubert! To your arms, and quickly!"

Even before he had finished speaking, there had come a horn's blast from the wood, and sharp upon it the thunder rush of horses' hooves. Out of the wood like a thunderbolt burst a tight mass of men-at-arms, their armor agleam and lances couched.

So quickly they came that de Brenn's archers were ridden down and scattered before they could more than draw bow. Then, without pausing, the French charged the English mounted men.

These were in no better state than the surprised archers. For the French were charging from the flank, and de Brenn's horsemen had barely time to wheel to face them, much less put their own mounts to the charge.

Before the momentum of that hurtling mass of steel and horseflesh, the English formation bent and broke. Horses were hurled aside or else knocked from their feet, and riders went crashing to the earth.

Now in the mêlée swords and axes were out and flashing. The narrow open space rang with the clang of steel on steel, the crash of body against body, the shouts and war-cries of the battling men.

"De Brenn! De Brenn! St. George for England!"

"St. Denis! St. Denis! D'Eu! D'Eu!"

"The devil take me if it isn't your same Frenchman, Old Wolf!" cried Red Hubert, as a silver and scarlet shield flashed momentarily in the battle.

But they had other things to think on just then, for having carved a way through the English line, a round dozen French knights came surging at the carts and bombards. In fact, the whole of de Brenn's men-at-arms were being driven back upon the bombardiers.

In the carts Robin and Wat the Armorer stood ready to fight off the attack as best they could. Red Hubert and Peter and John the Wolf had leaped to the ground, and with shafts hurriedly dumped at their feet, they were notching their arrows.

"At the horses, Old Wolf!" shouted Red Hubert. "Shafts are wasted against shield and chain mail. But sift a barb between the chargers' trappings, and you bring down both horse and man."

"Like that?" The gaunt archer loosed his arrow as he answered, and at the hiss of the shaft the leading horse went down, head over heels, flinging his rider ahead of him.

Red Hubert and Peter Joy were as sure of aim, and the feathered arrows sang. Not every one brought down its target, but the wounded horses screamed and plunged with the pain, causing a wild confusion.

However, some of the Frenchmen still bore down unscathed,

and Robin and Wat the Armorer found themselves hacking at shields and bobbing helmets, while desperately striving to fend off heavy blows with their own shields and blades. Too, the remaining Frenchmen had driven the rest of de Brenn's men down upon the carts now, and the bombards and bombardiers were penned in inside a furious circle of horses and warriors.

"Had we these bombards charged, as we should," panted Robin, "we might yet blast a way out! But not even a brazier is lighted for the firing skewer!"

"Said I not we put too much trust in de Brenn's guard?" retorted Wat, hammering away at the first casque within reach. "Mayhap we will know better next time."

THAT THERE would be another time, however, Robin had grave doubts, for the Frenchmen were gaining the upper hand on all sides. Then there was a sudden diversion.

Hubert and Peter and Wolf John, who had taken refuge beneath the carts from the first charge, were now out and scurrying beneath the horses' bellies, stabbing and slashing upward with their sharp knives as they ran.

Chargers plunged and went down, causing further disorder. The French tide of victory was still further stayed when de Brenn's archers, those that had fled, seeing the French all engaged, turned about and began to harry them with whistling shafts from the flank and rear.

Out of the mêlée then, and almost directly beneath Robin, emerged the gashed and dusty figure of Wolf John. He was dragging with him a figure in steel mail and casque, who struggled to rise at every step

"Ho, Wat! In the wagons with this one!" bellowed Wolf John triumphantly. "A Frenchman for ransom, and a baron at the very least!"

But as he hoisted the struggling captive upright, there was a bellowed oath, and a mailed fist all but drove the archer toppling.

"Knave! Dolt!" It was de Brenn's furious voice. "Know you

not an English 'scutcheon? Lend me a hand to horse again, and quickly!"

John the Wolf's amazed grunt was cut off then by a new surge of the ringing warriors. Out from among them reeled a battered figure, crest shorn from helm and shield hacked and dented. But straightway the figure turned and began to batter around on all sides with a great mace that swung like a circle of light.

"The Frenchman! By my bow, the Frenchman himself!" John the Wolf let out a bellow, and hurled himself forward. Fair on the warrior's back he landed, toppling him over and down among the threshing hooves, and instantly the dust rose and curtained them from sight.

At once Red Hubert and Peter Joy plunged without hesitation into that tumult. And at their going Robin thought that all was lost. Left alone to defend the bombards, he and Wat were sore beset on all sides. Already his arm was so wearied with constant slashing and parrying that he could scarce raise his sword for another blow.

Then there came a new uproar, shouts and the thunder of new horsemen arriving. Sir John Chandos with a near score of full-mailed knights following spurred up and threw themselves into the mêlée.

At that the Frenchmen, reckless as they were, gave back. They dealt halfhearted blows, and then turned to ride away, such as could. The clang of arms and the noise of battle gave way to the cries and groans of wounded and dying men.

CHAPTER V

THE WOLF SMELLS RANSOM

AS THE DUST settled, out of it once more came the three archers. They were dragging with them the knight in the once bright silver and red. But now his shield was gone and so was his mace with its steel-barbed ball. He struggled and struck out as he was carried along, though his only weapon was a broken dagger which the archers avoided with ease.

John Wolf was yelping in triumph. "A prisoner! A prisoner—and one of goodly value or I never drew bow!"

"Aye," shouted Peter Joy, "and ransom enough for all three of us."

The struggling Frenchman turned his battered casque from side to side, as if trying vainly to peer through his visor slits. His voice rose in fury, gasping in garbled Norman and English. "Is there no English knight here? No man of gentle blood to whom a baron of France may yield?"

John the Wolf shook him.

"Nay, you will yield to us, or we will off with thy helmet and slit thy throat forthright for thee!" bellowed the gaunt archer. "What say you—yield thy person to us or yield thy blood through a slitted gullet?"

The choice should not have been difficult to make.

But at that moment the Frenchman caught sight of de Brenn leaning wearily against the cart wheels, and so glimpsed his crested casque and golden spurs. With sudden desperation the French knight whirled, broke loose, and flung himself toward de Brenn, his broken dagger outheld, hilt first.

"I yield me to thee, Sir Knight! Here is my remaining blade—I yield me to thee!"

John the Wolf let out a roar, and sprang after, Peter Joy and Red Hubert hot on his heels, stabbing knives out and ready. So great was the uproar that Sir John Chandos spurred that way and threw himself between, and with him the knight who had charged alongside. Seeing the shield all gules with its golden fesse and six crosslets, Robin knew this latter for none other than the great Earl of Warwick himself.

"How now!" roared Sir John Chandos. "Hath this Frenchman not yielded himself to mercy? Wouldst slay a yielded prisoner in my sight?" He lifted his great three-foot Norman sword to drive them back.

But John the Wolf held his ground stoutly. "Nay, he is our own prisoner, taken in the battle with our own hands! We did but pursue him when he broke away—"

"My lord, he hath delivered himself up to me!" retorted de Brenn, who had accepted the dagger from the Frenchman. "See, I have even here the dagger which he yielded up. Whereupon these knavish archers set upon him to do him foul—"

"Yielded to thee?" Wolf John's face went red and then purple. "You were not even in the mêlée! Rather you were still sputtering out the dust of the horses' hooves from which I pulled thee not ten eye-winks agone! An I had not done so, you would have been either trampled or a prisoner thyself ere now!"

"Hold thy tongue, archer!" Sir John Chandos turned to Warwick. "If there be question as to whom this French knight did yield him up, surely he himself is best fitted to answer." Speaking in French, he addressed himself to the battered prisoner. "To whom then did you yield your person?"

"TO THIS knight here of the sable arms and boar's head device," responded the Frenchman promptly. Then he went on hurriedly: "If he be reasonable to ransom, a thousand *livres* shall be put in his hand as quickly as a messenger may gallop to my seneschal in Caen. And a thousand *livres* is reasonable ransom even for the person of Count d'Eu, viscount of Hogue and a constable of France! As Caen is little more than three leagues distant, my herald should be here with the gold ere midnight."

The Earl of Warwick nodded. "Methought it beyond reason that a Frenchman of gentle blood would yield himself to three forest running villeins. So I do judge him the rightful prisoner of our Lord de Brenn to whom the ransom is therefore justly due."

He turned to his squires. "Drive these bickersome archers hence, and do they make further outcry, then deal them such blows as will mend their manners!"

Though much of this had been in French and Norman, the

triumphant look on de Brenn's face and the movement forward of the earl's squires, swords ready, made the result plain even to John the Wolf.

He gave back, Peter and Red Hubert following, though their backward glances were scowls and their grumblings were withheld only till they were out of the squires' reach. When Robin interpreted the whole of what had been said, the gaunt archer's indignation knew no bounds.

"The constable of France, and a thousand *livres?* Then if this be barons' justice, I am of mind with Wat here! Full justice will no English freeman get until we have made an end of all barons!"

But Robin had other things on mind.

"Lucky it is, mayhap, that we are alive at all. The lesson is well earned and should be well-learned; we do not march again with uncharged bombards and firing skewer cold in the brazier. Lay hold to the powder ladle and ram-stick, then, that we be not taken unaware once more."

He would permit them no rest until the three bombards in the beds of the three carts had each been full charged with powder and ball and the braziers for heating the firing skewers lighted and fanned to a glow.

By that time dusk had come and Peter Joy had gathered dead limbs and built a cook-fire for their evening meat. All along the line of march other cook-fires were twinkling as the outposts were set against surprise and the remaining soldiers prepared to bivouac for the night.

SCARCELY HAD the five bombardiers finished their meat, however, when there was a trampling noise in the dark, and into the firelight rode the Baron de Brenn, with a squire and several men-at-arms at his heels. The baron's eyes gleamed sardonically, and at his nod the squire dumped down before Wat a stout sack which gave forth a metallic clank as it fell.

"Since thou art the master armorer of all England, and since I am appointed to command the convoy for these carts," said the baron, "thou shalt have the pleasure of tightening and repairing this casque and coat-of-mail from the battering they received this day. So to thy forge, armorer! An the mail be not as strong and good as new, come dawn, you shall receive two score lashes on the back as pay!"

He rode off again with his party, while the armorer stared and then cursed.

"Sooner would I fashion doublets for a pig than forge armor for this human swine!"

"Yet forge ye will, or take those selfsame lashes he made mention of," chuckled Peter Joy.

Wat nodded sourly.

"Aye, even so, even so. Nonetheless it is an evil choice which makes an honest man's blood to boil."

So saying, the armorer dumped the mail from the sack and gave the casque a kick that sent it rolling. Dragging from the rear cart his armorer's forge and bellows, he presently was pounding away with many rumblings and much surliness of stroke.

But by and by the grumblings and surliness ceased, the hammer clink quickened to a merry clang, and amazingly enough the armorer began to whistle.

Robin Santerre pulled himself to his knees and then stood up. "I have scant faith left in de Brenn's convoyance. Keep a watchful eye on the bombards, Wat. I go to see if Sir Allan Mayne will lend us aught of his masterless men for a second guard. Also there are matters I would take up with Algelt, the Flemisher."

No sooner was he out of sight than John the Wolf glanced to make sure Wat was busy, and then he nudged Red Hubert.

"See that low star yon, great ox? When it has reached twice its present height, it will be midnight. The Frenchman's herald will have returned from Caen, and the Butcher will be jingling in his own hands the thousand *livres* which should rightfully be in ours! How like you the thought of that?"

"As little as I like the thought of a swordblade spitting my paunch if we make further protest," answered Red Hubert lazily.

"The Butcher has the prisoner, and so the Butcher will have the ransom."

"Not until the herald reaches him with the gold," said John the Wolf. "Now it is reasonable that the herald will come by way of the best road from Caen. And even a French road should not be overhard to find."

"What?" The giant archer stared, and then slowly his eyes began to glint. "Thou are truly named, Old Wolf!"

Peter Joy's eyes too were sparkling. "But what of our own guards and outposts?"

"After dodging the warden's verdurers in the New Forest, if we can not slip through a few outposts and find the road to Caen in the dark, then we are no forest men!" Red Hubert sprang up. "Come then, Old Wolf, and make haste before Robin returns."

While Wat the Armorer still hammered at the dents in the Butcher's armor, the three archers melted like shadows into the night.

CHAPTER VI

BOMBARD GIRL

HALFWAY DOWN THE line of march Robin found Sir Allan Mayne, bivouacked among his ten score archers from the New Forest. Outlaws and masterless men the foresters might once have been, but under the tight discipline of the keen-eyed knight they made as brave showing as the best-trained soldiers in the army.

Cordially Sir Allan greeted Robin, and then listened intently to Robin's request. At the end he nodded.

"It is well thought. Tyrel and five score of the best in my company shall be there at daybreak, and march then as you wish. I will give Tyrel the order at once, that he may be sure to have it aright."

*Robin saw the French go down in agony
and death before the bombard's fire*

Feeling more cheerful at the promise, Robin sought out the siege train next, at the very rear of the column. And there, as he expected, in a canvas covered wagon lighted by a single taper, he found not only Joseph Algelt, the Flemish merchant, but his daughter, Katherine Algelt, as well.

Instantly the girl was up and pouring a cup of wine which she pressed upon Robin. Staring at the girl's dark eyes and red curving lips, Robin felt again that same hot throbbing of the pulse he had felt every time he had been in company with the girl since that first moment he met her.

Strange it might have seemed to some to find a young girl amid an army on the march, yet Robin knew that even the highest-born ladies in Christendom thought it no shame to accompany their husbands to the wars. And in the well-guarded siege train, there was safety as long as the army itself remained unconquered.

Stranger to Robin was the thought that a merchant of Flanders should be here. Yet had he not been here, neither would the bombards have been. For it was Joseph Algelt who had brought these strange new weapons with their powder and ball to England, and so proved their superiority over catapults and ordinary artillery that the Black Prince had leased them, with a full crew of bombardiers, for the great sum of ten thousand *livres*.

Now that fat-bellied, gray-haired merchant pulled himself from his wooden bench. Cursing the stiffening of his aged joints that had caused him to entrust his bombards to the youthful Robin, he inquired eagerly as to their safety.

"Safe enough, and under stout guard," said Robin, all the while drinking in the beauty of the girl to the complete neglect of his wine.

"But word reached us that you were under attack—that the French made a foray on the bombards!" The girl's eyes widened, and she laid soft fingers on Robin's hand. "You—you were not hurt?"

At the touch of her hand Robin's pulse leaped anew, so that he all but spilled his wine. "Nay—nay—not hurt," he stammered. "It was but a small raid, easily repulsed." He turned hurriedly to the old merchant. "It was that that I came to speak with your father about." And quickly he recounted the happenings of the day.

"**WE WILL** not be so easily caught off-guard again," he concluded. "But even with the bombards loaded, we have no certainty that they will halt a strong-pressed charge. Each bombard ball would without doubt cut a path through even full-mailed men-at-arms. But stout-hearted men would but close their ranks and press the charge home. And they would be upon us ere we could make shift to reload."

The merchant furrowed his brows and muttered in his beard, but it was the girl who spoke.

"You could not fashion flasks filled with gunpowder to light and hurl among them, as we did upon the galleys when they sought to board us that morning in the harbor?"

Robin shook his head. "The shards would have small effect against horsemen in full armor. Moreover they would be upon us at full gallop, such little distance can a flask be thrown."

Joseph Algelt pulled at his white beard. "On the morrow— mayhap on the morrow I will have a thought."

Robin set aside his cup and turned to go. As he drew back the hanging canvas at the back of the wagon, however, he realized that Katherine Algelt had followed him.

The taper in the wagon was dim and at her back. But even through the shadow Robin could make out the curving tracery of her lips, the dark mirrors of her eyes.

"You will take care?" she breathed. "You will take care?"

So near she was that he could see her parted lips, sense the fragrance of her breathing. And he fell a-stammering like any country lout.

"Aye, my lady. I will take good care. The bombards—they will be close under my eye. There will no harm come to them."

"Not the bombards!" she whispered swiftly. "No—I meant not the bombards!"

Then the canvas dropped between them, and Robin was stumbling back and away, as dazed as if the words had been full-swung blows of a battle-ax.

AT THE little bivouac fire Wat the Armorer was still pumping at his bellows and hammering the last blows upon rondels and ailettes and gusset-pieces, when John the Wolf and Red Hubert and Peter Joy stole back to the fire. He did not even give a glance to their coming.

Red Hubert was breathing hard and Peter Joy was panting both with haste and excitement, but John the Wolf dropped fresh sticks on the fire as calmly as if he had but just stepped outside to gather them.

"Underneath the powder casks, or in the sacks with the balls!" gulped Peter Joy. "Quickly with these! Make haste!"

"In my quiver—at the bottom, beneath the shafts!" muttered Red Hubert.

But John the Wolf only chuckled. "Nay, I have a better place than any of those!" He clambered into one of the heavy carts, was shadowed there for a full minute, and when he came back he was still chuckling.

"And in just good time," grunted Red Hubert. "For here comes Robin e'en now. And he would find little favor in our walk this night, I wot, if he knew aught of it."

It was indeed Robin who came tramping into the firelight again. His face was troubled, and he kept casting quick glances around and at the darkness.

"Were any of you away from the fire—any of you out there in the dark as I came up?" he inquired hurriedly.

"Nay," said Red Hubert slowly.

"Not I," echoed Peter Joy, casting a quick glance at the gaunt archer.

"Aye," said John the Wolf calmly. "I was out, gathering fresh firewood—a good hour agone."

Robin's face grew even more troubled. "Yet I had sworn I heard feet rustling, and saw some one skulking in the bushes' edge as I came up. And for a scant instant when I glimpsed his head turned against the firelight, I would have sworn it was that same skulking bowman, Will o' the Fens, you lashed with his own bowstave a few days agone."

Red Hubert drew a deep breath of relief. "His hide is yet too sore for his comfort, I wot, or for any risking of it further within our reach. Nay, it was not Will o' the Fens."

Then Wat the Armorer threw down his hammer with a grunt, dumped the last piece of the armor into the sack, and wiped the sweat from his forehead.

"There!" he said. "It is e'en ready whenever he come for it." He grunted again with strange satisfaction. "And much joy may he have in the wearing of it!"

CHAPTER VII

BRIGHT NORMAN SKY

SEEMINGLY, DE BRENN had taken the lesson to heart the next morning when the march resumed. He had reformed his escort into one tight group, his remaining archers just ahead of his mounted men. The whole escort held its station just a little ahead and to the left of the leading bombard wagon, where they could guard against onslaught from ahead or either side.

But Wat the Armorer regarded the arrangement with a sour eye. "Where then are the forest men whom Sir Allan was to send?"

But Robin only whipped the cart horses up. "They will be here when need arises."

Under the bright summer sunlight, the French landscape had never looked so lovely. The flatter land had given way to rolling rises and near hills, green garbed with forest foliage, and cut at intervals by purling brooks. Amid these the road to Caen wound like a silken riband, around hills and through glades, up one slope and down another. Occasional fields in full grain showed that the foragers had not reached thus far with their torches.

"Methinks here comes Sir Allan now," said Peter Joy.

It was indeed Sir Allan Mayne, the leader of the archers from the New Forest. But with him was a tall knight and several squires and mounted men-at-arms, their shields and pennons bearing the swan, the well-known armorial badge of William de Bohun, the Earl of Northampton. And by that Robin knew that they were the men of the constable of the army.

Swiftly and unexpectedly the constable's men ranged themselves athwart the road ahead, forcing Robin to halt. Then they swung from their saddles and approached.

"You are well come, Sir Allan," greeted Robin, though his brow was puzzled. "I know not what brings you here, but if it be the matter we discussed last eve, that hath been well attended to."

But Sir Allan's face was troubled, "Being of the van, perchance you have not heard. But last night there was such ill deed done that the shame thereof is come upon the whole army.

"For at midnight the Count d'Eu's herald, coming under herald's truce to ransom his master, appeared at the tent of the Constable of England himself, crying treachery.

"According to his words, he was set upon by foul villains upon the road, and not only pulled from his horse and grievously mishandled, but robbed of his master's purse as well."

"That was indeed an ill deed, an he came under herald's truce," said Robin, nodding. "But what concern have we of that?"

"It is the concern of all of us." The knight in the constable's livery made answer with darkened brows. "Not only my master but our royal liege lord, the King himself, is enraged at this stain on his kingly honor. So much so that he hath given order for every archer in the army to be full-searched even unto his doublet.

"And inasmuch as the villains' purpose seemed robbery, whoso shall be found in possession of the herald's purse shall be gibbeted in full sight of the army as a lesson to all who are tempted hereafter."

"But why the archers?" demanded Robin. "Why not the Irish and Welsh as well—the pikemen and other foot?"

"Because," answered Sir Allan gravely, "the herald made claim that his waylayers were surely archers, by their doublets and hose and steel caps, and because they spoke such low gibbering as would befit only forest men."

"Then methinks that still is no concern of ours," protested Robin, "since we are bombardiers, not archers."

"Nay, the herald gave other details," said the constable's knight tersely. "He described his assailants as three in number—one a huge man of great breadth, one slender, and one tall enough but of great gauntness."

The knight's eyes glanced eagle-wise over Red Hubert, Peter Joy, and John the Wolf, standing respectfully upright in their carts. Then he snapped a short command to his men. "Lay hand to them, and search them well!"

QUICKLY THEN the constable's men forced the three archers out onto the ground and made search of their garments and full accoutrements, even unto jerkins and quivers.

But when their search had discovered nothing, their leader waved his gauntleted hand toward the wagons. "The carts— search them also, and all their content!"

At that Peter Joy started, and even Red Hubert rubbed his red thatch nervously. But John the Wolf only chewed at a wisp of plucked barley between his teeth.

"Take care that ye slight not looking beneath the casks nor into the sacks of balls."

Yet though they thoroughly ransacked the carts even to the extent of plunging their hands deep into the sacks, the searchers at last descended to the ground empty-handed.

The constable's knight frowned and turned to Sir Allan. "There is naught here. So we must e'en continue our search throughout all the companies of bowmen. The King's anger is so great that he would gibbet the whole army if need be."

Remounting, the whole party rode away to where de Brenn's guard marched, and halting them, likewise began to search the archers there.

John the Wolf chuckled, and whipped up his cart horse until it dragged the heavy bombard cart along at a jouncing pace. "Get along with thee, thou bag of bones! Do you not smell Caen ahead, and perchance a fat French baron waiting for me?"

Robin could not but smile, although his brow was still clouded with both doubt and worry. "It would be strange thing that there are three other archers, then, in the army so exact of description as the herald gave for the three who waylaid him. Thou art sure, Wolf John, that the gibbet's cold shadow did not chill thy blood just then?"

"Not nearly so much as that we must depend upon the Butcher's watchful care against ambush or an out-sally," replied John the Wolf. "However, this seems one day that he will not steal prisoners from us. For an he not make haste, we will be in Caen long before him!"

Looking back, Robin noted that de Brenn had held his whole force back to wait for his archers, even his men-at-arms who were safe from search.

But his thoughts were drawn away just then by a sudden shout from Peter Joy. "Caen! Caen! It can be naught but Caen, for it is a goodly city!"

THE BOMBARD carts had topped a sudden rise. And there before them, clear and sharp despite the two leagues and more that still lay between, up-reared tall carillon spires, a turreted keep, and even the roofs of the tallest houses, though the bulk of the town was still shut from view by other slopes and ridges between.

With a yelp John the Wolf laid whip to his animal again, so that Robin had need to whip up his own cart horse to keep apace. Rattling and creaking, the heavy carts plunged over the slope top and down the rutted road toward a tiny winding stream that sliced the little valley below. Beyond the stream, the Caen road climbed upward again through a tall field of barley, still golden and heavy in the sheaf.

But all at once Robin became aware of still louder rattling, and shouts behind him. Turning, he perceived another cart racing and pounding to overtake him.

A villein in leather jerkin lashed at the horses, but on the seat beside him clung two passengers, one a slight figure in red mantle and with raven hair streaming unbound in the breeze. By that, even before he recognized the second passenger's hoarse shouts, Robin knew the arrivals for Katherine Algelt and her father, the Flemish merchant.

As Robin drew his own cart up to a halt and waved to the others to do likewise, the overtaking conveyance drew alongside. Joseph Algelt raised from his seat and began clumsily to clamber down over the wheel, cursing his age and his stiffened bones in the same breath. But the girl was on the ground as lightly as a feather, and already climbing into Robin's cart before her father had set foot to earth.

The Flemish girl's cheeks were red as good wine, and her eyes sparkling with the excitement of the chase. "You drive overfast, Robin!" she panted. "We had feared you would be at Caen before we might overtake you!"

Then the fat merchant was also alongside, and wanting with his exertion until Wat the Armorer gave him a hand up into the bombard cart. "Aye, we came in all haste," he gasped. "My head has been a-whirl all night, but it was only this morn that the thought struck me. A thought I must share with thee ere you perchance meet strong resistance from the French in Caen!"

"There was small need for such haste, then," said Robin, "for Caen lies still two leagues from here. We but glimpsed the spires and turrets from that last rise, a few moments agone. Nonetheless you are both welcome—and I am eager to learn this thought of thine, Flemisher. Hath it to do with the bombards?"

"Aye." The old merchant wagged his white beard vigorously. "This matter of a single ball not working such damage as would halt a stout troop of men-at-arms in their charge. The thought I had was that by use of a double measure of powder, each bombard might be loaded with twain balls, the firing of which would create double havoc among the Frenchmen."

"Two balls instead of one in each bombard, and fired with a double charge of powder?" Robin turned the matter over in his mind and nodded with interest. "The thought hath merit; it might well do such double damage as you reck.

"But on the other hand, it might do the damage to us, and

not the Frenchmen. I have mind that those flasks we filled with powder and closed with wads of dry bread, did not merely discharge the bread wadding from the flasks' mouths, but burst and shattered so that the shards flew in all directions.

"A double measure of powder and double weight of balls might be too great force for the bombard tubes themselves to withstand. In that case they might burst apart, even as did the powder-filled flasks for throwing, and so cut us bombardiers to bits with the metal splinters much sharper than any shards of pottery."

The girl let out a little cry. "Then you must not attempt it! You must not undertake the risk!'

"Not until we may make shift to try, without too great danger if the bombard bursts," agreed Robin. "Nonetheless, it is an idea of exceeding interest, and one I would like full well to put to test. An a bombard be cast stoutly enough, I doubt me not the double ball with double charge of powder would create double havoc, even as your father recks."

THE AGED Flanders merchant gave a grunt of disappointment. "Had double-charging the bombards enabled us to do greater destruction to the Frenchmen," he said covetously, "I had hope that we might ask an additional sum to our lease money from the King."

The girl caught at her father's arm. "It would be evil-earned money if the blood of the bombardiers were risked in the earning of it."

"Risk of our blood is part of the service of a bombardier," said Robin. "But there is no need to risk other blood as well, especially your own blood, sweet lady. So since there is no other thing to keep you here, and since there it still some danger if the French be nigh, I beg you and your father to return with all haste to the safety of the siege train in the rear."

But the girl cast a quick glance around at the green trees and peaceful field. "Nay, you said Caen still lay leagues ahead. And if the French have purpose to make a stand, surely they will withstand us there where they may have some protection behind their walls and houses.

"I am tired of the dust and dullness of the dawdling siege carts in the rear. Let us but ride a little way further with you, and we will return to the rear with good grace."

Looking into her dark eyes, Robin could not find strength to compel her departure. "Only a little way, then," he said. "No further than that little stream that lies ahead. The land in truth looks empty enough. And from that winding wood on the left I have no fear."

Wat the Armorer, however, blew upon the charcoal brazier he was nursing until the firing skewer he had thrust into the coals sputtered forth white-hot sparks. "Never is the wolf so still, as when he lurks beside the game path. And it seems to me that Butcher de Brenn delays overlong to overtake us."

"An he comes not up with us ere we reach the stream, I will wait there until he overtakes us," responded Robin. "He must surely come quickly now, for Sir Allan told me last night that Sir John Chandos marches close behind. And the Butcher would not choose to be caught too far off-station by a fiery-blooded man of Sir John's temper."

"Aye. But gold can soothe a man's wounded feelings right easily, even against the hot words of a Chandos," grumbled the armorer. "And I trust not this Butcher guard of ours. He hath had overlong to exchange words with that rascally Frenchman.

"Watch what may come of it."

"Loving us and our bombards as little as he does, he might be tempted by another purse of French *livres* to delay in coming to our rescue—and so bring down two falcons with a single shaft."

"Mayhap we might give the Frenchmen even greater surprise in that case than they give us," said Robin, casting another glance toward the fringe of wildwood to their left.

Then as the bombard carts took up their rattling progress down the slope toward the stream, he gave himself over to the pleasure of the girl's presence.

When they came to the sandy ford across the stream, however, with no man of the convoy guard yet in sight, Robin's face grew a little worried. "We will await their coming here," he said, pulling up and signaling the others to do likewise. "And it might be well that you have your firing skewers full-fanned and hot, Peter Joy and Hubert."

By way of reply the two archers in the other carts grinningly waved their sharp-pointed firing rods that were sputtering with heat.

Then as if that were but the awaited signal, the whole land of France seemed to come alive.

CHAPTER VIII

HARVEST OF STEEL

OUT OF THE barley field where they had been lying hid sprang up a multitude of men. Steel caps gleamed, arms flashed, and steel-ringed leather jerkins surged up in waves.

From the brown faces underneath the caps came such fearful battle-cries that Robin did not need the sight of the glittering crossbows to know that these were the redoubtable Genoese crossbowmen, hired by the King of France.

All that Robin saw at a glance, and he waited not to estimate their numbers, which must have exceeded three hundred. The next instant Robin had hauled mightily on the reins, jerking the cart horses around and up, at the same time that he plied the whip.

"About—turn about!" he shouted to Hubert and John the Wolf in their carts.

The wild yells of the Genoese no less than whip and reins brought the horses around, plunging till they almost overturned the carts. Hubert and John the Wolf had been no less quick.

Lurching and bounding, the bombard carts raced up that slope they had so recently descended.

But arbalest bolts can outspeed any horse that bears harness or saddle, and knowing that Robin drove with head turned over shoulder. At the sudden upward wave of Genoese hands and the glint of sun on leveled arbalests, he let out another shout.

"Down! Down into the carts, every man—and show not a hair if you value life!"

Dropping reins and whip, he seized the girl, threw her flat in the bottom of the cart; he crouched down, shielding her with his body. Wat the Armorer had been no more gentle in hurling the Flemish merchant to the same safety and then squeezing his own brawny shoulders alongside.

The next instant there came a mighty twang as three hundred crossbow triggers loosed at once. The air above the carts was filled with the whine and hiss of the deadly bolts they seemed to darken the sky, and the thud of those that struck the cart sides fairly was like the beat of iron hail.

Had anyone's head or even the tip of elbow or knee showed above the sides, it would have been riddled, so thick had been the flight of the arbalest quarrels. Had the cart sides themselves been of less than stoutest oak, the quarrels would have punctured them.

But the hissing and the pounding ceased, and Robin glanced around to find with amazement that not one of them had suffered wound.

BUT HURT of another sort they had suffered, and grievous hurt at that. For the deadly arbalest quarrels, skimming close overhead and around, had riddled the horses that drew the bombard carts, dropping them in their tracks. So all hope of flight was gone.

Knowing the crossbowmen must needs re-wind their ratchets before launching other bolts, Robin ventured to raise his head still higher.

Hubert's and Peter Joy's horses had been riddled even as his own, but the archers' staring eyes just above their cart sides told that they too had sought safety in good time. Beyond Peter's shoulder the gaunt face of John the Wolf showed like a thundercloud, and he cursed the Genoese and all their forefathers before them.

Now Wat the Armorer raised his own grizzled head, and found odd comfort in Wolf John's oaths.

"Had these bowmen been good English archers now, instead of slovenly Genoese arbalesters, we had been cooped below our cart sides with no instant even to glance around for help. For during the time required for the winding of a single arbalest, a good longbowman would have loosed a dozen shafts."

"And small comfort is there in that!" panted Robin. "For look—the crest of that little hill to the right of the bowmen! Are those not lances, and the casques of mounted men?"

Even as he spoke, over the ridge and down the slope beside the Genoese thundered a cavalcade of men-at-arms till the earth drummed with their coming.

"Now I see the end of the King's bombards—and all us bombardiers with them!" grunted the armorer. "For the Genoese will keep us to cover with their devil's windlasses while the horsemen over-ride us and cut us to pieces. And already the Genoese have their ratchets wound and ready to loose bolt again.... Down all heads!"

Again the hail of flying quarrels whined overhead and hammered at the oaken sides. When it waned and ceased, Wat drew himself to hands and knees, slipping his left arm through his shield-hold. Robin was doing likewise. Glancing at the other carts, he saw that Hubert and Peter Joy and John the Wolf had strung their bows and also made ready for their last fight.

"Down—keep down!" Robin ordered the girl. "We may hold them off a scant while, to the hope of rescue." He muttered to himself: "And scant hope of that, with de Brenn not yet in sight! And Tyrel and his forest men—what hath held them back?"

Then he was amazed to hear the girl's voice, almost at his

ear. "The bombards! Would not their discharge perchance hold the Frenchmen aback? At least surprise and delay them, till the coming of help?"

"Bombards?" All at once Robin gave a gasp. "The suddenness of the trap has addled my own brains. The bombards, of course!" Suddenly lifting his voice, he let out a great shout. "Hubert! Peter Joy! Drop bow and shafts, and lay to the bombards! And fire as soon as you sight the Frenchmen adown the muzzles!"

WITH A yelp Wat the Armorer snatched for the brazier only to find the girl already had the firing skewer gripped. Robin jerked at the fastenings that held the cart's tail-gate in place. As it fell, he could see that there was little time to spare.

Sure that their prey was helpless, the crossbowmen had surged down their slopes and across the stream, some winding their ratchets as they ran, others slinging their arbalests and plucking out their knives for the kill. Almost on their flank, the hundred or more men-at-arms were crowding and spurring their horses into the water and up the sloping bank on the near side.

"A murrain upon the Butcher and all the Butcher's men!" cursed the armorer. "Now it is almost sure that he hath delayed on purpose and for the Frenchmen's gold, for otherwise he had been here enow. And a murrain also upon Tyrel and the forest men, that they marched not as Sir Allan promised!"

Seeing the leading Genoese not five score paces away and racing like wolves, their stabbing knives brandished, Robin could well agree.

At that moment there came a tremendous crash and roar, and almost like an echo of it another thunder crash as the other two bombards bellowed. Through the boiling smoke that swept down Robin stared eagerly to see what destruction they had made.

But his heart sank at the sight. Forgetting the downward slope of the ground beneath the wheels, Red Hubert had fired without any elevation of his bombard muzzle, so that the hurtling ball had driven into the ground a dozen paces short of the charging

Genoese; it had skipped over the first three ranks and only cut a swath amid the rearmost ones.

Hastier still Peter Joy had fired without either lowering the end-gate or taking any glance as to the bombard's pointing. The ball shattered the oaken gate to splinters and then spun and bounced along the slope well to the side of the Genoese until it had imbedded itself harmless in the further bank of the little stream.

"The wedges! Pound in the wedges, Wat, beneath the front of this bombard sledge!" shouted Robin, snatching the red-hot skewer from the girl's hand and going to his knees behind the bombard tube.

With mighty hammer blows the armorer drove in the wedges, and the bombard muzzle seemed to rise in jerks. Then Robin, peering along the top of the bombard tube, saw full before him the onrushing waves of Genoese arbalesters, so near that he could even glimpse their wild eyes.

With a shaking hand he suddenly drove the red-hot skewer deep down the bombard touch-hole, and so into the powder charge within, then he flung himself aside just in time.

There came such a great thundering roar that it seemed the earth and sky had split apart. Like a live thing the bombard leaped from its sledge and hurtled crashing back until in its mad recoil it all but plunged through the stout oaken front-gate of the cart. The whole cart staggered and shook, and the sky above seemed to spin in circles above the belching smoke.

So mighty had been the thunderclap, louder even than the other two bombards put together, and so great the recoil and jolt, that Robin thought at first the bombard had burst. Dazedly he pulled himself up, amazed to find himself still alive.

But the bombard, when he looked, was still all of a piece, though completely off its sledge carriage. And Wat's voice, and then the girl's, as they stared through the smoke ahead, were crying in triumph. "The Frenchmen—they are down, they are mowed down and lying in swathes!"

As the smoke thinned, Robin saw along the slope before him such havoc that he was sickened.

CHAPTER IX

BUTCHER, WILL YOU RUN?

IN TUMBLED HEAPS the Genoese lay, either dead or dragging their bleeding bodies along the ground and screaming in agony. All down the slope and almost to the stream the torn bodies were scattered, so that it seemed as if the whole center of the Genoese had been mowed down in one wide swathe, with only the troops at the flanks and beyond the stream left alive.

"The bombard ball—it must have shattered at the muzzle!" gasped Robin. "For no single ball or dozen balls could wreak such damage."

"Nay," said Wat the Armorer. "For through the smoke I myself saw the whole ball driving through the center rank and so on and down the slope!"

The old Flanders merchant, who had been lying the while in the wagon bottom groaning and crying out to all the saints, ceased his moaning at that and sat up. "Mayhap in your haste of loading, last night, you by chance forestalled my very thought and charged the bombard with twain balls!" he said.

"Even so, it is not enough," grunted the armorer suddenly. "For they gather to come upon us again—and our bombard off its sled even if time remained for re-loading!"

Indeed the Genoese now showed the valor for which they were famed. Despite their tremendous casualties and the surprise and shock of this inexplicable death, they had begun to reform and advance once again.

As for the horsemen, they had been to one side and hence were unscathed. Their mounts had plunged and twisted at the thunder and smoke, but the riders with heavy rein and spur were jerking them into rank again, and sending them on up the slope.

But all at once, from the forest at the left that had been so silent, came the war-cry of five score forest men. Out of the fringing woodland stepped Tyrel's archers in long rank, their longbows raised and bent. And at full two hundred paces they suddenly loosed their shafts.

Now Red Hubert's scorn for crossbowmen as against the longbowmen of England was full sustained. For despite the great distance, the flying goose-feathered shafts drove full and hard into the arbalester's ranks, piercing leather and flesh and dropping the Genoese in their tracks.

Ere the first shaft had struck home, the next arrow was already in the air, and the third nocked on the string. For the forest men had set each a sheaf of arrows barb-deep in the earth before him, and they plucked their shaft without looking.

Against that swift, silent destruction not even the Genoese could stand. Dropping their arbalests and throwing their knives from them, they broke and turned in mad flight, stumbling over living and dead in their rout.

Yet the French mounted men were still spurring up the slope, their stout shields and full coats of mail proof against any but a random shaft sifting through an armor crevice. At their orderly advance Robin's heart sank anew. Then all at once there sounded a loud drumming almost at his ear, and he heard the armorer's shout: "Mayhap I have done the Butcher injustice, after all! For here he comes, and in the nick of time!"

CLOSE PAST the bombard carts and spurring to throw themselves into the fray galloped a solid troop of English knights and men-at-arms, with the unmistakable banner and boar's head of de Brenn in the van.

Nor did his baron's banner flutter alone. Among the charging knights Robin recognized the fesse and crosslets of the Earl of Warwick, and the blue boar of Vere. The Saracen crest of Sir

John Chandos raced to the fore, and his war-cry of "A Chandos! A Chandos!" rose above the thunder of hooves.

Alongside the gold and red shield of Sir John Chandos rode a slim figure in jet-black armor, and by his 'scutcheon of *fleur-de-lys* and the royal hue of his surcoat Robin knew him to be no less than Edward of Woodstock, the Black Prince himself.

With a thundering crash the smaller troop of Englishmen clove into the larger body of French with such force that they disappeared completely from sight. Then there was visible only a mad turmoil of men and horses, of slashing blades and hammering axes, that seethed and boiled like devil's brew.

"Quick, Wat! Call up Tyrel and his archers! And make ready to load the two good bombards anew!" shouted Robin to the armorer. "They are twice outnumbered by the French! The Prince himself will be taken or slain!"

But instead of obeying, Wat the Armorer coolly sat himself down atop the dismounted bombard, and shook his head with a grin.

"Nay, we have done our work, now let these highbred knights do theirs. This Chandos and these other nobles are so tender of their honor and chivalry, now let them make proof of it in open battle. Also I would see how our Butcher does bear himself in this affray!"

Red Hubert and Peter Joy came loping across with bow and quiver to hand, to perch themselves on the cart side nearest Wat. From there they regarded the clash of the horsemen with glinting eyes.

"Butcher he is, but he was no laggard in the charge," said Peter Joy. "For with my own eyes I saw him in the forefront as they clashed."

"And yet scant proof is that," retorted Red Hubert. "For he was caught in the forefront when the charge began. Needs he must remain there then, else he had been over-ridden and trampled by our own men."

John the Wolf now came clambering belatedly into Robin's

cart. But instead of joining his fellow archers on their perch, he turned upon the dismounted bombard, his face all twisted and his mouth shouting curses.

"A curse upon thee, and a curse upon all thy devil's brood! And a curse upon me for ever putting trust in thee! Gone, all gone—my goodly farm, my fat beeves, my casks of wine, my life of ease! All gone because of thee!"

And in his rage he delivered a great kick at the bombard tube. That, while it did the bombard no harm, caused the gaunt archer to howl and hop on one foot to even greater cursing.

Robin stared, certain that John the Wolf had gone bereft of his senses through some head injury in the fight. He was about to call on Red Hubert to seize him and so constrain him from further self-injury, when Wat the Armorer's sharp outcry drew his eyes to the battle once more.

"Our Butcher, our Butcher—Give eye to our Butcher! For methinks he hath his hands full and over-full!"

LOOKING OUT, Robin discovered that in its mad boiling and twisting, the mêlée like some whirlwind of steel, had turned and eddied over the sloping ground until it had circled nigh back to the bombard carts.

In fact, the trampling hooves of the chargers were treading among the heaps of dead and wounded where the charge of the Genoese had furthest advanced before it had been broken by the bombards and Tyrel's archers.

But what caught Robin's gaze was a most amazing thing occurring on the near fringe of the mêlée. There, unmistakable by his great size and shield device, rode Butcher de Brenn. His arm held his great Norman sword aloft, ready to cleave some hapless assailant to the waist. Yet amazingly the arm and sword remained aloft, though from both sides two French knights attacked, battering at him with both ax and sword. And the Butcher, crouched low beneath his great shield, jerked his charger this way and that, and seemed more intent to avoid blows than to give them.

Even as Robin watched, the Frenchman to the right side drove home such a great sword buffet on de Brenn's shield that it drove the stout buckler down and to the left. Whereupon his fellow with the ax hammered a blow on de Brenn's casque; the clang resounded even above the noises of the battle, and de Brenn reeled in his saddle. Still reeling, he reined his charger around and out of the mêlée, leaving the Frenchmen behind.

At that Wat the Armorer gave a grunt. "Shame it is if an ill-mannered horse flee out of the battle now, and so bring his master to shame and dishonor. Do thou bend they bows, Hubert and Peter, to the saving of this shame!"

Hubert stared, and then let out a great chuckle. Seizing his bow, he set shaft to string, even as Peter Joy did likewise. And before Robin could utter word, both bows twanged and both shafts sped.

De Brenn's charger was full-geared like its rider, its war harness of leather and steel rings dropping almost to its fetlocks. And those fetlocks were prancing and trampling. Yet so unerring were the shafts that each pierced a fetlock, and the charger went down as if its feet had been cut from beneath it, toppling its rider with a great clang to the ground.

Lying there on his back, Butcher de Brenn kicked and struggled desperately to hoist the great weight of his body and armor, so that he seemed like nothing so much as a hapless tortoise overturned onto its shell.

So comical was the sight that Robin could not but laugh. But the laugh died quickly on his lips.

FROM AMONG the heaps of tumbled Genoese suddenly upreared three skulking figures. Three unharmed arbalesters who, seeing death strike all about them from the bombards and the archers' shafts, had fallen to earth and pretended to be but other corpses amid the slain.

But now, catching sight of an English knight unhorsed and helpless almost at their feet, and thinking themselves unnoticed in the mêlée, they bounded out like wolves, to hurl themselves upon de Brenn.

Two of them hacked and slashed madly with their stabbing knives at the baron's armor. The third had snatched up a heavy battle-mace dropped from some wounded chevalier's hand, wherewith he hammered and pounded whenever he could find arm-space between his two companions.

"Nay, I had no thought to bring the Butcher to his murder!" suddenly growled Wat the Armorer. "I thought but to bring him to a sore headache from overmuch pounding. Peter—Hubert— turn thy shafts against these Genoese wolves, and in all haste!"

Hardly had he spoken the words, however, before Hubert's bow had already twanged. Spitted full through the throat, the wielder of the mace spun and fell, to be crushed almost immediately under the dying body of one of the knifemen whom Peter's shaft had toppled. The third Genoese turned to flee, but he had taken only a half-dozen bounds when Hubert's second shaft buried itself almost to the feathers between his shoulders.

"Now quickly with me, that we may fetch him in ere other Genoese wolves be out and at his throat!" exclaimed the armorer. With the words he was out of the cart and racing toward the unhorsed baron, Peter and the grumbling Hubert at his heels.

Laying hold to arms and legs, they half-carried, half-dragged the heavy burden back to the cart where they dropped it beneath and between the wheels. There was a great clank and a grievous groan from inside the casque.

Whether de Brenn was sore wounded or merely stunned, however, Robin had no time to see, for the mêlée on the slope in front was now finally resolving itself. Outnumbered though it had been, the English troop included men accounted among the first knights of all Christendom.

Sir Allan Mayne... Warwick... Vere of Oxford... and first and foremost Sir John Chandos, raging like a lion, dealing such blows with his great battle-ax that he hewed out a path for himself where'er he turned. Nor yet, despite his youth, was the

Black Prince outdistanced. Almost at Sir John's shoulder his jet-black armor gleamed, while his flashing sword dealt blow for blow.

Against such doughty warriors French could not stand. Slashing their way through, the English turned and charged back again. After the third charge the defeated French broke and fled, spurring their horses with such good will that the English made only brief pursuit. Upon Warwick's trumpeter sounding a blast near the carts for the rallying there, the English archers and horsemen flocked to reassemble.

CHAPTER X

RANSOM FOR THE DEAD

SIR JOHN CHANDOS and the Black Prince rode back together, their helmet visors now open to let in fresh air after the hot confinement of the battle. The other knights, riding up, raised their visors likewise.

Swiftly the Earl of Warwick ran his eye around, sighing with relief when he perceived the Prince alive and unwounded. "Who now among us has fallen? My Lord Stafford, it is sweet to see thee unharmed. Oxford—Hastynges—Sir John Chandos, still breathing fire despite such deeds as would befit a dozen stout knights!

"St. George and Our Lady have indeed been with us. But stay! My Lord de Brenn—where is our Lord de Brenn? Then he must have fallen. Send his squire to search the field."

At that Wat the Armorer suddenly spoke up from the bombard carts. "Nay, he is even here, beneath this very cart. Sore hammered he may be, but he is not slain for I did hear him groan event as we dragged him here to safety."

Two squires hurriedly dismounted and, pulling the heavy and clanking figure of de Brenn from beneath the wagon, hurriedly loosed the helmet to jerk it off. One of them let out a cry of amazement.

"Sore smitten he must be, near unto death! For see how the pounding did set this great pauldron rivet askew! And the gusset pieces and taces at his right armpit so sprung that in the overlapping they have fouled, one against the other. Though he might make shift to raise his arm, he could not deliver the downward blow, for the fouling of the pieces!"

Remembering de Brenn's odd actions at the beginning of the fight, Robin suddenly turned and shot a glance of keen suspicion at Wat the Armorer. It came to him then how surly the Wat had been when first ordered to repair the armor, yet how cheerily he had been whistling at the end.

There was no man in all England his equal in cunning at the armorer's trade, at the fashioning and fitting of rivets or plates. So if there had been ill-fitting of rivets or plates by Wat, it had not been by mischance but by purpose.

As if to prove Robin's suspicions, Wat's eye, meeting his, closed in a sly wink. "Our lord baron must indeed suffer a grievous headache, then, from this fearful pounding by the French," he said.

That this was so was soon evident, for with his casque off de Brenn moaned again, and stirred, and finally opened his eyes. But all he did thereafter was blink dazedly and rub his fingers across his bruised forehead and moan once more.

"Bear him to his tent, and gently," Sir John Chandos gave order to the two squires. "Well it is, though, that he bore himself so stoutly in the charge. For I had mind to upbraid him sternly in that he delayed so far behind the carts, and thus risked the safety of the very bombards he had order to guard."

THE SQUIRES lifted de Brenn to a horse and were bearing him away when up from the rear rode that same scowling constable's knight and his men who had searched the archers and the bombard carts that morning. Sir John received them with a chilly eye.

"Ye come overlate, sirrah, an ye seek honor and knightly glory. For the battle is already finished, and what honor there may be is already won."

But the dark browed newcomer shook his head. "I have naught to do with battles. I am the man of my lord Northampton, constable of the army, and have sole duty in the keeping of order in the army. The stain to the King's honor is not yet erased, for the plunderers of the French herald have not yet been found. It is the seeking of them that brings me here." He cast his surly glance upon Red Hubert and John the Wolf and Peter Joy.

Sir Allan Mayne stood forth angrily. "Thou hast already searched these, and all my other forest men. Go about thy duty then, and seek some other place where pillage and robbery is more likely to be found."

"But I have more recent information which makes it seem that our first search was over-hasty, and that these three archers are in truth the villains who treacherously waylaid the herald." Turning his head, the constable's knight called out. "Will o' the Fens! Stand forth, and repeat what thou didst say!"

Peter Joy's face went pale, and Red Hubert blinked, and John the Wolf grew red with rage. For with eyes glittering and face malignant, Will o' the Fens stepped from among the constable's men.

"Aye, these are the three!" he said boldly. "With my own eyes, last night, I saw them from the very fringe of their cook-fire. Saw this gaunt archer here take the herald's purse from beneath his jerkin, and hide it."

Sir Allan Mayne glared. "Thou art liar as well as knave! For the carts and bombardiers were well searched—"

"But not the bombards! Not the bombard tubes themselves!"

Sir Allan attempted to speak again, but a wave from the Earl of Warwick silenced him. "Search the tube, then, and quickly. And the purse be found within, and the thousand golden *livres*, I shall see that these three archers be gibbeted in sight of the whole army, so that all England and France may see how tenderly we guard our honor."

All this while Robin's eyes had been growing wider with amazement. Suddenly a great light burst on him, and he smiled, and with his own hands drew out of the cart the long-handled pole with its three metal prongs which was among the bombard's equipage.

"Here is the pole with which we withdraw the ball in case the powder miss firing. Take it and make search as you will."

Will o' the Fens seized the pronged pole and thrust it into the muzzle to the very bottom, and then thrice twisted it ere he withdrew it, but it brought forth nothing. Two others of the constable's men did likewise, to no more result than the discovery of a few charred grains of unburned charcoal which clung to the prongs.

"You see, my lords," said Robin.

Will o' the Fens' eyes were bulging. "But I saw it! With my own eyes—"

"Then thine eyes are as false as thy tongue!" cried the Earl of Warwick angrily. "Thy accusation is proved false. And that our force be not disrupted by false accusation, do you, my lord of the constable's men, see that this lying villain receive two score lashes laid lustily on his back."

Then to Sir John Chandos: "Take over the command here, Sir John, until we may send fresh horses for the bombard carts, and set a new guard over them in the march."

With these words he and all the other knights rode away.

SIR JOHN CHANDOS, who never wearied of studying a battlefield, rode slowly forward to where the tide of Genoese had rolled the furthest.

Robin Santerre felt the touch of soft fingers on his arm, and turned to find the Flemish girl's eyes worriedly on his face. "Ye suffered no hurt, Robin? Ye suffered no hurt from those quarrels that flew like hail above us? For I reck that ye guarded my own body against them with yours."

"Nay, no harm—no harm at all," said Robin. Remembering that even amid the rain of crossbow bolts he had thrilled at the nearness of her, he stammered now. "The cart sides—are of stout oak and of great thickness. It was they that guarded thee, and not I!"

Then John the Wolf's voice sounded in their ears, grumbling and cursing all anew. "My farm, my beeves, my casks of wine for my old age—all gone at one belch of this devil's bombard!"

"And thou dost complain at that?" growled Wat the Armorer. "Had it been otherwise, all three of you had danced on a gibbet by now. For that matter, the gibbet may get thee yet. For here comes yon fire-eating knight, and I like not the look in his eyes."

In truth Sir John Chandos was returning, and his warlike face was grim. He scowled at the quaking archers and no less at the bombards.

"Verily these bombards are the devil's weapons. They will bring an end to knightly warfare and honorable mêlée, even as I feared. Never have I seen men so riddled and cut to pieces, in all my days."

Even John the Wolf's face paled at that. Nor did he find comfort in the knight's next words, addressed to Robin.

"Little love have I for thee and thy bombards. For I foresee the day when bombards and bombardiers will be held of greater account than stout armor or all the good knights in Christendom."

Then all at once his eyes began to twinkle.

"But I love treacherous villeins and denouncers still less. So see to it that these three cunning forest men waylay no more heralds, and I will say naught to the constable's men about these Genoese being more riddled with golden *livres* than quarrels or longbow shafts!"

And with eyes still twinkling he turned away.

John the Wolf sat gawking after him a long minute. Then he turned sheepishly to Red Hubert.

"Mayhap thou art right. For I did feel the very breeze from

the gibbet cold upon my neck just then. Nonetheless, it seems ill waste that dead Genoese should now have those goodly *livres,* and not live Englishmen!"

But Robin's reply was as faraway as his look.

"Nay. For though the *livres* are wasted, the lesson is not. If a purse of gold pieces may be hurled from bombards so scatteringly and with such deadly effect, a sack of small steel balls or broken iron should be even more deadly. And that is a lesson which may save the lives of many good bombardiers in time to come."

FLIGHT OF THE GUNS

Today the English men-at-arms win a dubious glory by fire and pillage. But tomorrow only the Devil's weapons of these six bombardiers can answer the challenge of France....

CHAPTER I

FLAMING NORMANDY

FROM BARFLEUR TO Liseux in Normandy is four-score miles and ten, pleasant miles they may be in mid-July with the villeins toiling in the fields, the grain rippling in the breeze, and the apple trees bursting with late bloom and young fruit.

Yet Normandy was anything but lovely in this mid-July of 1346. For every blooming tree and peaceful ville that lay ahead, a pile of embers and a pall of smoke lay behind. Between Edward III of England and his cousin, King Philip of France there had risen a conflict over the provinces of Normandy, Guienne, and Aquitaine. Whereat Edward had landed at St. Vaast de la Hogue with full twenty thousand knights, men-at-arms, archers, and pikemen, and now was raiding the deep heart of France, burning and ravaging as he marched.

In three columns over a front of twenty miles the English marched, like destroying locusts. And that they might widen the path of their plague, they threw out on the sides a swarm of hobilars, light-armed men a-horseback.

Even the knights and squires and men-at-arms thought it no shame to over-ride and slay the dumb, bewildered Norman villeins of the fields, to lay the torch to peaceful villages and peasants' roof-trees.

Alone in all that horde of destruction, one small band of Englishmen marched and had no part in it. Well to the fore rolled and rumbled a half-dozen heavy carts on creaking wheels, while on either flank marched a score of seasoned archers, strung bowstave in hand, quiver and buckler at shoulder, short knife belted at side.

In the foremost cart Wat the Armorer, broad of shoulder and brawny of arm despite the fifty years that had grizzled his hair, turned with a perplexed frown to the youth that rode the cart seat beside him.

"Fire, murder, and destruction—my eyes are sickened of the sight. If this be war, Robin, why seek we not the Frenchman's knights and men-at-arms, or lay siege to his castles and strong points, rather than slay and burn where only defenseless villeins bide?"

Robin Santerre's eyes, too, were sickened, and a frown furrowed his high forehead that was more a scholar's than a soldier's.

On that battle ground
England's champion
met the French knight
in furious combat

"If I had known that such was war, I would have bethought me twice before leaving the honest halls of Oxford for this service. Pestle and mortar and books of the philosophers are more to my liking than blood and pillage.

"Yet I had thought—I had even hoped—that in these new bombards and their amazing powder might lie the end of all such burning and slaying. But look: Ahead of us lies a ridge, and beyond that ridge lies no man knows what.

"When we reach the crest it might be well that we halted and looked to our bombards and their chargings, that we run not afoul of just such ambush as was nigh our undoing at Caen."

IN TRUTH, when they topped the ridge, Robin's prudence seemed well advised. For there, directly before them, lay a swift and brawling stream pinched between sheer, rocky banks; sharp-toothed boulders ripped its waters into raging rapids.

On the left side of the stream lay a cluster of thatch-roofed houses, a small community that was unwalled and now seemingly deserted. On the other bank, however, and all but circled

by the snarling rapids, upreared a rocky peak. And on its very pinnacle, like an eagle's aerie, nested a frowning castle.

But the castle's drawbridge was up-drawn, moving helmets and pike-points glinted atop its battlements, and from its lofty keep the banner of the castle's lord fluttered a sullen defiance.

"Aye, you are right. Another Caen, mayhap," muttered the armorer, and halted for the remaining carts to come up.

Swiftly then, Robin Santerre leaped from his seat. As master-artilleryman and captain of bombards, he went along the wagons, dropping the tail-gates, inspecting the bombards. He tested the store balls seated in the muzzles, the powder beneath the touch-holes, made sure that the firing skewer in each glowing brazier was red-hot and ready for instant use.

From the other carts clambered down three men. One was a giant, red-headed and as freckled as a pied piper: the second a lean, scarred, grizzled man as gaunt as a gray wolf: and the last an agile fellow of no more years than Robin's own twenty. They each wore the habiliments and bore the weapons of archers.

"How now—how ride the bombards?" inquired Robin.

Red Hubert grinned and spat. "Well enough, eh, Old Wolf?"

John the Wolf scowled. "Nay, the roughness jostled me around until my insides are all but addled."

Peter Joy, the youngest, chuckled. "Our Wolf hath ever a sour temper. But give him a French lord to catch for ransom, and he will smile soon enough."

"Small chance for that, when these accursed knights and hobilars sweep clean even the pig-sties before we bombardiers e'en glimpse them," snarled John the Wolf. "If I had a horse I might fare better. But see—they ride into this Frenchmen's town before we scarcely more than sight it."

In truth, a party of full-armed knights and men-at-arms had come in sight on the left and was even now a-gallop toward the deserted village. Right after them came a yelping band of hobilars from the right who, at sight of the houses ahead, let out a shout and raced down with pike-points glittering.

"A fair race—and the devil take the hobilars!" Red Hubert grinned. "But see, they draw rein. And scant wonder. For if my eyes see aright, that black knight at the head of the others is none else than the Prince!"

Unmistakable indeed was the swart shield and armor of that Prince of Wales who was ever afterward to be known as the Black Prince. Open-helmed, rising in his stirrups and shouting like a boy, he led the charge upon the village. His was the eager hand that set torch to the first roof-tree, his the excited voice that shouted orders to knights and squires. For Edward of Woodstock was scant sixteen, making his first foray into hostile country, and all aflame with the zest and excitement of it.

Wat the Armorer shook his head. "Setting fire to a villein's roof-thatch is small honor to the Prince of all England. It had brought him greater honor had he challenged, instead, that great perching castle yon, where there might be blows received as well as given. But no—they fire the villein's roof and ride wide of yon Norman lord's stronghold."

BUT NOT quite was this true. For, leaving the flaming village, the Prince's party rode to the very stream edge where the stout wooden bridge, port-cullised at the castle end, led across the rushing stream.

But the drawbridge was open and portcullis dropped, and after waving defiant lances toward the stern battlements, the English knights contented themselves with firing the near end of the bridge and then riding on for further quarry.

"Said I not so?" demanded the Armorer. "E'en as at Barfleur, they rein full wide of stone nuts that may prove hard to crack."

"They have done us some good turn anyway," said Robin. "With the bridge fired, the Frenchmen in yon castle cannot sally out to cut us and our archers to pieces. But now we may even march on past the village."

"Past where the village stood, you mean," grunted John the Woll. "Already the hobilars are at it, like the scavengers they are."

When they creaked down the slope and neared the houses,

they saw that the grizzled archer had spoken aright. For the hobilars, some dismounted and some still a-horse, were dashing here and there, gutting the place of any belonging left behind by the villagers in their hurried flight, and laying the torch to every roof as yet unfired. Most eager among them was their leader, a dark, evil-faced man at sight of whom Red Hubert let out an oath.

"Will o' the Fens, or I never glimpsed yon varlet before! And changed from archer to hobilar!"

"Aye. Murder and pillage besuits him better than an honest archer's bow and quiver," grunted Wat the Armorer. "Sir Allen Mayne and his Masterless Men are well rid of him."

John the Wolf's gaunt jowls quivered wrathfully. "It irks me sorely to see the varlet a-horse and hence earning six pence pay a day as hobilar, when we honest archers and bombardiers earn but three. I have half a mind to sting him with a clothyard shaft."

"An one good French bowman lay hid in yon village, Will o' the Fens would not be so free with the torch," said Peter Joy. "One bowman could riddle half a dozen of yon hobilars ere they could drop torch for blade or pike."

His tone had something of regret in it, for between Will o' the Fens and the bombardiers there was no love lost. And reasonably enough, since, but a few days before, Will o' the Fens had almost got them all gibbeted by the army's constables for the matter of a ransomed Frenchman's purse.

CHAPTER II

THE KING'S BUZZARDS

HOWEVER, IT SEEMED that every able-bodied French-man had abandoned the village in full flight, for the hobilars pillaged and burned without hindrance. And foremost with the torch was Will o' the Fens and another great hulking hobilar of loud voice whose rose beside the leader.

Yet not completely deserted was the village, for all at once from out of a hut that had just been fired, hobbled a withered crone. She was bent with age and in rags, yet she beat at the fire with feeble hands and screamed curses on the hobilars.

At that the hulking hobilar beside Will cursed, and turning his horse, spurred with cruel force upon the crone. So quick was the rush that she could not hobble aside. Struck by the charging horse and man, she spun and fell beneath the horse's hooves, and lay thereafter writhing and screaming, her shrill voice ringing above the roar of the flames and the shouts of the hobilars. But instead of dealing quick punishment to the offending hobilar, Will o' the Fens merely sat his saddle and let out a great laugh.

At that Robin's face went white, and even the Armorer's lips grew tense. Red Hubert let out an oath and plucked a long goose-feathered shaft from the quiver at his back.

"Now that was an evil deed. For a woman is e'er a woman, even though she be Norman and not English. What say you of the distance, Old Wolf? A full two hundred paces, or perhaps an even score beyond?"

"Two hundred and a score, and forget not a half-pace for windage," answered John the Wolf, likewise notching arrow to bow. "Do you take the hobilar, and I will choose me Will o' the Fens."

But vengeance from another source overtook the hulking hobilar even before the red-headed archer could loose his shaft. For all at once from out the burning hut bounded an unarmed figure.

A plunging fury, this one.

With the second bound he was at the hobilars side, and before that amazed rider could turn, had gripped him by the leg. And so mighty was the jerk that the rider seemed fairly to fly from his saddle, to land in the dust with a thud. As swift as a terrier upon a rat, the newcomer was upon him, worrying him. The downed hobilar's voice rose in a shrill shout of fright, then the shout broke suddenly into a horrid cry, and was stilled.

So sudden was the attack that Will o' the Fens and the other hobilars had sat their saddles mute and amazed. Now they broke into shouts, curses, reined their mounts and strove to over-ride the Frenchman.

But he was unarmed no longer. Snatching the sword from the dead hobilar's side, he laid about him with great blows, bounding and twisting until the hobilars found their very numbers a disadvantage. Their blows and thrusts fell upon one another rather than upon their intended victim. So that their horses began rearing and plunging furiously.

But, Robin had not waited to see the end of all this. Leaping into his cart's seat, he seized whip and reins and belabored the cart horses until they broke into a frantic run down the slope, the bombard cart bouncing and clattering at their heels, while behind rattled the other carts with the archer escort racing alongside.

NOT LONG could one man hold out against so many, however; and even as Robin drove up, two hobilars, wiser than the rest, had dropped reins and pikes and leaped from their saddles down upon the lone Frenchman.

Even so, and hurled to earth as he was, he continued to twist and struggle until other hobilars swarmed upon him and so buried him beneath their bodies that he was unable even to move.

"Bind his arms and ankles!" ordered Will o' the Fens, his face purple with anger.

While this was being done, one of the hobilars knelt beside the rider who had been pulled from his horse.

"Dead as a smelt! And small wonder, for his neck is all but twisted into a knot!"

At that Will o' the Fens swung down from his horse, drew his sword, and advanced upon the bound and helpless prisoner who was staring up with anger and defiance and no fear.

Holding the naked blade before the prisoner's eyes, the leader of the hobilars gave a snarl. "Then let us see how thy neck will withstand an English edge. And thou should hold thyself lucky that we do not cast thee into the flames alive."

"And when that blade falls, so will this one also upon thine own fat neck!" Robin, who had leaped down from his cart and pushed his way through the crowd, had his own sword out. Robin's eyes shone with such fiery anger that Will o' the Fens stumbled back. Behind Robin came Wat the Armorer, his great hand on his sword-hilt.

But seeing only the two of them, and enraged at the interference, Will o' the Fens found heart and whirled around to his hobilars. "Out sword, and cut them down! Over-ride them!"

"That is somewhat easier in the saying than in the doing!" said a new voice.

Red Hubert stood erect on the cart seat, his bowstring full drawn and the barb of the arrow covering the leader of hobilars. John the Wolf and Peter Joy, in their own carts, likewise had shafts nocked and the bowstrings taut against the ear.

Without turning his head, Red Hubert called to them, "Do thou take the one beyond Will, Old Wolf—and Peter, you take the next."

"Nay, I will ne'er draw shaft again an' I not spit at least three of these varlets," growled the grizzled archer. "And Tyrrel here and his men should be good for at least two each. Eh, Tyrrel?"

At that the leader of the archer escort, who was panting from the speed of his running, nocked his own arrow to string.

"Thou wert ever a greedy old wolf, John. There will not be two apiece left for us, an' thou take three for thyself. We will spit these hobilars until they sprout more shafts than a hedgehog sprouts quills!"

Seeing a full score and more of shafts aimed at them, and knowing that every archer could drop his deer at two hundred paces, the hobilars began to give back, muttering among themselves. Yet there was still a surliness among them, which occasioned other words from the armorer.

"If clothyard shafts have no meaning for you, we still have the bombards ready for firing. So get you gone before we unloose them upon you!"

AT THAT there was no further hesitancy among the hobilars. For though not one in ten among the army knew the secret of this strange new artillery that cast great stone balls with vomiting fire and thunder, it was well bruited abroad that they were engines of the Devil's own making, against which not even mailed knights or barbican walls could stand.

Riders crossed themselves and muttered prayers to the saints, casting frightened glances toward the bombard carts, and then put spur to their mounts as they placed what distance they might between themselves and such fearsome engines. Only Will o' the Fens delayed, his rage overcoming his fear.

"Ye shall not free this Frenchman entirely from me! With one twist of his hands he brake the neck of Allard here, the stoutest man of my troop. E'en the Lord Constable would assess him death for that!"

"Nay," said Robin, "for the Constable's orders are that all unarmed villeins shall be brought in unhurt, for the building of the roads the siege train must use. And such a stout Frenchman as this should be greater worth than a half dozen dumb villeins of the fields." He nodded to Red Hubert. "Cut his ankles loose, Hubert, and stand him on his feet."

With one sweep of his knife, Red Hubert cut the cord that bound the prisoner's ankles, still leaving his wrists lashed for safety. Wat the Armorer had meanwhile bent over the limp form of the old crone. He arose, shaking his head.

"She is with the saints now, if it be that these French have saints. And clean flame is better than a hasty burying." So saying he lifted the scrawny body and gently thrust it into the leaping pyre of the hut.

The prisoner, however, had waited for no help, but had scrambled to his feet of his own accord. And now he stood, a stocky man of shoulder-breadth equaling even the giant Hubert's. His face was dark and rough-featured even to ugliness; his curious greenish eyes met Robin's without fear. So that Robin could not forbear a grunt of admiration as he turned to the hobilar leader.

"Take him back, then, to the master road-builder. An' he arrive not there alive, it will be to thy ill luck as well as his."

"Aye, and more than that," growled Red Hubert. "I shall come looking on the morrow. An' he have even so much as a sword cut on him, hobilar, your own carcass shall receive a like gash, but of just twice the length and depth!"

Then as the scowling hobilar rode away, driving the Frenchman ahead of him, the giant archer grumbled: "It would be better deed, methinks, even now to spit yon hobilar with a shaft, than to let him go."

Robin shook his head wearily. "There has been enough, and to spare, of killing. And since the sun is low, we would do well to drive only a little further along the stream, and then make camp."

Recapturing the reins, he whipped the tired horses up, with the other carts clattering after. So heartsick was he at the thought of the old crone's trampling, that he did not notice that John the Wolf had not resumed the driver's seat in the third bombard cart.

Instead, with a grin and a grunt, John had given the reins over to Tyrrel. Then, hopping lightly from the cart, the gaunt archer had vanished quickly amid the flaring roof-thatches and half-consumed walls of the village. Nor did he rejoin his cart until long after the others had already lighted the cook-fires for the evening meal.

ON THE morrow, however, they found a new and severe hindrance to their progress. For here the road wound among the lowlands and at times amid marshes fed by the stream's overflow. Even footmen and horsemen found the going difficult, and for the heavy baggage carts and other wagons of the train the road was completely impassable.

Picking his way gingerly amid the mire, Robin shook his head. "There is naught to do but wait in camp until the engineers have bridged a way. Our heavy bombard carts would sink to the hubs within a half-league."

"And that would suit our lords and knights, like Butcher de Brenn, full well," said Wat the Armorer. "They have no love for these bombards, seeing that, if the weapons prove themselves in this war, bombards and bombardiers may well displace that cumbersome armor of which these clanking knights are so proud. Even Sir John Chandos hath held that bombards have no place in the field, but should march only with the engines of siege in the train."

Robin was silent a long moment, his forehead knitted in thought. "Nay, the fault lies not in the bombards but in these heavy carts. Could we dispense with the carts completely, and merely fasten wheels onto the bombard sledges directly, we could go where any full-armed horseman could go. And that is an idea that is deserving of thought. But here come the *gynours*, for the bridging of this mire."

He pointed.

The engineers from the train in the rear were indeed coming up, bringing with them teams and carts, axes and rope and mauls, all the tools of their craft. Surveying the marshy road with keen, professional eye, the master *gynour* promptly set men to work, felling trees, gathering rocks, laying them side by side in the mire to form solid footing over which even the heavy baggage wagons and siege engines might cross.

These were valuable men indeed.

Now, too the reason for the Constable's orders about bringing in prisoners was apparent. Guarded and driven by armed bowmen and pikemen, great droves of French peasants were herded forward and set to felling trees and dragging rocks and timbers toward the low spots. Watching which, Wat the Armorer gave a sour grunt. In disgust he said:

"Now again I say that this war is but an evil and unfair thing.

The Magna Carta, on which we English set such store, hath it plainly writ that no English freeman may be set to *corvee*—to forced labor—nor other work without reasonable pay. And this is right.

"Yet we force these poor French villeins to felling of trees and dragging of rocks, with no more pay than a whip lash across the shoulders."

"Yet it hath ever been held in war that a captured enemy is at the full command and mercy of the captor, to do whatever he is bid," replied Robin.

"Aye, but when at Caen we captured the high and mighty Count d'Eu," retorted the Armorer, "was he put to felling trees and dragging rocks, with a whiplash across his back if he was lazy at the task? Nay, his bed and sup were of the finest, and he was even called cousin by our own Lord Constable, the great Earl of Northampton. For the rules of war are made by earls and counts and kings. When common, honest freemen like ourselves make the rules—But, hola! Who is this I see?"

CHAPTER III

ARCHER ON HORSEBACK

FOLLOWING HIS GLANCE, Robin glimpsed a stocky prisoner of tremendous breath of shoulder and ugly features who was straining at the thick butt of a green log. Then as the powerful shoulder muscles bulged, the heavy log lifted and fell into place with a loud thud.

Robin turned with curiosity to the English archer who stood guard with sword and strung bowstave. "How toils this stout Frenchman here? For meseems he hath the strength of three."

The guard grounded the end of his bowstave and scratched his head. "The strength of three, aye—and the surliness of six! I but rapped him with the end of my stave a moment agone, and he turned on me with such glare and scowl that I was glad I was a bow-length away."

"Art affrighted of an unarmed French villein, then?" inquired Robin. "That were shame to all English bowmen."

The archer scratched his head again, and then grinned. "Nay, it was not fear of him alone that moved me, but fear of a great, red-thatched archer of our own army who bespoke me this early morning.

"He gave me warning, did this great redhead, that did I so much as make gash or even bruise on this Frenchman's carcass he himself would do double-damage to mine own. And to add meaning to his words, this giant red-thatch squeezed my neck with but his thumb and fingers. My wizen is sore from the squeezing yet."

Robin knew that Red Hubert had been as good as his word.

Leaving the engineers and their prisoners, Robin and the Armorer returned to their own camp beside the rapids a small distance away.

But no sooner had they come in easy sight, than they both stopped dead still. And after a moment's sight, they both broke out into laughter.

In a little open space away from the bombard carts, Red Hubert and Peter Joy and John the Wolf were struggling with a plunging horse. Red Hubert and Peter Joy stood on either side, heels dug into earth and holding back with all their strength on two ropes that fastened to the horse's neck.

Alongside the horse John the Wolf dodged and twisted, letting out great oaths as he vainly tried to mount by means of the surcingle and looped straps he had knotted around the animal in lieu of saddle. Yet despite the two ropes that stretched his neck, the horse—a black, mettlesome animal with rolling eyes and back-thrown ears—plunged and kicked and twisted so that the gaunt archer had much ado to hold on. The dirt and tatters of his doublet and jerkin showed that John the Wolf had already mounted at least once, only to be as swiftly thrown.

"Now what knight's warhorse has this thievish John stolen?" inquired Robin as he ceased his laughing. "For assuredly such a mettlesome steed is more a knight's charger than a villein's plow horse!"

At that moment the animal had ceased plunging for a moment in order to regain his wind. Snatching the surcingle, John the Wolf was scrambling up and atop his back, digging his toes into the stirrup loops and yelling with triumph.

HIS TRIUMPH, however, lasted no longer than his first shout. With a bawl of anger at being so tricked, the horse went into such a fury of plunges and twists as made his previous efforts seem like kitten's play. The first plunge threw the dismayed rider forward on the mane and neck; the second dumped him spinning off and to the side.

At that Red Hubert and Peter Joy set up great shouts of jeering laughter, but they threw their full weight on the neck ropes anew to prevent the horse running free. The next instant their laughter changed to cries of alarm.

For in his fall John the Wolf, although freed of one stirrup loop, had become entangled of the other. And now with his head and shoulders in the dirt, he hung by the tangle foot, howling and vainly clawing to free his heel from the surcingle loop.

Nor was that all. With a great rear and plunge, the kicking brute had jerked one tie-rope completely loose from Peter Joy's surprised hands. Then as Red Hubert dug in his heels and set his great strength and body to the test, that rope snapped, sending Red Hubert spinning backward on the ground. Freed of the ropes, the horse whirled on his heels, and started to race wildly from the spot, his speed the more furious because of the bouncing, yelling thing that hung at his side.

"Quick, Wat! Catch him, catch him!" yelled Robin. "John's brains will be shattered out against the rocks." With the words he turned and raced toward the left to head off the horse which was plunging their way.

At sight of him, the animal curveted and circled to the right, where Wat the Armorer waited. With a desperate lunge the Armorer managed to lay hand to the surcingle, only to have it jerked from his fingers by another twisting plunge of the steed.

Then while Robin and the Armorer stood impotent, the horse, with John the Wolf still dragging from its stirrup loop, headed straight toward the spot where the *gynours* and the captives labored.

"Now is it in truth the end of John the Wolf," gasped the Armorer hoarsely. "For yon logs and rocks will crash his skull like an egg-shell. And naught but an arrow could overtake yon devil-brute now!"

"But an arrow may yet do it! An arrow may yet do it!" cried Robin with sudden hope. "See—Hubert and Peter are running for heir bow and quivers."

"Too late!" groaned the Armorer. "The horse is all but into the rocks and logs now."

Then in that instant when all hope seemed gone, an unexpected thing happened.

OUT FROM among the dazed guards and captives, rushed a bare-headed figure. His dark locks flying, his long arms outstretched, the Frenchman of the blazing hut raced toward man and horse.

He shouted in strange words as he ran. And amazingly enough the shouts seemed to distract the animal so that it pulled up short, even hesitated before resuming its flight.

That slight hesitation was enough. With that same tiger bound with which he had attacked the hobilar, the Frenchman was at the horses head. One of the long arms seized its muzzle, its foaming nostrils, jerked it down and around. Then the other hand reached back and jerked at the entangling stirrup-loop. With the second jerk the imprisoned foot came free, and John the Wolf dropped with a dull thud to the dirt.

"Now by my hilt, if Wolf John be still alive, I vow a full score of tapers of purest wax to the altar of St. Thomas in Bewly," exclaimed Wat the Armorer. "For, rude and sour-spoken as he is, yet John hath ever been a good friend and a stout archer when arrows fly."

"Nor must we forget this Frenchman," added Robin softly. "For it was his quickness that saved John the Wolf. I will speak to Sir Allan Mayne, to see if telling of this deed to the Lord Constable may win for this Frenchman the freedom that he merits."

He started hurrying toward the archer, thinking that at the very least they would have broken bones to mend. But amazingly enough rugged John was already hobbling to his feet, feeling of this limb and then that. After which he began to utter such a great bellow of curses as no man with a damaged skull could have bethought him.

Then from the Armorer, striding behind, came a surprised grunt, and a dry chuckle. "Nay, there is no need now to put in word with the Lord Constable for this Frenchman. For luck, the villein is even now attending to that little matter himself!"

Even as Robin looked, the Frenchman with startling swiftness had caught up the dragging neck-rope, looped it around the horse's muzzle and then his own left wrist. Then at a single bound and without even touching stirrup loop, he was astride the horse. He spun the animal around on its haunches. Disdaining to toe the stirrups, he drummed the steed's ribs with his heels, at the same time fetching him a great blow athwart his rump.

And before the dazed guards could reach for weapons, prisoner and horse were racing away across the uneven ground, clearing rocks and logs with mighty leaps.

"Now truly yon is a stout villein, e'en though he be a Frenchman and our enemy," exclaimed Wat the Armorer admiringly. "It is sad to see such a fearless man ride to his death. For see he rides straight for the river which no man could hope to swim, even an he survive the leap from yonder rocky bank!"

"Even should he enter the swift water alive, there is yet the crossing to be done," agreed Robin. "For Hubert and Peter Joy have bow in hand and arrows already notched, and they are deadly sure at twice the distance."

BY NOW the rider was charging with unabated speed to the very brink of the high rocks that rose almost sheer from the river's edge. Without so much as a backward glance, and with only a yell and a pull of the neck rope to lift the animal's head, the Frenchman hurtled from the rock, out and toward the boulder-studded rapids beneath. Robin's breath caught in his throat, as he strained his eyes for a glimpse of emerging horse or man.

And then he let out the pent-up breath in a little sigh. Far out in the foaming rapids a black shape had emerged, and then another. Swimming beside the struggling steed and guiding him by stirrup and neck-rope, the Frenchman was urging him on with encouraging shouts.

The guards came out of their daze then, and rushed toward the bank. But even as they gained it and notched their shafts, horse and man had scrambled out onto the farther bank. Bounding once more onto the animal's back, the Frenchman gave one last defiant shout, and the next moment was vanishing into the fringing forest.

Wat the Armorer shook his head, and spat. "If all the French knights and men-at-arms show as stout heart as this one villein, then our work is well cut out for us, I wot."

Robin's brow was wrinkled and thoughtful. "Didst note the way he rode without stirrups, and mounted at a single bound? It is strange that a villein of the fields should ride so well. And equal strange that a villein's plow horse should prove so mettlesome. I have a desire to inquire of John Wolf where he got such an animal."

But the gaunt archer, groaning and grunting as he counted the full meed of his scratches and bruises, only grinned sheepishly at the question.

"Had I known that it was Satan's own horse, I would have let him burn to his bones ere I led him out. But glancing at the crone's hut, yester-eve, while you were bickering with hobilars,

I did glimpse a little shed built onto it behind, and through a crack of the shed this horse's tail waving. So I did but creep back and lead him out, and hide him behind yonder woody copse until this morn."

Wat the Armorer scowled. "How now, art tired of being an honest bombardier and wouldst turn plundering hobilar?"

John the Wolf grinned even more sheepishly. "Nay, but it seemed a shame to leave all findings to these hobilars for no reason save they ride horseback and uncover all the loot before we men afoot can even come up.

"I did but reckon on keeping the animal to hand so that I might ride about and so perchance uncover some little thing before the hobilars. Not two days agone, so I heard, Will o' the Fens did catch a fleeing mercer with purse containing no less than twenty gold nobles."

"Hereafter you were better off to leave horses and pillage to the hobilars and keep to thy bombard and archer's arrows," said Robin, laughing. "But how comes it, Hubert, that you loosed not a single shaft at the Frenchman, e'n though he rode within half arrow-flight? And you too, Peter Joy?"

Red Hubert scratched his carroty noggin and closed one eye. "In truth I could not say. Except that when I drew shaft on the villein's back I could see naught but this howling old Wolf here, kicking and bounding; and so, strangely enough, my fingers would not let go their hold upon the shaft."

Peter Joy, too, looked somewhat embarrassed. "Even as Hubert says, my shaft refused to fly. But that may be because I had not even nocked it, much less drawn taut the string."

CHAPTER IV

SABLE CHAMPION

FOR TWO DAYS the *gynours* toiled in the mire before they
made the road solid enough for footing. Then once more Robin
set his bombard carts a-rolling, and so creaked across the marsh
and into the higher country on the farther side. And once again
the army spread out over the fair land, harrying and burning.

But now the Armorer's words seemed to have been spoken
with omen, for no longer did the raiders burn with impunity.
A band of hobilars, riding carelessly into a seemingly deserted
village, found a wolf-trap instead. Riddled with quarrels from
hidden crossbowmen, and then over-ridden and cut to pieces
by sudden charge of mailed horsemen concealed behind the
houses, they were lucky to ride back with one-tenth their origi-
nal number.

The news was brought to the bombadiers by Sir Allan Mayne
himself, the captain of the Masterless Men of whom the archer
escort was part. The young knight's face was aglow with excitement as he recounted the occurrence.

"Now we may find braver work for our swords than flesh-
ing them on witless villeins of the fields. For rumor hath it that
the leader of the ambuscade was none other than Bertrand du
Guesclin, than whom there is no stouter knight in all France."

"Du Guesclin!" exclaimed Robin. "Then I am glad the Prince
set you and the Masterless Men from the New Forest to be our
escort, in place of the Butcher de Brenn. For sooner would the
Butcher see us bombardiers cut to bits by this du Guesclin than
saved by any effort of his own."

Sir Allan's face clouded. "De Brenn is not the only baron in
our force who hates these bombards and their vomiting stone
balls, for the hurt they may do to chivalry. But I think you, as

well as my own forest men, may nurse your hate for de Brenn
too well. As Lord Warden of the New Forest, it was Baron de
Brenn's duty to render swift punishment to aught who poached
the King's deer."

"And never did the gibbet chains clank such constant music as
when the Butcher ruled the Forest!" said Wat the Armorer tartly.
"But, since you are our escort captain, what post in the army has
the Butcher now? An advanced and dangerous one, I hope."

"He hath been put in full charge of all the hobilars," answered
Sir Allan, laughing.

"And for once a fitting post!" retorted the Armorer. "For
pillage and plunder is more to the Butcher's liking, methinks,
than honest battle. He will be one of a feather with Will o' the
Fens and these other murdering hobilars."

AT THAT moment a thudding of hooves and a rattle and
clanking of armor told of a new arrival on their flanks. A troop
of almost two score full-mailed knights and squires was coming
up at a gallop. Seeing the golden field and scarlet pile on the
shield of the leader, Robin recognized him at a glance as Sir John
Chandos, reckoned as the best soldier in all England. Reining
up before the creaking bombard carts, the scarred veteran waved
a greeting to Sir Allan.

"You are well come, Sir Allan, with these carts. I am minded
for a little time to ride not over-far from these bombards. For I
wot that they may make excellent bait for the Frenchmen. Bait
that might trap Bertrand du Guesclin into fair encounter. And I
would deem it greater glory to cross blades with this Du Guesclin than with any other knight in all Christendom!"

"And may that glory be all thine and none of mine," muttered
Red Hubert who had come up just in time to overhear. "Bait for
the Frenchmen—bah!"

Robin turned in quick alarm lest the words have reached the
ears of Sir John Chandos who was as noted for his quick temper
as for his deeds of arms. But Sir John had already put spurs to

his mount and was galloping off to the east, his whole troop clattering at his heels.

Sir Allan's face was sober, however, as he turned back to Robin.

"You would be well advised if you set double-watch hereafter, and marched with bombards full charged and braziers lighted. For this du Guesclin is a doughty fighter, even as Sir John hath said, and gives little mercy to any Englishman he catches. When our supports reached the village where he ambushed the hobilars, they found no wounded there—only dead hobilars strung by their necks from ridgepoles and eaves."

"And mercy enough for hobilars, if Will o' the Fens is fair example," grunted Wat the Armorer. "I would have cast him alive to burn in the crone's hut, had I been Frenchman and he fallen prisoner into my hands."

Nevertheless they marched with redoubled caution after that. And well it was they did, for blow after blow the Frenchmen now struck, on this flank first, and then the other, making swift assaults and then riding away before stronger forces could come up to withstand them.

Alarm that was almost panic ran along the army, and it was rumored that the French were in league with the Devil himself. For had not three good Wessex knights been found pinned inside their armor, pierced through hauberk and burgeon and even shield itself by great four-foot shafts, yet not so much as a catapult or placement had been found in the place of ambuscade afterward?

So on the fourth day, finding before them another smokeless, deserted little village, Robin drew up his lead cart and rallied all the others around him.

"Look closely to bombards and braziers," he called to Red Hubert and Peter Joy and John the Wolf. "An we be bait, just such an innocent place as this would be well set for a trap."

"Nay," pointed out Wat the Armorer, "for see, yonder come Sir John Chandos and his men-at-arms in full sight. If there be any Frenchmen ambuscade in yon village, they will take caution at the sight and unspring the trap while they may yet flee."

"If trap it be, then better it is for us to bide here till Sir John's horsemen have unset the teeth," answered Robin prudently. Then he gave an exclamation. "And trap it truly was!"

FROM OUT the silent village ahead had suddenly ridden a compact little group of strange horsemen. Not more than a score in number were they, yet they advanced a little way and halted, lances in rest, as if fearless of Sir John's double force. These latter, at sight of the Frenchmen, gave loud shouts and set spurs to their chargers.

"Trap it may be, but its teeth will tear the Frenchmen's hides, and not ours," grunted Wat the Armorer. "Sir John's double score will make short shrift of them in the mêlée."

"I like it not," said Robin. "Quick! Swing the carts around till each bombard bears to the front. Then drop the tail gates and make sure that each firing skewer is red-hot and sputtering!"

But at that moment, from out the little troop of Frenchmen rode a single horseman. Full armed he was, from crested haume to solleret and spurs. Yet no hint of pennon fluttered at his lance tip, nor so much as a single device flaunted from his rich surcoat or breasted shield. Sable of arms and sable of steed, he sat there, a solitary and challenging figure, with none of his troop nearer than a dozen lance-lengths.

Seeing this, Sir John Chandos gave signal for his own followers to halt, and himself rode out alone in the van. Robin could hear the knight's voice calling to his squire.

"My eyesight is not as keen as it onetime was, Peyton, for I can not read this Frenchman's blazoning. Yet it is evident that he challenges to single combat, which is proof that he is thirsty for honor even as ourselves." And then he raised his voice eagerly. "Before we ride this course, Sir Knight. I would fain know thy name and title, for the greater glory of the tilt."

But the sable-armed Frenchman made no reply except to settle himself more solidly in the saddle.

At Robin's ear, Red Hubert's voice came sour and scornful, "Enemy he knows the Frenchman is, what more does he ask? Why do they not get at their bickering and have done with it?"

But Sir John waited another moment, and then called again. "I would also ask thy choosing—whether we run a single tilt with the lance before the general mêlée, or battle to the *outrance*, with sword and ax as well as lance, and afoot as well as ahorse?"

Again there was no answer from the Frenchman, unless it was his significant loosening of the great battle-ax that hung thonged at his pommel.

However, Sir John seemed to find that answer enough, for his voice rose clear and content. "Now I could well love thee for that, Sir Knight, e'en though you keep secret your lineage. To the *outrance* then it is—and glory to him that can win it!"

HE SETTLED his lance firm in couch, dropped its point, and drove deep his spurs. The strange knight in sable was no less prompt. Fair between the two troops they met, with such a thunder-crash of hooves on ground and steel on shield that it seemed no living man could withstand it.

Yet so true had each lance struck that they brake each in splinters and, though they reeled to the shock, each knight thundered on and past the other, only to jerk rein and whirl about at the end of the course. Casting aside their broken lances, they seized other weapons—Sir John his heavy, three-foot sword, the Frenchman his battle-ax.

Now they circled, stirrup to stirrup, dealing each other such buffets that the clang was like hammer on anvil. Yet so deft were they with blow and parry, and so evenly matched, that gashed shields and dented helms were the only visible signs of injury.

"Now if this be war, it is likewise foolishness," said Red Hubert testily. "That black charger's trappings fall to the fetlock, but I doubt me not that Peter and I and the Old Wolf here could sift an arrow through—or even between the rider's gusset-piece and burgeon. Then Sir John could make short work of the downed Frenchman. What say you, Old Wolf?"

"No shaft of mine will I loose, to lighten the blows on any knight's headpiece," growled John the Wolf. "Sir John would use us for bait, would he? Then let him gaff his own fish now that he has caught it. And a fighting fish this Frenchman is. Look, our man has already lost his shield!"

In truth, whether through accident or unusual force or cunning of blow, the Frenchman's ax had landed fairly at last, and with such strength that Sir John's shield was riven through from chief to foot, leaving the worthless halves a-dangle.

At that the remaining Frenchmen set up a yell of triumph which quickly changed to astonishment and dismay. For dropping the useless shield, Sir John had suddenly sprung from his saddle onto his opponent clutching him around the neck and dragging him to the ground where they both rolled over and over, slashing at each other with both battle-ax and poniard.

As if that were a signal, the waiting English knights spurred their mounts and hurtled forward, lances glinting. The Frenchmen charged to meet them, so that they crashed in a turmoil of man and horse and steel wherein the individual fighters were instantly lost in clouds of dust.

Exciting as was the combat, however, Robin did not center his eyes wholly upon it, but kept them roving constantly, suspiciously, over the terrain roundabout. Well it was that he did, for suddenly he started, gave a loud shout.

The sloping shoulder of a copsed hill a little way to the west had suddenly come a-bristle with gleam and glint of polished arms. And around the copse and over the hill-shoulder burst a full four score of Frenchmen. They hurtled triumphantly down upon the flank of the unsuspecting English knights.

DESPERATELY ROBIN shouted his orders. "Peter—Hubert—John! Quick to thy cart-wheels and slew them around! Point them to that low hut which marks the westward edge of the village. And that moment when you first glimpse horse and rider adown the bombard tube, thrust deep the firing skewers down the touch-holes! With good aim we may surprise yon Frenchmen e'en as they thought to surprise us!"

Even as he tugged at the wheel of his bombard cart, however, Wolf John let out a pleased chuckle. "Now mayhap our fire-eating Chandos may get his belly full of fighting, and more. He was over-quick to use us as bait, and now he is but the rat in the trap himself!"

"Hold tongue, fool, and save strength for thine own task!" retorted Red Hubert.

"An these Frenchmen over-ride our own knights they will be upon us next!"

Already the oncharging French were nearly up to the spot Robin had chosen. Then, running his eyes along the cast tube of his own bombard, Robin saw the front wave of the horsemen surging past it. Jerking the redhot skewer from the brazier that the Armorer held, he plunged it into the touch-hole and deep into the powder beneath.

But to his amazement there came no bellowing thunder, no belching smoke and flame, no jerk and crash of rebound. Instead there came only a slow hissing, and a murky wisp of smoke spurted from the touch-hole and curled skyward. The stone ball rolled out of the muzzle and hopped lazily onto the ground to stop within a dozen yards, while from the bombard's muzzle came more of that same slow hissing and wreathing smoke as had come from the touch-hole.

As for Red Hubert's bombard, it did not take life at all; it remained like a dead thing, even though the giant archer damned it with oaths and thrust on the skewer so hard that the slender rod bent beneath his fingers. Only from the bombard of John the Wolf, furthest of the three, did there come any real semblance of explosion. And that was only half-hearted at best.

There was more of smoke from the muzzle than of flame, and the muffled explosion threw the ball only halfway to the charging foe, so slowly that it might have been hurled by a rain-soaked ballista rope. In fact, so short the ball fell, and so muffled was the explosion, that the Frenchmen gave it no heed; without halt or swerve they continued their headlong charge upon the English knights.

With a crash they drove into the mêlée with such force that horses and horsemen were hurled sideways like nine-pins, and friend and foe alike overborne by the charge.

"The powder—it has spoiled, it has become ruined by weather!" panted Robin, shaking his head in bewilderment and dismay, "Yet how can it be wetted, since there has been no rain?"

"The reason is of small matter, so long as we know that it is ruined," said Red Hubert. He had leaped from his cart and was already snatching the long, goose-feathered shafts from his quiver. His freckled face was smiling with contentment.

"Bombards and their devil's powder may be well enough in their way, but to an old archer there is naught so sweet as the pull of an honest yew-stave in the fingers, and the whistle of the shaft upon the wing! Eh, Old Wolf?"

"Now it is thy tongue that is wagging, when there is better work to be done," retorted the gaunt archer as he likewise notched an arrow to the string. "At this range a man needs not even test for windage!"

Swiftly came the twang of his bowstring and the whistle of the barbed death. Red Hubert and Peter Joy were not whit slower. Struck between frontlet and body trapping, the mount of the nearest Frenchman screamed and went to its knees, plummeting its rider over its head. The second horse plunged and kicked, swerving out and wide of the mêlée.

But John the Wolf's arrow, not a hair's breath off its mark, struck home in the unprotected armpit of a French knight who had just raised his battle-ax to strike. With a convulsive jerk, the chevalier raised almost stiff-legged in his stirrups before toppling over and underneath the churning hooves.

CHAPTER V

BEWARE GOOD ENGLISH YEW

EVEN SO, THE outnumbered English were being beaten down and borne under, when the archers of the bombard escort came up at the run and ranged themselves in line with the bombards.

Jerking arrows from their quivers, they thrust them, barb down, into the earth at their toes, so that before each bowman the feathered ends thrust up waist high. Thus it was not necessary for any man to lower bow or give so much as a downward glance as he plucked each new shaft to replace the one just loosed.

The rounded helms and full-forged mail of the French chevaliers were of stoutest steel, so that any but the best-aimed shafts would glance away, but there were bowmen among the New Forest men who could bring down flying eagles on the wing. An upraised arm or misplaced ailette gave sufficient target for an arrow.

As for the Frenchmen's chargers, they were vulnerable at every swirl or ripple of their trappings. Even before a new shout gave Robin notice of the arrival of Sir Allan Mayne at the head of other archers and a score of pikemen in half-mail, the Frenchmen were beginning to lose heart for the fray, to rein their chargers out of the mêlée as speedily as they might.

Seeing the first signs of retreat, John the Wolf suddenly cast down his bow with an oath.

"Stay thy hand, Hubert, thou great ox. Or shoot at the riders and not at the horses, if thou must! For there are already horses for each of us, and more. And I have my eye on one e'en now that I swear no hobilar shall have!"

So saying, he drew his archer's knife, and with no other

protection than steel cap and archer's jerkin, he went leaping toward the stricken field. After one grunted oath, Red Hubert followed after, and Peter Joy came racing at Hubert's heels.

Sir Allan had set spurs to his horse and with a shout had hurled himself into the battle. But the French waited no longer. Those that were still ahorse rode off over the hill from which they had come.

There was no pursuit. Of the English no more than a scant half-dozen remained ahorse, and even those were battered and exhausted, as much from the stifling weight of their armor as from the blows they had taken and given.

Some were sore wounded; others lay in the crumpled sprawl of death. But Robin and Sir Allan were amazed and pleased to recognize the dusty and battered figure of Sir John Chandos stumbling amid the dead and wounded.

THEN, GLANCING toward the bombards, Robin perceived that the three archers had captured three warhorses with emptied saddles. Robin turned to meet them, his brow still furrowed and gloomy over the failure of the bombards. But John the Wolf was grinning with pleasure.

"Now we shall be as ready as any hobilar," he exclaimed. "Not only have we the means of riding into likely French villages, but the means as well for carrying away whatsoever we may find of worth therein. For I see Peter and Hubert here have been as lucky as I."

Hubert laughed. "All we had to do was to lay hand to the dragging reins of these beasts as they ran loose about the field. How got you that wicked looking steed you lead, Old Wolf? Methought you had had enough of such snorting beasts!"

The gaunt archer grinned. "In truth there was a battered Frenchman hanging to the reins and striving to mount, when I came upon him. But this Frenchman was so hammered in the mêlée that he over-toppled at the first push I gave him, though it was of no more force than to up-end a child. So I had naught to do but take up the reins and lead the beast here, e'en as you have seen."

"You had the rider to hand, and let him go free with no more than a posh?" exclaimed Peter Joy. "Hast forgot that a Frenchman may bring a goodly ransom?"

"And no ordinary Frenchman, by this figured saddle and these trappings!" added Red Hubert.

"What of it? Butcher de Brenn or some other knight would have taken him from me had he been of worth, even as they took from us that French *comte* at Caen," answered John the Wolf imperturbably. "Let them catch their own prisoners, an they want them. Also there was another reason. See you nothing strange about this horse?"

Red Hubert took another look and uttered an exclamation of surprise. "It is that very devil-horse that threw and nigh dragged you to death at the river, Old Wolf! Had not that lusty prisoner villein freed you, you would not be been standing here now."

"Aye, the same horse," said Wolf John. "And this rider of his that I let go—he had that same villein's long arms and barn-door shoulders, for surely not even in France could there be two sets of shoulders of such width!" He squinted one eye, and spat. "Now we are quits—he of me, and I of him."

"Since the Frenchmen are all gone and the afternoon already grows late," said Robin, "yon village seems a pleasant place to bivouac for the night. There will be shelter and, mayhap, water and grain for our horses as well. So tie your animals behind the carts and we will drive on into the village."

WITHIN THE hour they had the wagon teams unharnessed and fed, and a great fire roaring for their own evening meat, which Wat the Armorer set himself to cooking over the coals.

Red Hubert left to search among the deserted houses for any skulking enemy, and shortly thereafter Peter Joy and John the Wolf slipped away likewise, under pretense of fetching more wood and water, though oddly their footsteps died away toward the battlefield rather than toward the other houses.

Robin Santerre poked and prodded at the bombards, frowning worriedly, and he knelt to sniff at the muzzles and touch-holes. All at once he clambered into one of the wagons and, rolling out a powder cask, fetched it into the light of the fire and carefully broached it.

Dipping a handful of the powder from the top, he peered at it for a long moment before he dumped it in a little heap upon a flat board. Then he scraped forth a live coal from the cook-fire and dropped it onto the heaped grains.

But instead of taking fire with quick flash and flame, the powder merely sizzled and charred, sending up thick smoke and rank odor as the fire crept slowly along.

"Nay, we already know that it is spoiled and weakened," said Wat the Armorer. "Mayhap water has somehow gotten into it, even as it did aboard the ship when we crossed the Channel."

"Not water—for see, it is dry!" exclaimed Robin. Without waiting for answer, he dug his other hand deep into the cask once more, even to the bottom. And clutching a handful of the very bottom grains, he likewise examined them critically before scattering them on the board.

"Weakened it is, but not spoiled. Not spoiled for good, Wat! Look how the powder at the top of the cask is all black, and this from the bottom of the cask is gray and yellow. Yet in the first compounding it was all of a mixture. Do you not see?"

The armorer shook his head. "All I see is that it is still weakened and worthless."

"The coarse black on the top is the charcoal, Wat! Being lighter, it has lifted to the top in the jolting over the road, whereas the sulphur and the brimstone, being finer and heavier, have sifted to the bottom, I doubt not that the charges in the bombards separated from their compounding in like manner. Scant wonder is it that the powder sizzled and charred, instead of taking fire with speed and force."

The Armorer scratched his head. "Then what Sir John Chandos claimed is true—that bombards are better suited for engines of siege than for the field. For only by fresh compounding before each firing can we be sure that the grains will be well mixed, and in proper proportion."

But Robin shook his head, his eyes sparkling. "I remember that the wetted powder on board ship, when it dried, formed itself into little lumps in which the charcoal, sulphur, and brimstone were equally mixed. Here, give me a drop of water in my palm!"

Then into the wetted palm he dropped pinches of the powder both from the top and bottom of the cask. After mixing it well, he spread it out in little lumps on the board to dry.

Warmed by the heat of the cooking fire, the lumps took but a little while to dry. And this time, when Robin touched them with the glowing coal, each little lump vanished in a flash of flame and *whoosh* of spurting smoke.

"We have but to mix it wet and then dry it again in such little lumps," said Robin. "And I have another thought, too. If we measure it out beforehand, just enough for each bombard charge, and then sew each charge up tightly in a little sack, we will not have to measure each ladle into the bombard afterward every time we charge it. With a score of these charges already sacked, we can load and fire five times faster than we did before!"

"And good news, that, for honest men, but small comfort to the knights and barons," said Wat the Armorer. "For it hastens the day when common men with such bombards may overthrow all the armored knights that ride. I will bid Hubert look for linen or other cloth in these houses when he searches."

BUT ALREADY the giant archer was returning, and on his face was a puzzled expression. "Come with me," he said to Robin and Wat, "for behind this furthest house is somewhat that is great puzzle to me."

Going with him, they rounded the last house corner and then halted in amazement.

There, with two horses still hitched to it by harness, stood a curious thing on wheels. It had a long trough-like body, with two great poles protruding from either side, and a maze of ropes extending from poles to trough.

Robin let out a long breath. "A catapult! And not a fixed catapult for placement, but mounted on wheels for quick moving! Mayhap this is the very catapult that spitted those Wessex knights with its shafts, and then vanished as if on wings!"

"And look to the bowstring, and this cunning mesh of ropes and tackle-blocks," cut in the armorer admiringly. "Instead of an unwieldy windlass to be slow-cranked by men, the artillerymen have but to hook on yon horses to this tackle, and so draw taut the bowstring to its rigger in one tenth the time."

"The leader of these Frenchmen must be not only a keen soldier, but an ingenious man as well," agreed Robin.

He gazed again critically at the machine. "Even thus I had it in mind to mount the bombards. With a light frame and such strong wheels as these mounted directly under our bombard sledges, we would do away with the whole weight of the heavy carts, And with two horses harnessed to each bombard frame, we could maneuver as quickly as they moved this catapult. Think you that you could build such frames, Wat?"

The armorer nodded. "With the wheels from the carts, and the timbers from these houses, it would not be an over-hard task. Lucky we reached here before the hobilars, before they burned the village to the last roof-tree. I will set about it at cock-crow in the morning."

Returning to the fire, they found Sir Allan Mayne and Sir John Chandos there. Smelling the sputtering meat, the knights had been glad to stop and break their fasts. Despite the battering he had received in the mêlée, Sir John was in high spirits over the victory.

THEN OUT of the gathering dusk stumbled Peter Joe and John the Wolf. The gaunt archer's grumbling traveled even ahead of his feet.

"We had thought to search the battlefield for any good sword or armor or other little thing of worth. But Butcher de Brenn with Will o' the Fens and his accursed hobilars were there before us. Even now they are quartering the field like greedy wolves. So that all we found was his." He threw something heavy and clattering to the ground.

"A shield and an over-battered one at that." Wat the Armorer pushed it carelessly with his foot. "How did it chance that the hobilars did not get it before you?"

"Because it was in a little hollow off to one side, for one thing," said John the Wolf. "And for another thing they knew not it was there—which I did, seeing that it belonged to that same Frenchman from whom I took the horse."

"A shield all sable, and without blazon or quartering." Sir John Chandos stared at it. "That is strange." He took it up, studied it, and then with a quick cry drew his poniard and slashed its point across the shield. Whereupon the mystery was clear, for the black cloth that had been fastened across the shield's face came away in strips, revealing the bright lines of the quarterings and charges underneath.

At sight of them Sir John Chandos gave an even louder cry, and whirled on John the Wolf.

"Where found you this shield, archer? Quick with thy answer!"

"Where found I it? Why where its owner, the Frenchman, dropped it when I took his horse, e'en as I told you but a moment agone," answered the archer testily. "If you doubt me, you have but to regard the horse which is still tied to that cart over there. For the daubings on its saddle are the same as on this shield."

But Sir John was no longer heeding. "Du Guesclin!" he cried, turning to Sir Allan Mayne. "It was Bertrand du Guesclin himself with whom I tilted—and I knew it not!"

"Du Guesclin!" Sir Allan gaped with amazement. "Then we had him—"

Sir John Chandos' face fell. "Aye, he would have made a prize worth even the King's attention. For no Frenchman, unless it be King Philip himself, would have been so important or brought a greater ransom. If it be du Guesclin who faces us, we must haste with the news to the King and the Lord Constables at once!"

As they climbed to their saddles and clattered away, the bombardiers around the fire stared at each other wordlessly. The silence was broken by a great groan and a stream of curses from John the Wolf. Snatching off his steel cap, he beat himself with both fists over the bare head.

"In my hands—in my very hands, and I let him go! Ten thousand *livres*, mayhap twenty thousand! May I gut myself with my own arrow before I exchange quits with any other Frenchman!"

CHAPTER VI

THE RIVER OF JEOPARDY

BUT NOW WORD came of a threat even greater than a du Guesclin raiding the flank. For spurring messengers from the south brought news of a great French army there, full fifty thousand strong, marching up out of Aquitaine to fall upon the English.

Other messengers brought equally discomforting word that ahead, near Paris, King Philip was frantically collecting another great host including the King of Bohemia, the Duke of Lorraine, the Counts of Saarbrucken, Blamont, and Salm, and countless others with all their knights and levies.

Hearing which, Red Hubert gave a grunt. "Now mayhap there will be more war and less pillage, and the Butcher's hobilars will gather more blows than plunder. Certain it is that, an we stay here, we will be caught between these two huge armies like a nut between the pincers. Our King would do well to make haste back to the coast."

At Liseux, after sacking that pleasant city, King Edward did indeed change his line of march. But not back toward the Channel. Instead he headed almost due north, to the puzzlement of many.

It was Sir Allan Mayne who brought the explanation.

"We head toward the far north, toward Flanders, where our allies, the Flemishers, wait to join us in great force. With their help we may well withstand all that the French can bring against us."

"To Flanders, across all of France?" cried Robin. "But what of the two great rivers that lie between—the Seine and the Somme? For, if we fail to force the crossing of either, we are worse than rats in a trap!"

"Nonetheless to Flanders we go," answered Sir Allan grimly. "For me, after naught but burning and pillage, it would seem pleasant to find Frenchmen barring the way with knightly blows!"

"So said our old fire-eater, Sir John Chandos," said the red-headed archer. "And his head is still ringing, I wot, from those same knightly blows that he was so eager to exchange."

Toward the Seine, indeed, the army now marched. But arrived there, they found every bridge destroyed to its foundation, and the river itself too wide and deep to be forded. Scouting parties sent out to the left, toward the sea, brought back the same tale from there. There was naught to do but turn upstream where the river might narrow enough to be fordable. But upstream also meant directly toward Paris.

But still the news was all evil. At Elboeuf, the bridge was down, and the same at Mantes, and at Poissy. Even Sir Allan's face was gloomy, for Poissy was but one day's march short of Paris. And every messenger brought more alarming news about the vast army that was almost completely assembled there by now.

Although he sent his hobilars to burn St. Germain and St. Cloud, on the very outskirts of the French capital, Edward kept the main army all day in camp.

"Back we cannot go," said Sir Allan. "Cross this river we

cannot, for the bridge is burned. And to overthrow King Philip with his outnumbering French behind their own fortifications is beyond all hope."

"Then what remains that we can do?" growled John the Wolf.

"Why, naught remains but to make such a last fight as will be told about through all Christendom."

Red Hubert scowled. "A murrain upon it! I would liefer find a crossing and live to tell it myself, than be a dead hero told about even throughout Christendom!"

"Nay, there is no choice," said the knight, "for there is no crossing to be found."

Overhearing, Robin who had just come up from the river's side, caught his arm. "Come with me," he begged excitedly, "and see if you glimpse what methinks I do."

AT THE water's edge Sir Allan looked for a long time, and then shook his head. "I see nothing more than I have seen before."

"Not above the water, but beneath it," said Robin. "Stoop, and look close!"

And after that second glance, the knight started. "Piers—the stone foundations of a bridge!"

"Aye, and being stone they did not burn when the bridge burned," said Robin. "Could not our *gynours*, with timbers and felled logs, make shift to rebuild the bridge at least enough for our crossing?"

But already the knight was turning away with huge strides. "If they can, we may well escape this trap even now. Certain it is that word of your finding must be taken to the King at once."

And before noon the whole force of engineers was at work with hammer and maul and axe and saw, while archers and even knights and squires dropped bow and sword to lend a hand at dragging the great timbers. Only the hobilars were absent; the King had sent them out with orders to redouble their burning, that the smoke of the fired houses might make a curtain from prying French eyes.

A good curtain they made, for in the mid-afternoon two heralds came, with fanfare of trumpets, and with them a cardinal in full vestments. Met at the outskirts of the camp and so guided that they caught no sight of the river and the toiling *gynours*, they were led to the King's tent, and, shortly after that they went away again. A passing squire dropped the news in the bombardiers' ears.

"The cardinal was from the French King himself. King Philip, saying that we are caught in a trap without any escape, called upon our King to surrender, for the saving of needless bloodshed."

"And what said our King to that?" demanded Robin.

"He sent word back that we would never surrender without a battle, but that to save needless bloodshed he himself would gladly meet the King of France in single combat, the victor to gain both the crowns of England and France."

"Single combat, and to the *outrance?*" Red Hubert blinked. "Mayhap there is more courage underneath this clanking armor than I had given due."

"And mayhap," said Wat the Armorer dryly, "our King knows that he is much larger, stouter man than the King of France. Why did he not challenge the champion of all the French knights—this Bertrand du Guesclin, for instance?"

By now the *gynours* had assembled such a mass of timbers as seemed sufficient to make a footing for the whole bridge. And as soon as the evening shadows fell they were at work like beavers, standing to their waists and even necks in water as they laid and secured the great beams and planking.

So that by midnight the last plank was laid, and the van of the army already crossing. With a rumble and creaking, the bombards took the planks, the supply carts and then the great ballistae and other engines of siege following.

With the last cart and last man across, men were sent skipping back with torches to set to the new-laid timbers. As morning broke and the van of the French army, called by the smoke and flames, came up, nothing of the bridge remained but a seething line of fire.

At that the French sent up a great yell of rage and disappointment, lining the farther bank and shaking their fists.

Red Hubert grinned mirthlessly and shook his own fist in answer.

"Aye, curse!" he yelled. "Curse even louder, an it do you any good. For the same river that stopped us has now stopped you, and we are well away and safe."

But Wat the Armorer shook his head.

"Safe for twenty-four hours mayhap. But there are other bridges and fords in plenty up-river, beyond Paris, I doubt me not. And these Frenchmen will be up and crossed and hot after us ere we have gone a two-days' march."

THAT THE armorer had spoken truth was soon made evident, for on the second day scouting horsemen brought word that the French had crossed the river and were already in hot pursuit.

And now instead of a raid, the march of the English became a flight. A flight, toward the northern coast.

"And the Devil take the hindmost," grunted Red Hubert. "Or if not the Devil, at least this testy, hard-riding du Guesclin. And of the two, I am not sure I would not choose me the Devil."

Robin glanced with satisfaction at the bombards, now riding high and easily on the simple frames and tall wheels that the Armorer had built. "An the Frenchmen come up fast, our ballistae and heavy wagons in the siege train will be hard put to stay ahead. Lucky it is that we conceived these new bombard mounts."

But at that moment Sir Allan rode up with a troubled frown. "The King has ordered all the archers, including our New Forest Men, into the van. Bombards and bombardiers are to fall into the rear and march with the train."

"In the train?" John the Wolf snarled. "A knightly reward indeed for discovering the bridge piers and so providing a crossing! For with the French army raging up behind, the rear is the most perilous post of the march."

"And hence a far likelier place for the seizing of that Frenchman whom you are so eager to catch," said Red Hubert, grinning. "You may yet have chance to meet again with that du Guesclin who is worth twenty thousand *livres*." He turned to Sir Allan. "But if you and the forest men march in the van, who then will guard us and the train?"

"Five hundred picked men-at-arms," replied the knight. "Also de Brenn and his hobilars, since though mounted they are light-armed and hence quicker to ride against threatened raids."

"The Butcher de Brenn?" John the Wolf spat out an oath. "Now indeed my neck already begins to ache with the feel of the Frenchmen's gibbets. For the Butcher and Will o' the Fens would quicker desert us than guard us,"

"That may be," said Red Hubert, "but Will o' the Fens' neck will ache quicker than thine if du Guesclin catches him. So hold thy growl, Old Wolf, until there be somewhat to growl about."

Past Pontoise, Grisy, and Auneil the army raced, not even lingering to fire those luckless towns. Instead of five or six miles per day, the army was now averaging twenty. Full twenty of the heaviest carts that could not keep up with the pace were left behind.

Baron de Brenn rode past the next day with a black scowl on his face, the reason for which presently came to the bombardiers' ears. Full twenty hobilars who had sacked and burned the abbey of Beauvais had been summarily gibbeted by King Edward's orders.

"Ho!" grunted John the Wolf, "we gibbet our own hobilars for sacking and burning, do we? 'Tis strange how hot pursuing Frenchmen make good Christians of us all at once!"

"Nay, that is not the reason for the gibbeting." Wat the Armorer shook his head. "More likely it was that in the pillage these hobilars delayed the march."

THE FRENCHMEN were already hacking at the rear-guard

when the English reached the Somme at Pont-Remi. Knowing there was a bridge there, King Edward had already sent ahead a strong force of men-at-arms and archers to try to force the passage.

But the alarm had outsped the hurrying English, and they found such a strong force of Frenchmen from the nearby towns gathered on the opposite bank that the advance force was beaten back with over five hundred Englishmen killed or captured.

The bridge-heads and fords at Long-Pré and Picquigny proved likewise impregnable to assault. Like a wounded lion gnawing at his paws, King Edward turned left and along the Somme bank, looking vainly for a passage.

Looking at the over-widening river, Wat the Armorer shook his head. "Now we are in even worse trap than we were at Paris. For here the river is more than twice a-wide, and every bridge or ford is guarded on the opposite side by increasing bands of Frenchmen. Yet we cannot turn upstream where the river might be narrower, for that would but bring us full against the whole French army."

Only one comfort had the change in conditions brought to Robin. Now that the bombards traveled with the train, they were in among the siege wagons and the supply carts. And among the supply carts traveled the Flemish merchant, Jacob Algelt, and his black-eyed, red-lipped daughter, Katherine.

Strange as it was to find a pretty girl of sixteen marching with an invading army, her presence was no stranger than was the position of her father. For the bombards which Robin served were not the King's, nor were they any part of the national artillery.

They were the private property of the old Flemish merchant, from the bombard tubes down to the last ball and ounce of powder. At his own cost the merchant had had the bombards cast, the balls cut and the powder manufactured. Then as a private venture of profit rather than patriotism he had brought the weapons to England, hoping to sell them to King Edward for his war on France.

Yet so distrustful of these strange weapons were the King and leaders of the army that only because of the good word of the Black Prince had they consented to use them, and then only by lease until they had well proved their merits.

As for the girl, she was an only child, and whether her father had brought her with him because of this or because she would not remain behind, was more than Robin could say. Yet her knowledge of the weapons and the compounding of the powder, as even Wat the Armorer admitted, was greater than their own, and perhaps equal to her father's.

It was more than this, however, that set Robin's heart to pounding at every glimpse of her. From the first meeting, he had found the girl's sparkling eyes and red, laughing lips, more deadly even than the bombards themselves.

HENCE WHEN he found himself marching alongside the light, canvas-covered wagon in which the Flemishers rode and lived, he was taken again with that fierce pounding of the heart. Then the tarpaulin edges lifted, and the impish face of the girl looked out at him.

"You are well come," she cried in her odd Flanders accent, "for I had feared lest you perhaps had fallen behind and been taken."

At her seeming solicitude Robin felt the hot blood flushing his face, and so fell a-stammering. "Nay—nay, sweet lady. With Wat's tall wheels we have kept ahead of the French. And, praise God, I am here and safe."

Whereupon she laughed. "It was not *you* I worried about, Sir Captain—it was only the bombards!"

The tarpaulin fell between them once more, but behind it he could still hear her laughter, which in no way improved his feelings inasmuch as he knew Wat and Red Hubert had heard the talk.

"An a maid laughed at me like that," said the red-headed

archer, "I would buss her until she had no breath left for laughing, or else I would use a stout bowstave to the same effect."

Even the armorer smiled. " 'Tis pity that in those books of his which you studied at Oxford, Roger the Monk discoursed only of levers and powder, and mentioned naught of the even greater force that sometimes lies in a woman's eyes."

Since Robin could make no answer to that, he gave himself entirely to the progress of the bombards, calling so many orders and finding so much fault that the bombardiers changed their laughter to grumbling.

But when they halted at sunset to bivouac for the night, there were other and more important things to think on. For by now the river had widened until it was more than half a mile across, and so near to the sea had they come that they could see the black brine of the tide swirling on top of the water.

Wat the Armorer shook his head. "Now in truth I wot that we have come to the end. We are cornered between this great river and the sea itself, with the whole French army closing the way behind."

"Perhaps," said Robin, "the King has word of some hidden ford here, for surely he would not lead into such a trap with open eyes," Yet, glancing at the vast width of the river, he could not speak in aught but gloomy tones.

CROSSING TO the canvas-covered wagon, he called to the Flemisher inside. After a moment the merchant appeared, his skullcap perched above his grizzled locks and his black robe clutched tightly about his paunchy stomach.

"An the French attack us here," Robin said, "whip up your horses at once! Put as many wagons as possible between yourselves and the battle. And keep crouched well below the wagon sides, both thee and thy daughter, for shelter against arrows and crossbow quarrels."

The merchant's face whitened and his lips went thin. He moistened them nervously with little lickings of the tongue. "And what of you and the bombards?"

"I have plan to draw them up and facing outward," said Robin, "to wreak such destruction with them as we can. And, for that reason, I plan to double-charge them with two balls instead of one."

"Two balls? Double-charge?" Despite his fright the fat merchant let out a little cry of covetous dismay. "But the double-charge may burst them! They may be ruined. For they have never been proved against such great charge and weight of ball."

"Better that than being over-ridden and cut down," said Robin grimly, and he turned back to the bombards.

But, after swinging the guns around until they pointed outward, he had another thought.

"Not with two balls," he exclaimed to Hubert and Wat. "Double measure of powder, yes. But I mind me now how great was the injury to those crossbowmen at Caen when we did fire upon them that bag of gold coins which John the Wolf hid there after stealing it from the French count's herald. So charge each bombard with one ball, and on top of that ram home such arrowheads as you have in your pouches and to spare."

While they were doing this, there was a trampling of hooves, and Baron de Brenn rode by with two horsemen. One of the riders was Will o' the Fens, at sight of whom John the Wolf spat out a sour oath.

The other rider, though a Frenchman by his dress, rode not as a prisoner but with free rein. And his dark face wore, instead of alarm, a look of covetousness and greed. With spurred horses, the three rode hurriedly toward the King's tent.

No sooner were the bombards reloaded, then, than John the Wolf, with his habitual curiosity, was off to find what it was all about. He returned with his eyes glinting.

"It was as Robin said. Our King heard rumor that there was a ford somewhere near. So he spread word that he would give an hundred gold nobles to any man who would reveal the place. Will o' the Fens found this Frenchman, Gobin Agache, who claims to know the whereabouts of such a ford. So he and the butcher are hurrying the traitor to the King."

"Ho, ho!" jeered Red Hubert. "And the French traitor expects to live to spend this gold, with Will o' the Fens having knowledge of it? If so, he is fool as well as well as traitor! But there is a ford here, then?"

"Aye. It seems that the river hath a bar of chalky ledge running completely across. By reason of its white bottom the ford is known as *Blanche Taque*—the White Stones."

"It doth sound incredible," said the Armorer, gazing dubiously at the wide stretch of swirling water. "But if there be a ford, why do we not begin the crossing at once?"

"Because the King does not choose to venture the crossing in the dark, and also because the crossing is possible only at low tide. That will not be until tomorrow's dawn. But at that time, so this traitorous Frenchman holds, the tide will be so low that men afoot as well as on horseback may cross."

CHAPTER VII

TRUMPET TO BATTLE

ALL NIGHT LONG the army bivouacked, yet no man slept, feeling full well that the morrow might bring their last day on earth. And when at dawn they looked across the Somme, hope dropped low. For on the other side could be seen the glinting arms of thousands of Frenchmen, cavaliers as well as levies afoot.

Then the trumpets blared before the King's tent and mounted messengers spurred throughout the whole camp, ranging the army according to the King's orders. Five thousand archers with the pick of the knights and men-at-arms were to lead the way and try to overthrow the French defenders on the farther side. The rest of the army was to follow in order, with the hobilars bringing up the rear with the train.

"The Butcher's own idea, I wot!" grunted the Armorer. "Then if this du Guesclin falls upon us before we are all crossed, the Butcher will throw us and our bombards and the train wagons to him to save his own skin. For plunder is e'er a retarding device."

"Yet mayhap we are not so unlucky after all," said Robin. "Mayhap this French traitor leads the army into a trap so that, over their heads in water, they can be quickly cut to bits."

"Which would still have us behind in another trap." John the Wolf pointed with his hand. "But this French traitor will not out-live the trap, if trap it be. The King has left him with the hobilars to be the last man across. And at first sign of treachery they have order to pull his head from his shoulders!"

There indeed, among the hobilars, sat the French traitor between Butcher de Brenn and Will o' the Fens. But his reins were no longer free, for they were tight clutched by a grim man-at-arms. And another man-at-arms on the farther side kept tight hold on a hempen rope that was noosed around Gobin Agache's neck.

Now the cry of "Archers to the front!" was running down the line. Sir Allan Mayne waved as he rode past at the head of his Masterless Men from the New Forest, each man holding high his great bow that it not be wet and ruined by the water during the crossing.

Knee-deep and then waist-deep they waded into the river, the Irish and Welsh stabbers surging at their heels. And then with clank of metal and snort of chargers, the knights and men-at-arms followed.

"We will be lucky, an the water come not over our bombards and powder, and so wet them to their ruin," said Robin, as with troubled eyes he watched the deepening of the river around the archers' waists. "Peter Joy, do you see that the powder in the powder carts is piled on top of the balls and other stores to be as high out of water as possible.

"And do you all, when we start to cross with our bombards,

hold high your braziers and firing skewers, that they be not quenched in the crossing."

All this time the advance archers and horsemen were wading almost waist-deep. Then as they passed mid-stream, even as Gobin Agache had said, the water began to shallow. Whereupon the forest men let out a great shout and hurried forward, notching arrows to their bowstrings.

SO GREAT was the eagerness of the Frenchmen on the farther side, however, that they could wait no longer. Instead of holding back to charge the English as they slipped and scrambled up the river bank, the French knights spurred recklessly into the water to meet them.

Which was a grievous mistake, for the archers shot not at them but at their mounts. The animals, stung if not deadly-stricken by the barbs, plunged and pitched with such force that many unseated their riders. Pulled down by their heavy armor, these latter sank like so much lead; many a good knight drowned in that moment without either having received or struck an actual blow.

Having loosed a half-dozen shafts each, the archers now spread apart to let the men-at-arms behind them ride through. These, with ready ax and sword, fell upon the already shaken French chevaliers and cut them down or drove them ahead in full rout.

Meantime the archers had started shooting anew, but now they aimed their shafts at the French crossbowmen and foot levies who still stood in battle array on the bank. Riddled by a rain of shafts, these levies fell in windrows, or else threw away bows and pikes as they fled in wild panic.

All this the bombardiers had watched with keen excitement from the other bank, John the Wolf even standing up on top of his high bombard seat. "The crossing is won!" he cried. "The Frenchmen break and run, our men after them! I can see Tyrrel—Sir Allan—"

"Turn thy eyes the other way, and see if you can catch glimpse of du Guesclin behind us which is more to the point," growled Wat the Armorer. "The army is almost across safely, but we are still on this side with du Guesclin and the whole French army. Ha! said I not so?"

Even as he spoke, from the rising land to the south came the loud thunder of galloping hooves, and then a great shout. Immediately after there broke over the slope a flashing wave of men and horses, the gleam of swords and lance-tips making a white crest to the wave. With yells of rage at sight of their quarry escaping almost under their noses, the French horsemen drove down on the hobilars and the train. Out in front on a great red charger rode a knight in sable mail.

With one glance at that charging horde, Robin spun about with terror in his face. But it was terror for someone else, and not for himself.

Then hope sprang anew as he sighted close to him the canvas-covered wagon. Standing up in it, frantically lashing the reluctant horses into the river, was the old merchant, Jacob Algelt. And clinging to the seat beside him, her hair flowing behind her but her eyes sparkling with excitement, rode Katherine.

"Into the water and whip them on across!" shouted Robin encouragingly. "We will remain with the hobilars and hold them off as long as we may!"

"Which will not be long, if we wait for the hobilars!" said Wat.

"Nay, the hobilars will not wait for us, so I will not wait for them!" John the Wolf cursed, and laid his cracking lash to the team drawing his bombard. With a jerk and a jolt the animals surged forward, dragging the bombard carriage at a run down the bank and into the water.

So unexpected was the jerk that the gaunt archer was hurled from his perch. Clawing at empty air, he spun head over heels, to land with a thud in the dirt. Limping and cursing, he rose to his feet and stared wildly about him.

"THIS WAY, John! This way!" shouted Robin, with his heart in his throat. For the rushing wave of horsemen had burst over and through the outlying wagons like a giant comber, and everywhere mailed men thrust and slashed at the fleeing wagoners. Full upon John the Wolf were driving a score of Frenchmen, at their head the sable-armed knight on the great red horse.

"Curse this bow!" Red Hubert was gasping, and out of the corner of his eye Robin could see the red-headed archer clawing for quiver and bow which he had slung over his back to have freer hand with his reins.

Now the giant Frenchman was standing in his stirrups, his gleaming battle-ax already uplifted for the blow. Yet John the Wolf stood frozen in his tracks, the dazed look still on his face as he turned it, bare and unprotected, up toward the Frenchman.

But the blow never fell. Almost at the last moment, the Frenchman suddenly dropped his hand, swerved the great roan with knee and wrenching hand on the reins, and hurtled on past toward de Brenn and his hobilars.

The shock of his passing seemed to bring John the Wolf out of his daze, for he suddenly let out a yelp and dodged like a hare beset by hounds.

Twisting and ducking, he threaded between the chevaliers, so that only the outermost one got a fair stroke at him. The stroke did not land, for just as it was being delivered a belated arrow from Red Hubert cut the horse out from between the Frenchman's knees.

"This way, John—this way!" shouted Robin again. Turning, the gaunt archer raced that way, ending in a bound that landed him breathless and clawing atop the bombard muzzle.

Simultaneously Robin felt his own arm gripped, heard the armorer's voice in his ear. "Hold fast, Robin! There is naught more we can do here now and we have our own skins to save!"

With the words came the crack of the whip as Wat laid the lash to the horses. Bouncing and jolting, the bombard rattled down the slope and into the water. Almost wheel to wheel raced Red Hubert's bombard as the red-headed archer plied the whip.

They were axle deep in the river before Robin caught his

breath and had time to glance around. Then he realized the truth of what the armorer had said.

Besides the bombards and their companion carts with the powder and ball which Peter Joy was urging on ahead, only half a dozen other wagons out of the whole train had escaped. But Robin's heart leaped as he recognized one of these, just a half-length ahead and to the right: it was the canvas-covered wagon, with the old merchant lashing the horses, and Katherine Algelt clinging at his side.

Then, grunting and panting, John the Wolf came clambering along the rocking bombard to the seat where Robin and Wat sat. To Robin's amazement he still had his bow clutched tight in one hand. He grinned sourly as he looked at it.

"I knew not that I still held it until just now, and then it was too late to throw it away."

"You may find good use for it yet," said Wat the Armorer. "For did I not say the Butcher and these hobilars would not stay to risk their skins for ours? Look!"

ROBIN SAW de Brenn and over half of his hobilars spurring and urging their horses along in the water. Nor was that all. Back at the bank the Frenchmen had begun to spur into the water and splash after them.

John the Wolf cursed, but it was at the hobilars and not at the French. "Now by my bow, if I were not still shaking from the nearness of that black Frenchman's ax, I would send a whole quiver of shafts among these cowards a-horseback!" he cried. "They pause not even to make a rearguard fight."

But heedless of the curses, the hobilars and de Brenn spurred on past and continued to press their mounts toward the farther side.

Wat the Armorer grunted. "Mayhap there is some justice to it, after all. For you glimpsed, did you not, that Will o' the Fens and the traitorous Frenchmen were not among these that got away?"

Robin Santerre, however, was not concerned with hobilars

nearly so much as with the pursuing Frenchmen who were already splashing stirrup-deep in pursuit.

"Hand the brazier and firing skewer to Wolf John here," he ordered the Armorer, "and do you splash over and give hand to Hubert with his bombard. If those Frenchmen gain much closer on us, we will e'en see if these bombards will fire in water as well as on land."

With John the Wolf fanning the brazier, and with the Armorer atop the other bombard seat alongside Red Hubert, Robin caught a moment's breath. But then to his right and almost abreast of him he saw the Flemisher's canvas-covered cart.

Whether his horses had been frightened by the water, or whether they had been confused by the wild screams of the driver, Robin could not tell. But they were losing ground, and bade fair to stop stubbornly where they stood in mid-stream.

The old merchant, his robe flying in the wind, was plying the whip with desperate curses, and casting terrified glances back at the oncoming Frenchmen behind. But the girl Katherine smiled and even loosed one hand to send a wave to Robin.

"Praise be to God, you are still here and safe!" she cried. "And this time I mean thee and not the bombards—"

Then Robin saw her look suddenly upstream, and her whole face seemed to freeze in horror. "The boats!" she screamed. "Look upstream, Robin! The boats!"

Robin spun around, at first not able to take in the sense of her words, understanding only the sound of alarm that rang in her tone. She pointed wildly and his eyes swiftly followed her fear-laden gesture.

There, swinging swiftly down from around a point which had hitherto concealed them, came three large boats filled with armed men. Rowing and poling, they drove straight for the ford and the bombards, their bows and gunwales lined with glinting bills and pikes, and the darker metal of chainmail and steel caps. The shouted threats and curses all but drowned out the oar-beats.

The sunlight slanted through the trees in golden spears of light, and struck up harsh, pricking glints as it hit the Frenchmen's glittering armor. Near at hand, Robin could make out Wat's harsh mutter, and Katherine still stood frozen a graven image of terror and hopelessness.

"Now indeed is this a devil's malady for which there is no physic," said John the Wolf, his face taut. "For they can row faster than we can drive. And from the boats they can chop us to bits with those bills without ever coming in reach of our swords."

Robin's lips were thin and tight, and his eyes agleam. "They have not reached us yet. Hold tight, now John, for there is no way to bring the bombard to bear except to turn the horses themselves."

CHAPTER VIII

FOR A DEVIL'S MALADY....

LASHING THE OFF horse at the same time that he threw his whole weight on the reins, Robin endeavored to jerk the animals' heads around to face downstream. He set up a shout to Hubert and Wat on the other bombard: "Do you train your muzzle on those Frenchmen from the shore, and fire so soon as it bears! These boats we will try to care for of our own selves!"

But the bombard horses would pay heed to neither reins nor lash. Setting themselves into their harness, they drove straight ahead toward the farther shore.

At that Robin's heart sank, and the Frenchmen in the boats set up a yell of triumph and redoubled their efforts at the oars.

The next instant Robin saw Katherine Algelt standing up on the seat of the Flemish cart. She poised there, then she flung herself out and down. Her outstretched arms caught the neck of the nearest bombard horse, and clung. A moment later she had pulled herself up and over, and was standing on the insecure footing of the bombard pole, while she jerked and tugged at the head-harness of the snorting horses. Her efforts, aided by Robin's pull on the reins, made the horses give way, and they turned downstream turning the bombard after them. Quickly Robin dropped the reins and grabbed the hot firing skewer out of the brazier which John Wolf had continued to blow upon. Holding the point just above the bombard touch-hole, Robin glanced along the muzzle.

Not three score yards away, the leading boat was swirling down, the others clustered close behind. Robin could see the fierce scowls of the Frenchmen, could see the hands already tensing on the halberds. Then with a lurch the bombard muzzle swung to bear straight upon the boat. And Robin thrust the skewer deep and true.

The next instant he seemed fairly hurled into the air. He came down, knees and elbows crashing against metal and wood; his brain reeled and his nostrils filled and choked with the smoke and stinging fumes. When the smoke cleared he found himself clinging half to the bombard seat and half to the bombard, while John the Wolf lay in similar plight alongside, his forgotten bow still clutched in one hand.

The Frenchmen had been struck by a tornado of steel and death. The stone bombard ball, true-aimed and at pointblank range, had ripped through the leading boat's bow, crushing it like an egg shell under an axe. What Frenchmen had not been killed by the ball or the flying arrowheads, were already splashing in the water which ran red with blood.

Nor was the first boat the only one smitten. For the steel arrow-barbs that had been rammed atop the ball had scattered and whirled on all sides. They had spread disaster among the tight-packed Frenchmen in all the boats, especially the polemen who, standing erect for better leverage, had thus offered greater target.

FOR AS much time as it took Robin to scramble back to a firm seat, the stricken boats lay and drifted. Then while the screams and groans of the wounded filled the air, those Frenchmen still alive were seized with sudden panic. Dropping their weapons, they seized upon oars and poles and splashed away as furiously as they had come.

But even in that moment of triumph and with Wolf John's shout ringing in his ears, Robin felt a sickness of heart that was worse than any pain. For the horses were lifting their heads again and snorting, and the bombard pole on which Katherine Algelt had stood was empty now. The girl was not anywhere in sight.

Then there came a splash, and a panting laugh close beside him. And out of the water, which dragged her hair back in sodden streamers, rose Katherine Algelt; she caught at the bombard wheel and pulled herself erect.

"Now in truth both thee and thy bombards are passing rude," she gasped. "For they make no difference between bombard ball or lady. I am quite sure that I was hurled as far by the lurch as was the stone ball by the discharge!"

His heart singing with joy, Robin caught her hand and pulled her up to the seat beside him. And if in his delight he held her very close, she seemed not to mind. For ten heartbeats he held her thus.

It was John the Wolf's sour voice that brought him back to the present. The gaunt archer was shouting a jeer across at Red Hubert and Wat the Armorer.

"Are ye so shaking, then, that ye cannot fit skewer into touch-hole? For I heard no bombard's voice but our own!"

"Since the mere sight of us pointing their way set the Frenchmen running for the shore," answered Red Hubert, "why waste the ball?"

"Nay," said the armorer. "The real reason was that there was a deep hole in this accursed ford. And into it our wheels dipped so deeply that this bombard gulped a whole bellyful of water.

So that our powder is as wet as the bottom of the ford itself, and no whit easier to set afire!"

Looking toward the shore, Robin saw that the Frenchmen, either frightened by the fate of the boats or by the bombard turned upon them, had turned and were splashing back frantically.

Then he perceived something else. Ashore where two tall trees with outstretching limbs grew close to the water, a knot of French horsemen and footmen had gathered. Foremost of the horsemen was that sable-armed giant on the red horse; he was shouting directions to men who were climbing squirrel-like into the trees.

"It is a long bowshot, though I have seen you shoot further, Old Wolf," called Red Hubert. "Were that Frenchman bare of head, instead of full-helmed, you might repay the reckoning for that ax that nigh split you in twain a while back. For unless I mistake that black-armed Frenchman is the same who raised his ax above you while you stood chittering like a frighted rabbit."

But John the Wolf shook his head. "Chittering mayhap I was, but not from fright. Rather it was with astonishment at seeing before me that same knight whose horse I stole when I pushed him away after he had out-hammered Sir John Chandos. And he was more; he was that same villein who loosed me from the devil-horse's stirrup!"

"Du Guesclin!" Robin gave an exclamation. "Then it is in truth du Guesclin? But what is it that he is doing now?"

The answer came even as he spoke. Suddenly the French knight waved his hand, and there was a scurry of movement, and then two black and kicking shapes shot from the ground to the tree-limbs where they hung and spun, still kicking.

"Will o' the Fens and that traitor Frenchmen, Gobin Agache, I wot." The armorer crossed himself. "Though one be traitor and the other murderer of women, it is a hard end to come to. This du Guesclin is a hard man."

"Aye—he pays his debts." John the Wolf suddenly turned

and caught reins and whip from Robin's hand, and lashed the bombard horses into frantic motion, "it has just come to my mind that he has paid *all* his debts, and so is now free to start afresh. Sir John Chandos may have him an he wish, but I want no more of him in any fashion!"

As the horses drew the bombards through the shallower water toward where the main English army waited, Robin touched the girl's hand. "When the tide comes low again on the morrow, I doubt not that they will follow us. But for this day, thanks be to God, we are still alive and safe."

There was a twinkle in the girl's eye as she answered. "Aye, thanks be to God I was sorely troubled a while back—for the safety of the bombards!"

ABOUT THE AUTHOR

LIKE MANY ANOTHER sailor I was born and brought up quite a piece o' ways from blue water—a town of one thousand down in the backwoods of Georgia, to be exact, where I ran wild among the "cricks" and swamps and hammocks until I reached college size. Then I had a lucky break and won an appointment to the Naval Academy at Annapolis. By more lucky breaks I managed to graduate with fair marks in professional subjects, but with better grades in boxing, broadsword fighting, etc. Even as a midshipman I'd had a look-in at the Vera Cruz affair of 1913, and was at Monte Carlo in 1914 when the Big War broke. I can still remember the Austrian cruiser that scooted hell-bent out of the harbor of Villefranche just in time to beat the opening gong. After that we played hide-and-go-seek in the fog with British destroyers all the way down to Gibraltar and then put in a week off Morocco holding down the international peace while France replaced her veteran Foreign Legion with rookie regiments.

After graduation I drew a cruiser and was shot straight to Haiti, where we were just straightening out the Haitian revolution of 1915—the one the Haitians began by chopping up their president into teeny bits in the French consulate.

After that, just the usual round of Naval officer duties, including service on cruisers, battleboats and gunboats—also some staff duty and even an assignment to the President's yacht. Had a look at quite a little water and land—and started to write my first yarn while snowed in on the old frigate *Constellation* at the Newport Training Station.

Roy de S. Horn

Put in most of the Big Fight on battleboats and cruisers, writing Washington regularly for assignment to the destroyers or aviation, and getting told equally regularly to "'tend to the job assigned me and shut up!"

Had bad luck firing battle practice while commanding Number Six turret on the Arkansas and came out of it with "low visibility" in one eye. Too low to pass exams, so they retired me out.

After that turned to writing as a profession, and knocked around pretty much over the country—Michigan and Wisconsin big timber country—Eastern big towns—and West from border to border. Watched 'em make the movies in Hollywood for a year or so—then jumped the country and went as second mate on a four-masted bark carrying "Jap Squares" from Puget Sound to Australia. Wasn't much of a square-rigger man, I don't expect, but I picked up a lot of stuff from the best deepwater skipper and mate in the trade to-day—at least I think they are. Got cut down Christmas night off the corner of Australia by a dumb squarehead steamer that had sent its lookout aft to read the log in dirty weather—weather that had already made us take in royals and upper to'gallants. Having sound bulkheads and a lumber cargo we managed to weather it out until off Sydney, where a couple of tugs took us in.

Knocked around Australia for quite a while and then the South Seas on the way back. For the past few years I have been writing yarns in whatever time I have left after editing a couple of magazines myself.

And that's that!

THE ARGOSY LIBRARY ™

SERIES 7 INCLUDES:

* BRAND * TUTTLE * BECHDOLT *
HORN * MCCULLEY * ROSCOE *
* HALL & FLINT *
* BEYER * MCCALL *
* MONTGOMERY *

THE BEST FICTION
FROM THE FRANK
A. MUNSEY LINE